DECLAN

LUCKY IRISH SERIES 4

ANNA CASTOR

ISBN: 9789083046297

❀ Created with Vellum

CONTENTS

INTRODUCTION TO THE LUCKY IRISH SERIES - AUSTIN

F amilies in book 1 - 2:

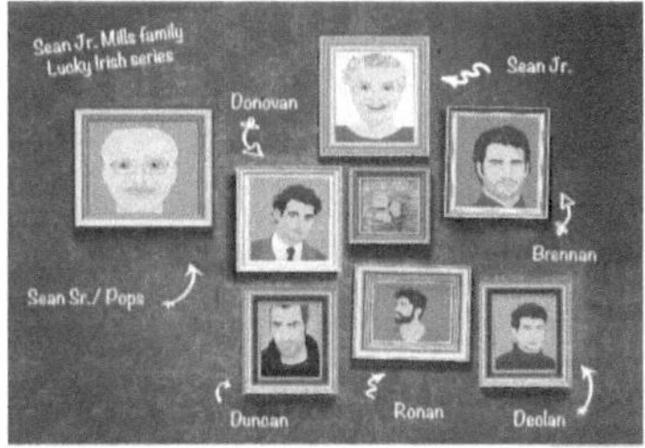

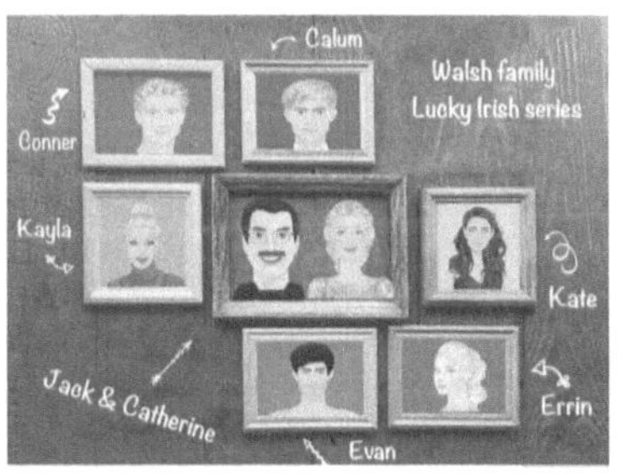

Additional families from book 3:

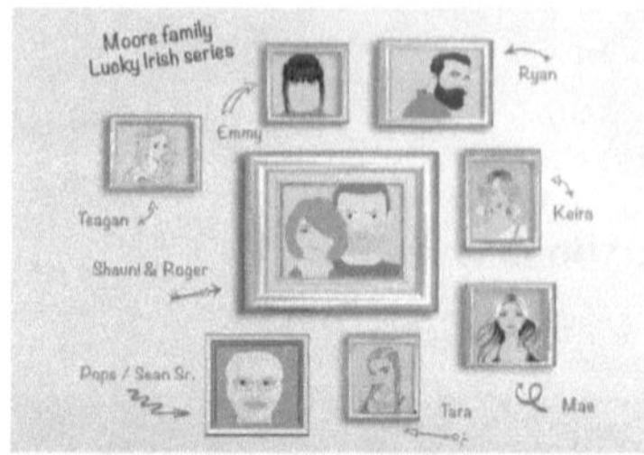

Additional families from book 4:

Rob Walker family
Lucky Irish series
Nora
Cat
Kieran
Brenda & Rob
Ross & Abigail
Devlin
Finn

Ron Walker family
Lucky Irish series
Aaron
Ryleigh
Liv & Jessie
Luke
Ron & Emily
Ross & Abigail
Billie

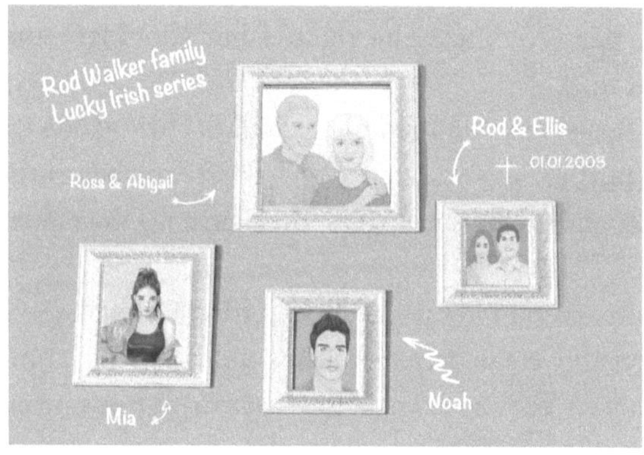

Rod Walker family
Lucky Irish series
Ross & Abigail
Rod & Ellis
✝ 01.01.2005
Mia
Noah

PROLOGUE

Prologue
March

Tonight was the night. No more self-doubting and pussyfooting. Bree checked her lip gloss once more in the vanity mirror of the sun visor, flicking her tongue over her pearly whites. She righted her shoulders and took a deep breath.

The Texas heat engulfed her rich dark curls as she exited her beat-up purple sedan. After a few short brushes through her bouncy strands with her fingers, Bree gave up the effort to tame her hair.

She'd parked in her usual spot, behind Dec's black Chevy on his impeccably clean drive way. How did he find the time to pull out all those weeds and tackle the overgrown mess when he was still renovating inside?

She'd been here almost every day and most nights for the past three months. At first, she'd helped Dec clean out all the junk left behind by the former owner. The house had been a steal, but not without reason. It had been a dump. A smelly, dingy two-story house in southeast Austin.

Never one to shy away from hard work, Bree assisted the Mills brothers and cousins wherever she could as they helped Dec in remodeling the two-story house. It had been fun learning some tricks of the trade from Dec's cousins Keenan and Aiden who worked for their father's construction company.

Bree used her hand to shield her light blue eyes from the lazy evening sun. She glanced up at the freshly white painted house and smiled. Finally, they were entering the stage of making this place beautiful again. They all had enough of tearing down and throwing away the old, rotten elements of the house.

Bree stopped in her tracks. The red paint of the small porch pained her eyes. That damn stubborn ass. After all the color-coding and Bree's efforts in persuading him to go for a more gentle looking pale blue, Declan still went ahead with this God-awful vermillion.

Dec needed his head examined. She righted her little black dress and stomped in her high heels over said ugly red porch as Dec opened the door.

"And? What do you think?" he smiled a mile wide and opened his arms, showcasing a job he figured well done.

"You never listen, Dec."

She shook her head as she walked up to him. Because if he would really listen to her—or take notice, he'd known how her stomach flip-flopped at the mere sight of his dimples. How her heart skipped a beat at his smiling gray eyes.

Damn, she was a mess. She would even put up with this hideous porch if it meant she'd live here with him, waking up every day in those muscular tanned arms.

"Squirt..." he said, and Bree winced at his nickname for her. She wasn't the six-year-old tomboy following him around anymore. In front of Declan stood a twenty-six-year-old who just had an emergency video chat with her sister Gwenn about her outfit tonight.

She was on a mission. The normal 'one-of-the-guys-Bree' wouldn't cut it. Tonight, she wasn't the girl next door and Dec's best friend in her favorite sweater and jeans. No. In front of Declan stood a WO-MAN.

Yes. She emphasized it out loud in her head and his smile faltered. He could always read her mind. So, how he didn't read the signs of her pining and lusting over his Irish ass was the greatest mystery of all times.

Maybe he didn't want to hurt her feelings by addressing it. Or he was afraid to have the same conversation she was about to have with him. Telling him how she felt might ruin their friend-ship. They both avoided this topic. Well, either way, tonight would be the start of a new chapter in their relationship. Hope-fully, a chapter filled with lots of clothes ripping...

"I know, I know..." he said as he held up his hands, making his black stained T-shirt creep up from the top of his dusty jeans. She bit her bottom lip at the sight of his dusty trail of hair going down beneath his belt buckle. Bree cleared her throat.

"The color is gross, Dec. It's—"

"Yeah, I know. You're right. I should have listened to you. But at least for now, it has a coat of paint." He shrugged before he opened his arms for her to step into. She couldn't remember the time he wouldn't invite her into his arms for a hug.

Even wearing a new dress for this special occasion couldn't hold her from hugging his dirty torso. Clean, manly sweat and wood dust. She placed her cheek on his chest to get her fill. He squeezed her tighter for a moment and stepped back to travel his eyes over her.

"You seem different. What did I miss? Didn't we talk this morning? What's up?" Declan said as he took her biceps in his calloused hands. The observant cop side of Dec scrutinized her expression as he narrowed his eyes.

"Geez. I'm wearing make-up? Maybe that's it?" Bree said as she tucked a curl behind her ear.

"No. That's not it. It's something *in* your eyes, not *on* your eyes. Your eyes always speak volumes to me. And they're telling me there's something going on you'd rather not say. What's the matter?"

Bree sighed and shook her head. Why was this so hard? He was her best friend. She usually told him everything. Well, perhaps not that she'd masturbated this morning after hanging up the phone with him. His raspy voice after he'd just woken up had gotten her all hot and bothered. She'd needed some kind of relief before going into work and had made do with the showerhead.

Oh, how she longed to feel the real deal instead of getting off on just the thought of Declan. They stood so close she could almost taste him. Bree took a deep breath, full of his scent, and closed her eyes for a moment.

Okay, let's do this. It's now or never.

"Dec..." she said as she opened her eyes. His name came out in a pained whisper.

"What is it?"

His eyes searched hers for answers. As he cocked his head, his charcoal longer hair on top swished over his frowned forehead.

She swallowed the big lump in her throat and said, "I'm in love with you."

His brows shot up, and he took a step back from her. His hands let go of her upper arms. Losing his warmth and the lack of a verbal response made her involuntarily shiver. She looked up through her eyelashes and winced at his expression.

Dec rubbed his neck, exposing his hard bicep next to his ear. A smear of ugly vermillion paint graced his elbow. He shook his head in disbelief.

"Fuck, Squirt. I..."

She swallowed back the tears threatening to overflow her eyelids. After a few hefty blinks, the first damn tears descended. Declan wasted no time and beat her to it as he wiped them away with his thumb.

"Shit..."

He took her cheeks in between the palm of his hands and for a moment, she was sure he would lean in and kiss her. His stormy eyes locked onto hers, but she couldn't read him. How could he control his emotions like this? Didn't she affect him as he did her?

"Say you feel this too, Dec," Bree said. The pleading in her voice was clear.

"I... yes, I love you."

Bree's heart rate went sky high, but his pained stare demolished all hope. And his next words shattered her heart into a thousand pieces.

"But not in that way. I'm sorry, Squirt."

3

DECLAN

"Twins? But Ronan is so big and... rugged."

Declan narrowed his eyes at his giggling date, Stacy, as she flung her hazel hair over her bare shoulder. Stacy tried to catch his twin's eyes, but Ronan ignored her and nudged Declan's leg with his knee under the table. "Told ye, Dec. These fine ladies like bad boys."

Fine ladies, his arse.

He raked his fingers through his hair and sighed. This was the last time he would let his brother talk him into going on a double date.

Ronan barged into Declan's home this evening, declaring enough was enough with his moping. Declan agreed to tag along, although he much rather spend the night at Bree's with her curly head resting against his shoulder.

Like a second home, Declan used to go over to Bree's cozy apartment any time during the week. The former best friends would talk about their day, lounge together on Bree's sofa and binge-watch the latest horror show.

She would tease him about being jumpy during the scary parts. He would tickle her side before pulling her in to rest her head on his chest.

Like a cat, Bree loved to curl herself around him. No words were needed. Until Bree declared her love for him six months ago and even being in the same room turned awkward. Let alone lying entwined on her sofa.

He tried to be considerate of Bree's feelings for him, but his actions hurt her. He kept his distance so he wouldn't lead her on. And to be honest, the distance also made sure he wouldn't give in to his own feelings for Bree.

He'd promised himself a long time ago to never let any romantic feelings mess up the best thing in his life. He'd witnessed the nasty break-up between Ronan and Bree's sister, Fianna. It ruined not only their friendship; it divided both families for a long time.

But this distance between him and Bree ripped his heart right out of his chest. And the longer their status quo continued, the harder it got to get back to being best friends.

Long, fake nails trailed his hand. Declan gripped his beer bottle so hard, his knuckles turned white. He pulled away from Stacy's touch and brought his beer to his lips.

He was glad he'd driven separately tonight. Normally, Declan would make the most of his evening. Even during a bad date. He would try to keep the conversation flowing by broaching solely safe topics and laugh at the right moments.

However, Declan's date showed more interest in his twin. And knowing Ronan, he wouldn't mind going home with both ladies. His king-sized bed has seen more action than Chuck Norris, Bruce Willis, and Jason Statham combined.

He held back a snort when the two women cackled at another dumb joke from Ronan. Declan loved his twin. But man, did he have a big head. Undefeated in his weight class, Ronan's attitude got worse by each win.

With his next MMA fight three months away, Ronan indulged himself with the groupies circling him like flies on shit.

"What do you do, Declan?" Stacy asked.

He titled his head and wondered where this sudden interest came from. They sat in a packed Velvet Club for almost half an hour now. Until now, Stacy merely answered with 'yes' or 'no', never asking him anything in return. She listened in on her friend's conversation with Ronan and often joined in when Ronan made his date laugh.

Declan wasn't insecure. He never lacked attention from the opposite sex. Perhaps, in this crowd, Declan was the dull and dutiful twin. The two women at their table were here for a good time between the sheets, not for good conversation. And that's okay. But it definitely ruled them out as Declan's type.

Maybe Bree would still be up and he could swing by her place tonight. Perhaps enough time had passed and they could work on getting close again. See if she'd already started on that new zombie show.

Stacy cleared her throat.

"Erm, sorry. I'm a police officer."

He crossed his arms and watched closely for her response. It could go either way; although he wasn't worried that she'd start a discussion about police brutality or riots. Stacy struck him like the kind that would—

"Hmmm. You can cuff me anytime and to anything, Officer Mills..." she licked her bottom lip before she leaned in from her side of the table. His eyes traveled from her mud brown eyes, down to the cleavage on display in a tight shirt that barely held her tits inside.

"Damn," Ronan said next to him.

Declan rapped the table with his knuckles and pushed out of his chair. One shared look was all it took to let Ronan know he wasn't going to the bathroom but hightailing it out of there.

Stacy shot from her chair, and it was then he realized he'd never answered her stupid remark about cuffing her.

"I'm off, Ro. Ladies, pleasure meeting you."

"Wait!"

Declan turned and held Stacy steady with his hand firm on her bicep, halting her swaying arse from tumbling down on her high heels.

She blinked up at him. "Thanks. I guess I had a bit too much to drink."

"No problem."

Stacy leaned in and said, "I'd love to catch a ride in the back of your patrol car…"

"You'd better join my brother and your friend. I'm not into role-play. But I'm sure my brother has an entire collection at home for you all to play with."

He hoped he'd successfully diverted her sudden attention.

Her eyes went wide, and she giggled. "Tessa told me about Ronan's mirror. I'm not surprised he also uses toys."

"Yeah, that damn mirror above his bed is notorious."

He locked eyes with his brother over Stacy's shoulder. "You got her?"

"Yeah, man. We'll take her home. Talk to you later." Ronan waggled his eyebrows and Declan rolled his eyes.

He took the fastest route and twenty minutes after leaving the Velvet Club; he knocked on Bree's front door.

After the longest minute in history, Bree opened with a scowl on her face. Not her usual greeting.

"Hi, Squirt."

"What are you doing here?"

"I… I wanted to see you." He took a small step in her direction, but when Bree didn't budge, he halted. She was dressed in her standard work attire; black pencil skirt, light blue button-down shirt with the top two buttons undone.

He wondered why Bree hadn't changed into her sweatpants like she usually did right after coming home. Had she also been out tonight?

Bree fisted the door like it was her lifeline. "Why?"

"Do I need a reason to come see you?"

Bree tucked away a stray inky curl behind her ear. She shook her head. "No. Not really. I'm just surprised that's all."

"So, can I come in?"

Her hesitation devastated him. He tried to give her a genuine smile to persuade her. But his smile fell flat the moment he realized she could see right through him.

"What's up?" she asked.

He massaged the back of his neck. "I miss us."

Bree's eyes widened, and she let go of her firm hold of the door. She gave him a shy smile before she bit her bottom lip.

He placed his hand on her front door, and Bree took a step back. Her eyes traveled over his outfit and she frowned.

"First you wait months to come see me, and now you show up at almost eleven at night. Where have you been, anyway?"

He glanced down to his gray slacks and black dress shirt. Shit.

"I was out with Ro and some people at the Velvet Club."

He didn't want to throw his double date in her face, but it didn't surprise him how well Bree could read between the lines. She jutted her chin at him and righted her shoulders.

"Ah, let me guess. Your date sucked—as in her personality sucked. No surprise there if Ronan introduced—"

He held up a hand.

"Bree—"

"No, no. You're right. I don't care, anyway. Look. I'm tired and was just about to turn in."

"Squirt..." He didn't know what to say. Why couldn't he continue to give her the space she needed? A whisper in the back of his head said he knew why he stood here in Bree's hallway, rather than cuffing Stacy to his bed right now.

It was the same reason he punched Joey Calvari in the face when he boasted how he'd kissed Bree under the bleachers. Or why his gut churned each time Bree talked about meeting some guy in college.

Obviously, his rejection of her love already ruined their friendship. Standing at the crossroads, they could further drift apart or Declan could finally listen to that whisper in the back of his head.

Bree grabbed the door handle. She narrowed her eyes and said, "I don't get you. How do you figure it's okay to come over after one of your dates? I've told you how I feel about you. It's so insensitive. And rude. Here I thought Ronan was the asshole twin..."

With that parting shot, Bree slammed the door shut.

"Open up, Bree. It's not what you think."

She didn't respond. He whipped out his phone and dialed her number. She didn't pick up; instead she turned off her phone and the ringing behind the door stopped.

"Shit."

4

BREE

"Oh, that always breaks my heart," Kate said.

Bree glanced up from her hands, trying to unstick Billy's dinosaur jacket from his zipper. She peered over St. Helena's Kindergarten's schoolyard and searched for whatever Kate meant.

A flailing Tommy shouted, "I'm not going. You can't make me!"

Declan's cousin Keenan held his son Tommy in his arms and rubbed his back while whispering to him.

"Can you take over Billy's zipper from me?"

"Sure." Kate took Bree's place in front of the five-year-old.

"Thanks, Kate. I'll be right back, Billy."

"Okay," Billy said.

Bree took a few steps in Tommy's direction before he noticed her. He wormed himself from Keenan's hold and ran into Bree's waiting arms.

Tommy snuggled into Bree's chest and said, "I don't wanna go."

Bree lowered Tommy and got down on one knee in front of him.

"I'm so glad you're here. I know it's your first day today, and you're probably scared. But you know me, Tommy, and I'm so happy to have you in my class."

Tommy grabbed the end of his sleeve and wiped the snot from his upper lip. "I still don't wanna go."

"I know, Tommy. But we're going to have so much fun, I promise."

"Hi, Bree."

Bree broke eye contact with Tommy to meet Keenan's worried eyes.

"Hey, Keenan. How are you?"

"Long time no see, Squirt." Keenan's upper lip pulled because he knew how much she hated the nickname his cousins gave Bree.

"At school, my name is Bree. *Miss Bree*, for Tommy."

She placed her hand on Tommy's shoulder and winked at Tommy.

"*Miss* Bree?"

"Yes, Tommy. When we're at school, I'm your teacher and every student calls me Miss Bree."

Tommy scrunched his nose. "Dad and uncle Declan didn't tell me."

The mention of Declan left a searing pain in her heart. She'd ignored his calls and texts for two days. But after he kept calling her, she was afraid he would show up on her doorstep again. So she finally told him he needed to give her some space.

Declan's audacity baffled her. After months of ignoring her, he finally took the effort to seek her out. And for a moment, she'd let her hopes run away with her, thinking he really missed them being an *us*.

But then it clicked. Declan had been going around town on dates, while she was at home nursing her broken heart.

It had been the final straw when she realized he only meant he missed her as a friend. Declan would never love her like she loved him.

Although she'd pined over him these last months, she now agreed that he did the right thing by keeping his distance. Because the moment she opened the door and gazed into his gray eyes again, her heart whispered, *'He's here. He's finally ready to love me back.'*

All her hopes shattered for a second time, leaving her numb. The one man she thought would never hurt her, did exactly that.

"Tommy, I know you'll have fun in *Miss* Bree's class," Keenan winked at Bree, "So, let's get you inside. Uncle Aiden is waiting for me."

"I want to go with you," Tommy's bottom lip trembled.

Keenan pulled Tommy in for a hug and tears filled the man's eyes. Working at construction sites all day made Keenan a bulk of a man. Seeing him swallow back his emotions had Bree joining him as she swallowed a big lump in her throat.

Keenan wasn't just another parent bringing their child for their first day at school. Keenan and Tommy felt like family. As a kid, Bree had spent more time with the Mills brothers and cousins than she did at home.

Seeing Keenan on the brink of crying had Bree almost joining father and son with her own waterworks. Bree swallowed again and stepped over to Tommy.

She ruffled his blonde hair and leaned in. "Can I tell you a secret, Tommy?"

Tommy stopped sobbing for a moment and tilted his head so he could nod.

"You'll not like school all the time. Sometimes, school's stupid. And that's okay."

"Bree." Keenan arched one brow.

"It's true, Keen. I know you always hated school."

Keenan's raven hair brushed his frowned forehead as he titled his head. He narrowed his green eyes and stared her down from his six foot three.

"You're not helping here, Squirt."

Tommy giggled.

"Why did Dad hate school?"

"Because he'd rather help grandpa Niall. He wanted to build houses instead," Bree said, and smiled at the memory of a young Keenan walking around with a hand-me-down tool belt from his father.

Tommy grabbed his father's arm and jumped on the spot.

"I want to go with you, Dad. I wanna build a house too."

Keenan gave Bree a pointed look.

"Now look what you've done."

But Bree wasn't discouraged. "Do you know what your dad did?"

"No?" Tommy's eyes went over from Bree to Keenan and back again.

"He sucked it up and went to school, and so will you." Keenan grumbled.

"What did he do, Miss Bree?"

Bree smiled at Tommy, already picking up on addressing her with Miss.

"He made a lot of friends at school. And some of those friends are still in his life. And you know what? You'll make a lot of friends here too. Think about all the play dates and fun you'll have with some new friends."

She never could tell a lie to save her life. So yes, school would probably suck sometimes and she wouldn't tell Tommy otherwise. As a teacher, Bree brought the kids in her class up to speed with the alphabet or the difference between a square and a rectangle.

But what really brought a smile on her face were the moments she could help the kids whenever life threw rocks into their ponds to ripple the surface. She wanted to guide them.

Perhaps that's the reason she'd become a teacher. To help other little Bree's who need a listening ear and a soft guiding hand while growing up. Her dad sure hadn't been around. And her mother? Well, 'complicated' and 'demanding' couldn't begin to cover a description of her mom.

"That's right, son. I'm still friends with a lot of kids from my school." Keenan wanted to say something else, but his phone interrupted him. He glanced at the screen and declined the call.

"I need to get going, Tommy. Aiden's calling to see where I am and I'm sure Miss Bree wants to start her class."

Bree watched Kate take over her kids for a few minutes as she stood watch in the hallway and directed both classes to go take their seats. It often came in handy as their classrooms sat side by side.

"Come, Tommy. Let me show you to our classroom."

Bree plopped down in her chair and kicked off her black pumps under her desk. Today had been a good day with a lot of small victories. Anthony finally asked Bree for her help with his alphabet assignment. And Tommy made a friend on his first day after an hour of sitting on the side, watching others play and work.

A soft knock on her wide-open door drew Bree's eyes to her colleague Craig. He often checked in with her after school hours.

"Had a good day?" He walked into the classroom and perched himself upon two tiny desks in front of Bree's desk. Craig resembled a linebacker, so it was probably for the best he divided his weight over the two desks.

"Yeah, I had the best day. And you?"

Craig's eyes lingered on Bree's hair when she tried to tuck another unruly strand of hair into her ponytail. Her bouncy curls were all over the place today and she remembered she needed to pick up some new curl creams.

He cleared his throat and said, "Yes. It was great. We had a lot of fun with the sensory bins."

"Oooh, did you use the props?" Bree leaned in and for a moment she thought Craig eyed her cleavage. She instantly sat up straight again.

Craig laughed and said, "Yeah. Those fake spiders and lizards were a hit."

"Good."

A moment of silence passed, and Bree wondered if Craig waited to ask her something. He shifted on the desks and cleared his throat.

"So, I wanted to ask you something." He held up his palm and waved. "And it's perfectly fine to say no...."

Bree's heart almost beat out of her chest. Craig loved to joke with Bree ever since he first started working with her two years ago. He flirted, she laughed it off.

But one night, about three months ago when she was still heartbroken about Declan, he gave her a brief kiss after a faculty softball game. She'd regretted the moment Craig's lips had touched hers, and she instantly had backed away. Craig hadn't flirted with her since.

She let her eyes take her fill of his muscular arms, his broad chest and finally, his tanned, smiling face. In front of Bree sat a total opposite of Declan. Maybe she had been stupid to dismiss him so easily after that kiss.

Craig is blonde where Declan has black hair.

Craig is bulky. And although Declan's twin Ronan is bulky, Declan is more lean and muscular.

But most of all, Craig was interested in her, and Declan was not.

"I'll go out with you," she blurted.

He laughed and said, "I wanted to ask you if I could borrow your pattern snakes to work on with Liv tomorrow. But hey, if a date's on the table, I'll take it."

She smiled at his joke. "Right."

"I really wasn't going to ask you out on a date." Craig placed a hand on the back of his neck and gave her a pained expression.

"Why not?" Bree placed a hand in front of her mouth, as she couldn't believe how snotty she sounded.

Craig laughed and said, "That night we sort of kissed in Lucky... I ehm, I got the feeling you wasn't really into it?" His cheeks colored red.

"Oh." What was she to say? He nailed it right on the head. She wasn't into him at the time. But maybe she could be now? Things could grow, right?

He shifted on the desks. "Look, I then asked Kate about your friend."

"My friend?" Bree scrunched her nose.

"Yeah, that cop who hates my guts."

Bree giggled but hastily cleared her throat when Craig didn't laugh along with her.

"Sorry. He doesn't hate you. You two don't even know each other."

"Well, I've seen him a few times in that Irish pub and he's always watching you and giving me the stink eye. I wanted to check with Kate that I wasn't stepping on anyone's toes. She'd said it was a long story, so that wasn't really encouraging."

"I'm sorry, Craig. I guess in retrospect, my heart was indeed with Declan."

Why did she have to tell him that? He must find her so attractive as she pined over some other guy. Geez. She had no idea how to play the dating game. Bree had reluctantly dated some guys in college. It was right after Declan asked his ex, Susanna, to be his girlfriend.

A petite blonde with no spunk, Susanna had been the total opposite of Bree. Whenever Bree talked to Declan on the phone while away at college, she zoned out the stories about Susanna.

When he'd broken things off with the blonde after six months, Bree hoped things would turn around and he would finally see her differently.

She came home for the summer to find Declan dating a doppelganger of Bree. That hurt even more. Because then she'd asked herself if he wanted someone like Bree, he could have picked her. So what was wrong with her? Why didn't he want *her*?

Bree got back from college and worked at St. Helena's Kindergarten. Declan didn't have a girlfriend in the past few years, and they grew even closer as friends. Bree had fought a long internal battle before she finally confessed her love for him last March.

"And is your heart still with him?"

She shook her head. She didn't think so.

"But my heart is still healing. I want to be honest with you, Craig. I'm still getting over him and it will take me some time. So, I'll understand if you'd rather blow this whole thing off. I know you didn't want to ask me out. Forget I said anything."

She slipped her feet in her heels under her desk and pushed out of her chair. She needed to get out of here. She grabbed her bag and walked in the door's direction. Craig halted her as he stepped in her way.

"I'm picking you up at seven on Friday. We'll do something fun. Okay? We'll take things slow. But I can't let you walk out of this door without giving us a shot."

Bree's cheeks heated when Craig leaned in and gave her a soft kiss on her lips. She tilted her head to get better access and they bumped noses.

"Oomph, sorry," she said.

Bree placed her fingers on her lips.

He smiled at her. "No worries. I'm sure sparks will fly on Friday."

5

DECLAN

"Why didn't you tell Emmy to hold the onion rings? Yer always stinkin'—"

"Shut your face, Dec. And while you're at it, take a walk. Against the nearest tree," Caitlin said.

She slammed the passenger door to their patrol car shut. Declan winced. He had to stop baiting Bree's oldest sister. It wasn't Cait's fault Bree wanted nothing to do with him.

It had been almost a week since that night he showed up at her apartment. Bree still ignored him and had asked him for some space.

Cait shifted in her seat and buckled up. After rummaging around in the green takeaway bag with the yellow Lucky logo, she handed Declan his shot of cholesterol.

"Thanks." He unfolded the foil and bit down into the warm bun. He closed his eyes and groaned at the rich taste. Ever since his cousin Emmy worked as a chef at his family's pub The Lucky Irishman, Declan and his partner Caitlin detoured several times a week to grab some lunch from Lucky.

The grease of the juicy hamburger trickled down the corner of his mouth. Declan wiped it away with his thumb and licked it clean.

"Why can't you eat a hamburger like a normal person?"

Declan laughed with his mouth full.

Caitlin's sneer warped into a wide smile as she watched him make a fool out of himself by dropping some pickles from his mouth onto his lap. Luckily, they fell on his napkin. He took the pickles in between his thumb and index finger and slurped it into his mouth.

"I never understood what Bree saw in you."

Cait joked, but it soured him right up. He wrapped his half-eaten burger back up in its foil. She placed a hand on his arm. "Sorry."

"I'm sorry too for causing this whole situation. I know I've said I wanted to avoid all talk about Bree. But I need to know, since she doesn't let me in anymore; how's she holding up?"

Cait's light blue eyes shifted from his to the windshield and back to him. "I... I'm not sure what to tell you, Dec."

"You can answer my question." Declan took a sip of coke from his white straw and eyed Cait as she bit her fingernail.

"Well... erm, yeah."

"Ah, spit it out, Ryan."

Caitlin rolled her eyes. He knew she hated it when he called her by her last name like everyone else at their precinct did. Perhaps because they grew up together, it seemed distant somehow.

"Okay, *Mills.* You asked for it. Bree is going out on a date with Craig."

He sucked in a breath and waited for the sudden nausea to pass. His throat felt tight and his heart pounded against his chest.

"Craig? Who's Craig?"

Caitlin shifted in her seat to grab her drink. She sure took her time answering as she slowly brought the straw to her lips. She reached the almost empty bottom of her drink, making slurping sounds that irritated the fuck out of him.

Finally done, she said, "Her colleague. You know the one... it's that buff guy."

His eyes went wide. "That blonde fucker?"

"Yep." Caitlin seemed highly entertained by Declan's reaction. She took a bite out of her stinking onion ring and waved the half-eaten thing in his face.

"Time to wake the fuck up, Mills. For all the hurt your stupid ass caused by turning her down, you deserve to do some groveling."

Rejecting Bree's love for him had been the right thing to do. It hadn't been easy, but life isn't easy. Right?

"You know why I turned her down, Cait."

Caitlin propped the remaining piece in her mouth and huffed.

"You know why..." he repeated.

Caitlin snagged another onion ring from the bag and narrowed her eyes at him.

"Pff. You're just scared. And let me tell you: scared isn't a good look on you, Dec."

His brother Brennan had said the exact thing. Declan gazed out of the windshield and his eyes followed an elderly couple passing their patrol car.

The only Mills brother who had supported him in this whole situation had been Ronan. His twin said Declan had dodged a bullet by turning down a Ryan girl. It should have been the first clue he'd made a mistake when only Ronan supported his decision.

"You know how it worked out between Ro and Fi. Fianna even went as far as moving to Colorado for a while to live with my uncle Frank's family."

"So?" Caitlin cocked a brow.

"*So?* So, I didn't want to lose Bree as a friend when all would have turned to shit."

"Who said anything about things ending between you and

my sister? For all you know, you two might have lived to be a hundred together. I still can't believe you didn't trust your gut. You just went along with whatever Ro was spewing. I don't understand how you two are even twins. Unlike Ronan, you would never hurt my sister. At least, you didn't before you turned her down."

"Ro still claims that Fi and him were on a break while he was with that girl."

Caitlin bristled at Declan's lame excuse for his brother's behavior.

"He's nothing but a liar. Ronan Mills only cares about himself. You on the other hand... You're all about caring for others and doing what's right. I know that somewhere in the back of your twisted mind, you thought you were doing Bree a favor by turning her down. But if you'd reach deep down into your soul, you'll know that you've made a mistake."

He wanted to steer away from all talk about Ronan and Fianna and asked what he'd wanted to know from the moment Cait said Bree would go out on a date.

"Is she really into this guy?" It would hurt like hell to see Bree finally move on.

"She's going out with him tonight, Dec. If I were you, I'd—"

"I love Bree, Cait. I'm not messing things up for her and—"

Caitlin held up a hand and shook her head. "And because of your love for Bree, you need to step in, Dec. You don't seem to realize the importance of this date. This Craig-person is the first guy she's going out with since college."

Caitlin leaned forward and emphasized the word 'college'. Damn, that was a long time. He always tried to avoid talks about going out on dates. In hindsight, he must have known Bree didn't like seeing him with other women.

And he knew where he stood in thinking of Bree with some other guy. He hated the idea, but luckily the situation never came up in the past few years. Now he realized it was because

Bree didn't want to go out with someone else. She'd only wanted Declan.

"I hate to say it, but I think there's a possibility she really likes the guy."

Not what he wanted to hear right now.

"Then it's good for her to go out on this date. She needs to move on." He wasn't sure if he was persuading Cait or himself.

Cait threw a half eaten onion ring through the cabin and it smacked him on the side of his forehead.

"What the fuck?!"

Declan grabbed a napkin from his lap and wiped himself clean. If she'd done something this childish to his twin, Ro would have released a food fight on her arse.

Declan narrowed his eyes and in one swift move, disabled her from her ammo as he snatched the takeout bag from her lap. "Give me that. Damn woman, what are ye doin', throwin' food at me?"

"I needed to get your full attention and I've been trying to get through to your thick skull for quite some time now. And nothing has worked so far!" Caitlin threw her arms in the air, making her long brown ponytail swish over her shoulder.

"I've tried to avoid bringing up my sister to make you miss her more. I've tried talking you into following your heart. I've tried the silent treatment whenever you went on a stupid date because of Ro."

Caitlin's bottom lip trembled as she was so pissed at him she was about to cry. Cait only ever cried if she were pissed off. He furrowed his brows and leaned in to place his hand on her shoulder. She shrugged his hand off and jutted her chin at him.

"Enough is enough. Wake the fuck up, Dec. My sister is going on a date with a guy who could mean the world to her. He could be the guy she would binge watch those stupid shows with. Not you. He could be the guy she'd call for help. Not you.

"Craig is going out with her tonight and will show Bree

exactly what she's been missing all these years. He's after her heart. The guy is serious and is in it for the long haul. He could end up as her man. Not you."

His chest tightened, and he couldn't get enough oxygen suddenly. Declan sat upright, clenching and unclenching his fists while concentrating on his breathing. He closed his eyes for a second. Cait's hand on his shoulder made him look up.

"You wouldn't have this reaction if you weren't in love with my sister, Dec. Why are you fighting this? Please... I don't get it." Caitlin's voice was small as she pleaded with him.

"I promised her... I promised Mom, when she—" His voice broke and he tapped a fist to his chest while he cleared his throat.

"You know I was six when she died." Cait nodded but didn't respond. He hated to talk about his past, but because Cait grew up next doors to him, he didn't have to tell her about what happened after his mom died of breast cancer.

Cait knew all about his father ghosting on his five sons for sometimes weeks at a time. Cait's family had moved in next doors when Declan's mother had been gone for almost two years.

Caitlin had her own shit show for parents checking out on their kids. She knew exactly how he felt. It made it somewhat easier for him to talk.

"It was on my mom's deathbed when she took my face between her cold hands and said that I would make the world a better place. She loved how I never put my own needs before others.

"After my mom died, I did everything I could think of to make my mom proud of me. I kept Ro from fighting as much as I could. And I helped Brennan out around the house since he was the oldest in charge."

He glanced at the windshield in front of him and took a deep breath.

"Bree was the reason I smiled for the first time in two years after my mom died." He shook his head and the corner of his mouth lifted.

"She tried to race me with that purple bike of hers. All along the way back to my house, she was boasting on how she'd kicked my Irish butt. Even though I let her win."

Cait snorted. "Of course."

He stabbed a tear from the corner of his eye and chuckled when he looked over at Cait, who also dabbed her eye with a napkin.

"Who would have thought the little Squirt from next doors would bring me back to the land of the living? I needed her, Cait. And you and I both know Bree needed me just as much. We were not just two kids sitting out a storm together. Bree is a part of me.

"I tried so hard to fight any feelings I had, and for so long. I just couldn't risk having that part of my chest ripped out."

Caitlin nodded. "Thank you, Dec, for sharing this with me. For the first time in months, I finally see where you're coming from. But can't you see, Dec? Your mom would have loved Bree for you. And she's probably up there somewhere," Cait waved her hand above her head, "and getting really annoyed with you depriving yourself from the love of your life."

A smile ghosted around his lips at the thought.

"You can't always play things safe, Dec. You might think you're doing Bree a favor by holding on to the past. But you're not only hurting yourself here. She's hurting too. You're no longer best friends. Things have already changed. For the first time in your life, you need to go after what *you* want."

6

BREE

"It's nice here, isn't it?" Craig asked as he placed his bulky arm around Bree's shoulders. He smelled like citrus. It could go either way with citrus. It could remind you of fresh, homemade lemonade... or in Craig's case, air freshener.

Bree deftly took a step aside to walk over to the first hole.

"The goal is to get the ball through this Moulin-rouge looking windmill, via that border, and into the hole," Craig said.

"Hmm-mmm."

It wasn't exactly rocket science. But she held her tongue. If she were here with Dec, they would pick a dare for the loser right now. They would rib each other and she would try to get on Dec's nerves, just to make him lose concentration.

But since she was here on a date with Craig, she placed her golf ball on the tee and gave her swing a little more grit than necessary. The golf ball flew over the windmill and came at a complete standstill right next to the hole.

"Wow! And you'd said you've never been here before."

"I haven't." Bree smiled as she walked over to her ball. She gave it a little nudge and filled the hole.

"Is there anything you can't do?" Craig grinned as he shook his head. He placed his golf ball on the tee and made a big show out of taking an aim. After swinging back and forth with his putter, he finally made contact, and the ball flew against one of the windmill blades.

"Ah, that's unfortunate," he said, sucking air between his teeth.

"Yes, very unfortunate." Bree rolled her eyes. What was she even doing here tonight?

He'd told her he wanted to do 'fun stuff' together. And just go from there.

No pressure.

Going to the miniature golf course wasn't exactly 'fun stuff' in Bree's book, but it beat sitting home alone, thinking about Declan.

"Shall we make this game a little more interesting, Bree?"

She perked up at his words. Maybe she'd been too harsh on Craig. Perhaps he was her kind of guy after all. Craig was gorgeous, with his blond locks of hair and blue eyes. He was bulky, but not so much it bothered her. The sweet aura surrounding him was the first thing that drew her to him.

Because the one thing she searched for in a guy was trust. She wanted to know she could rely on her partner above anything. She trusted Declan with her life, but no longer with her heart. She really wanted to make it work with Craig.

But their kiss in her classroom had been... meh. Maybe during this date there would be more sexual tension between them?

She placed her hand on his muscular, tanned underarm and leaned in.

"What do you have in mind?"

"The winner gets to pick the restaurant," Craig said.

Bree let out a deep breath and said, "Ookay..."

"What? Did you have something else in mind?" he asked with worry in his voice.

"No, no. It's fine."

She walked over to the second course and stood in front of a giant wooden shoe. "What's up with these props?"

"It's owned by an old Dutch couple. Don't you think it's kind of sweet?"

"Hmm." Bree started her backswing but held back the last minute because she didn't want to hit Craig as he came to stand close to her. Her putter kissed the golf ball for a second.

"First stroke!" Craig said.

"Excuse me?"

"Your putter contacted the ball."

"That was an accident! I backed out of hitting it because I didn't want to knock your head from your torso!"

"It still counts as the first stroke. You began your backswing and in the regulations it says," he put his next two words into quotation marks with his fingers, "'The Players', are ready the moment you begin your backswing. If the putter contacts the ball from that point, the stroke counts."

Bree shook her head. "You're kidding."

"No, Bree. According to the World Mini-golf Sport Federation—"

"You know what? I'm done." Bree stomped through the golf course with Craig hot on her four-inch heels.

"Bree, you can't be serious."

"Oh, but I am, buddy. I'm done."

He grabbed her shoulders and spun her around. He smiled down at her since he had a lot of inches on her, even with her in heels.

"Are you usually this fierce?"

She looked from his full lips to his smiling eyes. "Whatever. Craig, I don't think—"

He leaned in and kissed her mid-sentence. His lips coaxed her to open up for him, and when she did, he turned his head and their teeth clanked together.

"Oomph," she said.

Craig cleared his throat and said, "Sorry."

"I'm sorry, too."

He leaned in for a second round. But all she could think of was how she would see him at school on Monday. And how she would have to act normal.

They went from a kiss without a spark in the classroom, to a kiss that sparked because their teeth ground against each other. She giggled against his mouth.

"What is it?" Craig said.

"I'm sorry, Craig. It's not you, it's me."

"Well, that's not very original of you, Bree." Craig said with a wry smile.

"I'm sorry."

"You keep saying that." He chuckled.

She smiled and took a step back.

"Yeah, I know. Don't mean to."

"Is it that guy you were talking about earlier?"

"Hey, are you two done here?" A teenage boy said as he walked up to them next to the tee.

"Sure, buddy," Craig said.

The teenager scoffed and said, "Thanks, *buddy*."

Bree took Craig by the arm and led them to the terrace in the center of the golf course.

"You know I'll still wait for you, Bree."

She halted mid-step and shook her head. She pulled her arm from his. "No, please don't wait on me. I know my head is not here tonight. But even without *him* in the back of my mind, I think we're better off as friends."

"But—"

She pressed her lips against his.

"See?" she whispered. "Nothing... It's like kissing a dead fish."

He jerked from her and she laughed at his surprised expression.

"Come on, you feel it too. I mean, you *don't* feel it too," Bree chuckled.

"Damn, but I want to feel it," he said. He took her in his arms for a warm hug.

"Me too." She meant it. She wanted to feel the spark with Craig. She wanted to be happy with this handsome man. This reliable man who can cook like a chef. A Kindergarten teacher, good with little children.

This guy would treat her like nobody ever treated a Ryan girl before. He would worship the ground she walked on. Okay, not exactly, but still...

But she had to spoil it by thinking about Declan. Her former best friend who didn't give a fuck. Who'd rejected her. Made her feel small for saying she'd loved him.

After reassuring him that her sister Gwenn would pick her up, he'd left her at the terrace of the miniature golf park. Sitting in between families and couples in love, she grabbed her phone and went through her texts.

KATE: How's it going? Did you make a par or something like that?

She smiled. Kate had moved from Jersey last June and worked with Bree and Craig at St. Helena's Kindergarten. They had instantly clicked, although Kate had been skittish at first.

But it didn't take Bree long to break the ice between them. And because Kate was lusting over Declan's brother Donovan, they were both stuck in the same boat.

BREE: Nevermind par. I almost nailed him in the head.

KATE: Haha, oh no! What did he do?

BREE: I was out with his alter ego tonight.

KATE: Clumsy Craig was on a roll, eh?

Bree smiled at Craig's nickname they'd given him. He truly was a sweetheart, looking out for his colleagues and helping wherever he could. But the man often dropped things on his toes and bumped his head against whatever surface was near him. He'd even tripped Kate once accidently in the schoolyard.

BREE: Yep. I almost hit him with my putter... we clanked our teeth, kissing...

KATE: You KISSED him? AGAIN?

Bree sighed as she typed.

BREE: It's never going to happen. Ever again. E.V.E.R.R.R.R.

KATE: Haha. Okay. Stop shouting in your text ;)

BREE: You started it, remember?

KATE: Do you need me to pick you up?

BREE: No, Gwenn will be here in a few minutes. Thanks! Talk later?

KATE: Yes. And I'll see you Monday. Your turn to drive.

Bree smiled as her fingers worked the screen:

BREE: Okay!

"Hey, Hotness. Want me to cool you down?" Gwenn said in a low voice, pretending to be a dude. Gwenn sat down on one of the three vacated white plastic chairs on the terrace. She handed Bree a cone with two scoops of chocolate ice cream and one scoop of strawberry. Gwenn licked along her wrist to clean the trail of chocolate.

"Thanks, sis." Bree said. "Hmm." Her younger sister always knew how to fix her mood.

"I got you," Gwenn said with her mouth full of bright yellow ice cream.

"What flavor's that?"

"Lemon custard."

"Yuck."

"Pffft. Don't knock it till you tried it."

"Thanks for picking me up."

"No problem, sis. You let me stay at your place and let me use your car. It's the least I can do. So, where's Mr. Perfect?" Gwenn said as she took another bite out of her neon colored ice cream. Her straight, long brown hair spilled into her cone, making her swear out loud.

Bree chuckled. "He's too sweet. Too... well, you know..."

"I get it. He's not Dec. That's wrong with the poor guy. If we could give him some of that Mills Irish fire, he'd be perfect, right?" Gwenn smiled.

"I guess," Bree said before taking the last bite out of her cone.

"Didn't you have dinner tonight? You're gobbling like it's the first thing you've eaten all day."

"It almost is. I called it quits before dinner."

"Haha, it must have been real bad tonight," Gwenn said with a twinkle in her azure eyes.

"Not that bad…" Now she felt bad for Craig. She didn't need to be bitchy about him.

"Bad enough to miss out on dinner. And I know how you can eat."

Bree shoved her sister playfully, making her miss her ice cream cone as she leaned in for another bite. "Hey!"

Bree laughed out loud, when her sister gave her a playful shove of her own. "Come, let's get a move on. Kera is coming over tonight."

"I thought she was spending a few nights at Caitlin's?"

"No, she called and said Fi was driving her crazy already," Gwenn said as they walked over to Bree's purple sedan. Gwenn and Kera have both returned home from their deployment in the military yesterday. Gwenn completed one tour in Afghanistan, and their sister Kera had been a field medic for several years now.

"Fi is on a roll, eh?" Bree said after clicking her seat belt in place.

"Yep. Don't know how Cait can stand living with her. She's our sister but…"

They both laughed. Ever since Fianna had retired from show jumping with her horse, Stormchaser, she had a stick up her bum. Like living in the spare room of her sister in Austin, Texas wasn't good enough.

"I swear, if I hear her yapping about the Mills men one more time, I'm putting her down in a headlock," Gwenn said after changing lanes. She wasn't kidding. Bree could easily see Gwenn do it. Working in a male dominated environment had made the youngest Ryan sister strong, although still feminine.

"Ro still get's her riled up, Gwennie."

"Well, maybe she just needs to get over it. I'm sick and tired about hearing these same stupid arguments between them. Like any of it all matters. There are far more important things in this world...."

Gwenn cleared her throat, and silence filled the car. Bree knew her sister had encountered awful situations abroad. Being in the military had changed her, not particularly in a bad way. But it had toughened her, made her grow up in a really short time.

A few times, Bree had asked her about her experiences, but Gwenn had said she'd rather not talk about it. So for Gwenn to mention misdoings in the world was a big thing. Bree glanced over at Gwenn. "What are your plans now?"

"I'm thinking about doing one last tour, Bree."

Bree's heart skipped. She fisted her seat belt and took a deep breath. All the Ryan women had been thankful Gwenn and Kera had made it back in one piece. It had been just yesterday that they've hugged each other for the first time since months and months. And now Gwenn was throwing it out there that she was putting her life on the line again?

"I know. I didn't want to blurt it out like that. I'm sorry," Gwenn said.

Bree looked out of her window. She was searching for the words, but minute after minute passed. She jumped when a car door slammed shut. She looked over at Gwenn's vacated seat and then over to Gwenn, who walked in front of the windshield. Apparently, Gwenn had parked the car in front of her apartment building without Bree even noticing. Damn, she was a mess.

She followed her sister in. Kera greeted them when they entered Bree's apartment on the second floor.

"Hey, sis! I've grabbed your last bag of chips, hope you don't mind." The second oldest Ryan sister had made herself comfortable with a bottle of wine and a half filled glass on the coffee table in front of her. Her legs were crossed and a bowl of chips sat on her lap.

"It's okay, Ker," Bree said.

Kera scrutinized Bree's foul mood and placed the bowl of chips next to her glass of wine, almost tumbling it over. She rose to her feet. "What's the matter? Did something happen with that guy?"

Bree chuckled. "No, no problem. If anything, I've almost assaulted *him* with a putter."

Gwenn snorted and took the seat next to Kera on the sofa. The one-bedroom apartment wasn't all that much, but it was what Bree could afford on her teacher's salary. She took two steps forward and sat on a bar stool at her kitchen counter.

"Did you know Gwenn wants to sign up for another deployment?"

Kera shook her head, and it made her coppery bob swish. "No? What are you up to, Gwenn? Tomorrow is our welcome home party at Lucky's and you're already thinking about going back?"

"I don't want to talk about it," Gwenn said and crossed her arms.

"You better talk about it. You can't get us all worked up and then say nothing. Are you going or what?"

Gwenn sighed. "It's just... I know I'm going to get stir crazy over here. Doing nothing. Pretending to be normal. When I'm not. I can't see myself working a nine to five. Do you?" Gwenn took Kera's glass and chugged it.

"Just give it time. I know what you mean. I've been to the desert. I've seen a lot of shit too, you know. Don't you think for one second I don't get you. Because I do. More than any of our sisters." Kera looked over her shoulder to Bree. "No offense."

Bree took two wineglasses from the counter and filled herself and Gwenn a glass of wine. "None taken."

"When you're in that hellhole, it's all you know… It's all you'll *have* to know. Coming back home often spooks some of us more. The reality of being back home, in somewhat tranquility, scares the living shit out of some of us."

Gwenn nodded her head as she stared in front of her. Kera laid her hand on her sister's shoulder and nudged her. Gwenn blinked a few times and looked over at Kera. "Sorry, wasn't really going to enlist again. I mean, I don't think I would…"

"Just give it time, sis," Kera said.

"Maybe the party tomorrow will do you some good," Bree said.

"Yeah, well, if it wasn't for Mom going to Brazil for a few months and renting her place out, I would have stayed there instead of staying on your sofa. At least then I'd be able to tune everyone out," Gwenn said.

"Ah, so you don't want to trade places with me and stay with Cait and Fi?" Kera chuckled.

"No damn way!"

The three sisters laughed at Gwenn's outburst.

DECLAN

"Who do you think I should take home with me tonight?"

Ronan nudged Declan's shoulder with his knuckles. When Declan still didn't answer his twin, Ro finally had enough of his sulking.

"I know I'm supposed to be the fun twin—and normally, I don't mind. Because hey, it gets me lots and lots of pussy. But ye don't have to make it so easy for me. What crawled up yer arse?"

"Ye know what's botherin' me," Declan said.

"Shit. Not that again. I'm outta here," Ronan said and slid from his seat at their booth in their family's pub. He marched straight to the bar, joining the group of women he'd eyed moments ago.

"Hate to say it, but Ro's right, Cuz. Snap out of it," Aiden said. Declan stopped staring at the tabletop he'd littered with the peelings from his beer bottle label. He shot a glance at his cousin Aiden, who brought a hand to his faux-hawk.

He slid his fingers through his inky strands. Aiden usually did this before saying or doing something he'd rather not. It was almost as if the motion somehow calmed him.

"I heard Bree went on a date with her colleague last night?"

"Yeah." Declan watched Bree talking with Pops on the other side of the pub. His shoulders slumped. Bree was laughing at something his grandfather said and acted like she had the time of her life.

"Cait said Bree might be interested for real in this guy."

"Nah, I don't believe it for a minute, Cuz," Aiden said before he shook his head. He grabbed his beer bottle from the table and took a gulp. Declan gazed around the welcome home party for Gwenn and Kera. All the Ryan sisters were here, as were Declan's brothers and most of his cousins.

Bree's mom was still in Brazil for work and unfortunately missed out on everything. He wondered how emotional Bree's sisters at the airport had been two nights ago. Normally, he would've known because he would have trailed along with Bree to pick up her sisters. And if he couldn't make it because of his work, Bree would have checked in with him throughout the day. How he missed her calls in the morning. Waking up with Bree's voice... it was the best thing. And then he fucked it all up.

"I don't know how to fix this. Fuck. I'm normally real good at fixing things. Mending critical situations, bringing people together—it's what I do for a living," Declan said, shaking his head.

Aiden ran his hand through his hair again. "Bree's hurting. She keeps her distance. But she's obviously still in love with you. Anyone with eyes can see that. I always wondered how you didn't see it."

"Maybe I did see it. I was a dumbass for not acting on it.... But it doesn't matter anyway if she always loved me and if I always loved her back or not. Bree's no longer in love with me. She's dating that chump from work."

He looked over at Bree, who stood at the bar, now talking to Fianna. Bree's raven curls were bouncing over her breasts while she waved animatedly during her story. Her black dress showed off her curves, and he took his fill. Declan couldn't look away when she glanced over her shoulder and their eyes met. Bree broke their eye contact first and started a conversation with Aiden's brother, Keenan, who'd joined them.

Declan drowned the rest of his beer and clanked his bottle on the tabletop.

"Aye, stop staring and get yer arse over there."

Declan winced at the booming sound of his grandfather's voice. Pops sat his colossal frame down at Ronan's vacated spot and swirled his whiskey glass in his calloused hand on the tabletop. After narrowing his bushy gray brows at Declan, he jutted his chin at him.

"Can't stand seein' our Squirt with anyone other than ye, Dec. It not only pains me eyes, it hurts me heart."

Declan's own heart squeezed the moment Bree's nickname fell from his grandfather's lips. Their families were still close, and it made their situation even more difficult.

"She's happy, Pops." It pained Declan to admit.

"Bollocks."

Declan searched his grandfather's eyes that showcased such confidence, like he had some inside information.

"Did you have a talk with Bree?"

"Yes. Seems like I'm doing all ye work, boy. Talked with her just now."

Declan followed Pops' eyes in Bree's direction. Bree's eyes widened, but she almost instantly turned her head from him. It spooked him she'd been out last night with her colleague. His talk with Cait had made him see maybe he could go after what he wanted. But tonight wasn't the most ideal night to talk with Bree.

"Told her what I've been telling ye arse: youse two belong together." Pops slammed his fist on the tabletop, making Aiden and Declan jump in their seats.

Pops shook his head. "Don't know why ye out here, sittin'

with ye cousin. Or out talkin' with ye twin. I'm comin' for Ronan next. All those lasses... not one will make him forget Fianna."

"He should know by now, he's had plenty of girls since—" Aiden chuckled before Pops gave him a smack to the back of his head.

"A damn disgrace is what it is. A girl like Fianna. Or Bree. How can me own boys hurt them both like that? First Ronan cheats on Fianna. Breaking me lass' heart. Then ye go on and tell Bree ye don't love her. I'm telling ye... If I die of a sky rocketed blood pressure, it will all be yer fault."

Pops' round cheeks were blazing red, and his eyes sparkled with fire.

"Somewhere along the way, we all messed up in bringin' ye boys up to manhood. How could me boyos do something like that? I just don't understand." He clutched his hand to his heart and Declan shot off his seat to kneel in front of him.

"Pops!"

"Nothin' the matter, Boyo. I just need to calm down. Didn't mean to scare ye."

"I don't like this. Are you feeling pain in your chest? How about your arms?" Declan assessed his grandfather like he would any other person on a call. He could give his grandfather CPR, but he'd rather get him to the nearest hospital straight away.

"Don't treat me like I'm sick. I'm just upset!" Pops roared.

"If ye had spoken to Bree, yer heart would have been broken too."

"Pops..." Declan started, but he couldn't find the right words.

"What? Am I wrong here? Am I the only one who saw little Squirt and G.I. Joe runnin' after each other ever since they were yee high?" He waved his hands in the air at the height of two small children. Pops talked like they were still the same children. But Bree was a twenty-six-year-old woman now. She was dating her colleague, Craig. And Declan... he was still secretly pining over Bree.

"Pops, I know that you've always wanted us to be together. But—"

"But what? Don't tell me, ye don't love her. Don't ye dare lie to yer grandfather."

"I'm not. I love Bree. It's taking me this long to see that I've always loved her. I was stupid in thinkin' we shouldn't be together because of what happened with Ro and Fi. I didn't want to mess up our friendship like they did." Declan sighed and shook his head.

"But it's messed up either way, Cuz," Aiden said.

"I know. Now we're not even friends anymore. She's hurt. I'm hurt. Damn." He looked over at Pops who folded his arms in front of him, on top of his rounded belly.

"So make it right," Pops said. "Get back yer best friend and gain yerself a lover and a soulmate."

Bree kept her distance tonight. He looked over at Pops once more and when his grandfather shooed him, he finally stood.

"Aye, that's it, Dec. Go on," Pops said.

"Good luck, Cuz."

Declan nodded at his grandfather and cousin. He stepped up to Bree and Cait, while Bree had her back turned to him. Of course, Cait saw him coming from a mile away, but she was helping him out by not giving him away.

"Bree, can we talk?"

Bree's shoulders tensed before she turned around. A cute blush crept over her throat and ultimately pinked her cheeks. Bree always hated it whenever her body betrayed her and showed her embarrassment.

It had been the first time she had this reaction to Declan, and he hated it. She never felt embarrassed around Declan before. He was going to close this distance tonight. Enough is enough.

"Hi, Dec."

"Hi, Squirt. I know now is not the best time to talk, or the place to have a talk."

He exhaled as she gave him a smile and a nod.

"You're right. Maybe, we can meet up later this week for drinks?" She bit her bottom lip and her beautiful blue eyes pulled him in.

"Or... you can go home with me tonight." As her eyes narrowed, he quickly added, "I mean, you haven't seen my place now that it's finished." Damn. Why was he so nervous?

Bree watched Cait's back as she retreated from their conversation. Bree tucked a curl behind her ear and said, "Okay. I... guess it's fine. Can I catch a ride with you? I drove here with Gwenn, but she's obviously staying since it's her party tonight."

His palms got sweaty, and he swallowed the lump in his throat. This was it. They were going to be alone together. She would sit on his couch in his home. They could talk and... He croaked his words, "Sure. I'll drive you."

After saying goodbye to some of their friends and family, he gently placed his hand on her lower back and directed her to the back entrance of Lucky. Why did it feel so different when he touched her now? His hand on her back almost burned from the spark this simple touch ignited.

They reached his truck and halted their steps next to his vehicle. He stepped in closer. Heaven. Her smell, her rosy cheeks, the almost pitch-black curls falling over her shoulders and resting over her ample breasts.

As he leaned in to kiss her, her eyes went wide with shock. Like he was crazy. How stupid had he'd been for turning her down in March? Could she really not believe he would kiss her now?

She took the smallest step back and opened her mouth. Probably to talk him out of it. But he closed the distance and kissed her. He entered her mouth and played with her tongue.

Hesitant at first, she softly worked with him. Goosebumps traveled all over his skin.

Declan grabbed the back of her head and the kiss became even more intense. He was kissing his former best friend, but there was nothing friendly about this kiss. He'd experienced nothing like this.

The first time he fantasized about Bree, he'd been a horny teenager. She may have been his best friend, but he hadn't been blind. He blamed his hormones and Bree's growing curves.

He loved how eagerly she returned his kiss. Her fingernails bit into his shirt that clung to his biceps. He trailed his other hand over the small of her back, familiarizing himself with the feel of the curve of her apple butt. After a hungry squeeze, she moaned against his lips. He pulled her against him and she gasped at the contact of his erection against her belly.

"Let's go home, Bree."

His voice sounded pained. He needed to let go of all the worries he'd had before. Just feel and don't overthink things. It had been one advice his oldest brother, Brennan, had given him.

She kissed his jaw before she laid a sweet kiss against his throat. "Okay…"

He nodded in response and took her hand to lead her into his truck.

They had idle chitchat during the drive about Bree's sisters and the welcome home party. He parked the car in his driveway. Both didn't make a move to get out of the truck. The silence became heavy.

"Even in the dark, it's ugly," Bree said, looking over Declan's porch. She let out a giggle.

He agreed. The color was a thorn in the flesh. The vermillion reminded him of the day he'd finished painting his house. It was the day Bree came over and told him she loved him and he'd fucked it all up.

She crossed one toned leg over the other and her short dress crept up even further. If he hadn't been paying attention, he'd missed the black lace triangle, peeping from between her upper legs. But he made damn sure to pay attention.

He leaned over the console and placed his hand on her thigh. He stroked her goose bumped flesh with his thumb.

"I'm going to repaint it."

They sat in the dark with only the dim light of the navigation illuminating the cabin of his truck. Bree swallowed, and other than a quick nod, she didn't respond. Bree kept staring at his house in front of her.

His hand on her thigh held the question from Declan if touching her like this was okay. And it revealed Bree's permission.

He trailed his hand upwards. Slowly. His fingers were imprinting a map of her body and memorizing every bit of caressed skin. Bree slightly opened her legs to give him room for his quest.

The sexual tension was palpable. It felt new and exciting. Because in this moment, as their roles shifted from friends to lovers, Bree was a total stranger to him. He had yet to discover her pleasure points. Her likes and dislikes. Her fantasies...

Bree's heavy breathing filled the cabin of his truck. She grabbed the door, but didn't make a move to get out of the truck. She tilted her head against her seat and wet her lips with her tongue.

He leaned over and kissed her plump lips. He teased and nibbled her tongue and slid his hand between her thighs. She was hot. Wet. And oh so eager as she ground her wet panties against the heel of his hand.

He slipped a finger underneath the slick lace and found home. He groaned against her lips. He hadn't meant to do this. Not here in his truck, on his driveway, even before they talked. But it couldn't be helped. It was like now he'd received the green light from Bree, he couldn't wait a single minute longer to touch her again.

She nipped him as she moved beautifully in her need to come.

"I'm so close, Dec."

"Yes. Let me take care of ye."

She let her head fall back against the headrest, and her mouth fell open. No sound. But that beautiful face screamed of ecstasy as her mouth formed an 'O'.

Bree seemed almost in pain at the forceful way she tried to keep her eyes closed. Her chest heaved, and she panted after finally finding her release.

He dashed to her side of the truck and swooped her into his arms. She seemed a bit embarrassed and wouldn't meet his eyes. He carried her inside and took the stairs two steps at a time.

Bree giggled. "Someone's in a hurry."

"Damn right. I can't wait any longer." He smiled as she kept giggling. He walked her straight to his bedroom and laid her on top of his covers.

He watched closely as Bree eyed the room. Her gaze traveled from his king-size bed, over his sandy colored walls, hardwood flooring and finally to his walk-in closet. "I like what you've done with it, Dec."

"Thanks."

No matter how many times he'd wanted to ask her to come over, he never did. What an idiot he'd been.

He stripped out of his shirt. Bree watched his fingers work on the buttons of his shirt, never giving him any reason to stop. He stepped out of his shoes and made quick work of his jeans. Bree swallowed when he came over to the bed and grabbed her ankles.

He pulled her flat with her back on the bed. She let out a surprised squeal, but before she could start her gorgeous laugh, he leaned in and smelled her. After letting out a pained groan, he nudged her pussy with his nose.

"Oh my God!" she said.

He chuckled and reached under her black dress with both hands. In one brisk tug, he ripped her black lace from her body. She surprised him by raising her voice. "Yes!"

He leaned in and made room by gripping her knees and pulling her legs wider. She let her legs fall open for him.

"Oooh, Dec." Her heavy breathing made her words come out in a whisper.

He licked her slit from bottom to top. Lapping at her juices. So sweet. So salty. Like Bree. A bit of sweet and a bit of spice.

"Hmmm," he said.

She moved her pelvis against his mouth, seeking more friction. He put two fingers through her folds and found her entrance. He worked her like she'd possessed him with learning her body's reaction at every spot he'd touched.

After going in her entrance higher, he fingered her upper wall. Bree's hips shot up as her walls clamped down on him.

She fell back unceremoniously, with her arms spread out over his white covers like a starfish. He brought his boxer briefs down, freeing his painfully hard dick. While resting his weight on his right underarm, he leaned over Bree.

He wanted to free her tits, bite on her nipples to make her scream. But the urgency to feel her clamping around his hardness instead of his fingers was too much. He grabbed his cock and lined up against her entrance. Bree's eyes opened up at the touch.

"Say you want this."

"I... I want this. But don't we need a condom?" Her wide eyes held his stare.

Shit. Why didn't he think of that? He always used protection. Always.

And now he hadn't been prepared, and he had no condoms lying around.

"Fuck. I… I don't have any condoms."

He leaned on his forearms and made a move to get off of Bree, but she threaded her fingers into his hair and tugged him closer.

"I'm safe. I mean… I'm clean and protected." Her eyes searched his for a moment.

"I'm safe too. But—"

"Please, Dec. Let me have this. I need you to make love to me. I don't want you to stop. Please."

He kissed her throat and made a line with his tongue from her jaw to the top of her dress. Bree moved again with him as she lifted her hips, trying to find his erection between her legs.

Bree brought her hands over his shoulders and crossed them behind his neck. She pulled him down, pressing her breasts against his chest. She whispered in his ear, "I want you. I've always wanted you."

He pierced his dick into her the moment she'd said she'd always wanted him. Because that truth was sweet as fuck to hear. His chest expanded at her confession. He wanted to own her. To take reign of her body and her soul.

"I can't hold back, Bree."

"I don't want you to hold back," she said in a breathy voice.

He tilted his head back and rocked into her with more force. His muscular arms shook with the strength it took to hold back.

"Finger yer clit, Bree… I'm going to come. I want ye there with me."

She did as he asked and moaned at the touch. She looped her legs around his waist and he thrust in deeper.

"Yes. That's it. Take me deep, Bree. I want you to feel me everywhere." He moaned the last word as he jerked and shuddered. He kissed the top of her nose. She opened her eyes and gave him a blinding smile.

"Fuck, yer so gorgeous." He rolled to her side and took her in his arms.

Bree snuggled closer and rested her head on his collarbone. She placed a sweet kiss against the side of his throat.

"Cait told me about your date. Thinking about you and some other guy drove me absolutely crazy."

Bree tensed at his words. He found it odd, but when she didn't respond he let it go. It probably wasn't the best time to bring it all up now. Better talk to her about it tomorrow.

Her breath evened out against his skin, and she was almost asleep.

He squeezed her tight in his arms, and whispered against her hair, "It's so good to have my best friend back."

He reached for the light switch above his bed stand and engulfed the room in darkness. He smiled a mile wide as he played the night over in his head.

Damn, he couldn't wait to have breakfast with her tomorrow.

Finally, Squirt was home.

8

___

BREE

B ree tiptoed around Declan's home, letting her fingers trace the walls of the stairway on her way down. She didn't want to wake Declan, so she'd left the lights out. She locked the door and pulled it closed behind her.

She crept to his rocking chair on his porch and glanced at the time on her phone. Seven a.m. She called the first person she knew could handle a situation under pressure. And above all, one who could keep a secret.

"Bree? That you? What's wrong, sis?"

"Gwenn, I need you to pick me up," Bree whispered.

"What? I can't hear you!" Gwenn said. "Speak up!"

"I can't talk any louder." Bree looked over her shoulder into the window next to the rocking chair. The living room was still dark.

"Where are you?" Gwenn asked.

"I'm at Dec's. I texted you last night."

"Oh, right. Sorry. You woke me up, so I'm not really sharp right now."

"You need to come get me. Now." Bree said on a stage whisper. She winced, worrying she'd been too loud. She glanced behind her again, but everything was still quiet.

"I'm coming. I'll be there in twenty. Stay inside and wait for me."

Bree groaned. "I already locked myself out. I'm sitting outside on his ugly ass porch."

Gwenn sighed. "That's not smart, Bree. What were you thinking? Dec's place is safe. Now you have to wait outside for me to—"

Bree hushed her sister. "Well, next time I'm creeping out of someone's home after a good fucking, I will think back to this conversation. Will you just get your butt in gear?"

Gwenn laughed, and Bree winced.

"Can't believe you said that out loud," Gwenn said, knowing her sister. Bree heard a door closing in the background. "I'm walking over to your car. Call me if you need me. Be there soon." Gwenn said before she hung up.

Dec always insisted Bree to park on an exact spot right under the streetlight. He'd deemed it the safest in the parking lot of her apartment building. He'd showed Bree three other spots, just in case that 'safe' spot had been taken. Always looking out for her. That's Dec.

Like a stupid teenager, she hadn't cared they didn't use protection last night. She just wanted him to never stop. Too afraid he'd come to his senses and turn her away again.

Bree groaned at her own stupidity. She'd just started on the pill again. So she wasn't worried about getting pregnant. She was also safe. She hadn't been with anyone since her last year in college. She had an all clear test done after Blake, who'd been her first and her last. Hmm, Declan was her last now.

She looked up at the Texas sky and puffed out a deep breath. Orange, yellow, and pink clouds painted the sky as the sun rose. Why on earth had they had sex last night?

She realized it had been a mistake the moment he mentioned Craig. Ugh. He said he hated the thought of Bree with Craig. If that were all it took for Declan to finally notice her, she would have started dating years ago.

She shook her head. Declan dismissed her feelings so easily last March. Like he couldn't believe she would tell him she'd loved him. Sure, he'd been understanding and sweet. But he'd never led her to believe he'd felt the same way.

Not even once in the past six months had he shown an ounce of regret. It was like he'd turned her down, and that was that. He wanted to stay friends. But who was he kidding, anyway?

Like a kicked puppy licking her wounds, she'd tried to move on. It hadn't been easy. Their paths crossed everywhere. At his brother's dojo where Bree took self-defense classes. At Declan's family pub, Lucky. At Cait's apartment.

Everywhere.

Agreeing to a first date with Craig had been a milestone. Declan only felt jealous because she wasn't lusting over his ass anymore. Now someone else had grabbed her attention. Pfff.

Little did he know that she'd told Craig they'd better be off as friends. For all Bree knew, Declan thought she was still dating her colleague.

And he took her home with him, anyway. And maybe because of it. He hadn't made a move in the past half year. So why now?

She almost missed his whisper before she went to sleep last night.

It's so good to have my best friend back.

That was exactly not what she'd wanted out of last night. Being back friends again was never an option for Bree.

The one thing she'd learned from the past six months was that she deserved someone who would go for her completely. Not someone who tried to win her back as a best friend. Or tried to mark his territory when someone else was sniffing around.

She hated to say it, but she couldn't trust his intentions. And trust was the one thing she needed. After all that her family had been through, she would never settle for less.

She didn't need someone who's uncertain about his feelings for her. Or someone who'd only want what he couldn't have anymore.

Her sister pulled into the street and lowered her speed the closer she got to Declan's two-story home.

Bree picked up her heels and sneaked off the porch. She'd left her shredded panties behind on the bed. With messed up hair, her heels in one hand, and crusted cum between her thighs, she practically ran to the passenger door.

Look up walk of shame online.... enter photograph of Bree this morning.

She couldn't believe she was walking out on him like this. But what was the alternative? Going through the awkward 'next morning convo'? Give him room to hurt her feelings all over again?

Bree opened the passenger door and stepped inside. After fastening her seatbelt, she looked from under her lashes at her sister.

"You reek of sex," Gwenn said with her nose turned up.

"Oh my God, stop it. Don't even mention it." Bree brought a hand through her wild hair and got stuck in her dark curls. Gwenn busted out laughing.

"Oh, this is priceless. I want to take a picture so bad."

"Gwenn! Get a move on. Drive," Bree shooed her sister before looking out of her window. She held her hand against her pounding chest. Luckily, there was still no sign of Dec.

"Tell me everything," Gwenn said after turning the car around on Dec's street.

Bree shifted in her seat, pulling the hem from her dress down.

"Why are we making a clean getaway? You practically

jumped into this car, flashing your pussy all over the damn neighborhood."

Bree surely hoped that Keenan, who lived across the street from Dec, didn't have to wash out his eyes because of Bree's show this morning. "You can take the girl out of the army.... but never the army out of—"

"Ah, suck it. So tell me what happened."

"Okay, picture this... Hot, sweaty sex. No, not just hot... MIND-blowing sex," Bree said.

"Yes! About time."

"I guess...." Bree stared out of the window as they drove past one and two-story houses with green strips of grass lining each driveway. Dec really did well for himself. His house would make a magnificent home someday for him and his family. The thought pained her.

"What's wrong, sis? Why are you here with me, when you could go for another round with Dec?"

"You know why." Bree whirled in her seat and narrowed her eyes at her sister.

"I can't let him get to me. He's just afraid I'm not lusting over him anymore, so he wants to pull me back in again. He doesn't want me, but he can't have me being with somebody else."

Gwenn stopped at a red light. She mirrored Bree as she whirled in her seat. Her azure eyes narrowed even more when Bree didn't flinch. "You know Dec's not like that. Come on, Bree."

"No. I don't know that."

Gwen laughed. "You know Dec's in love with you, too. Anyone can see that."

"I must be blind," Bree said.

"Or stupid."

"Hey," Bree said as she shoved her sister's side.

Gwenn didn't budge an inch and grinned. She brought them home safe and parked the car in Declan's 'safe spot'.

After a shower, Bree found Gwenn in the kitchen, two eggs

in the skillet. Bree climbed upon a barstool and placed her phone next to her glass of orange juice. Her head pounded as she jumped from her ringtone.

INCOMING: DECLAN CALLING

She hit the red button and picked up her glass. Bree downed her orange juice in a few gulps and clanked her glass on the kitchen counter.

"You'll have to talk to him at some point, Bree."

Bree filled her glass for a second time with juice and ignored her sister. Because she needed to do some damage control, Bree picked up her phone to text Declan.

BREE: Last night was a mistake. It needs to stay between us.

Not a moment passed before he typed his response.

DECLAN: The hell? It was NOT a mistake and you know it. Pick up your phone.

He kept calling her. She solved the problem by turning off her phone.

"Sooo, and you go to Kindergarten every workday to do what exactly? Are you a teacher or a student there?" Gwenn smiled above her coffee cup.

"Shut it. I just can't deal with him now." Bree stood and walked a few steps. She looked out of her window and noticed that everyone was going on with their day. Like nothing enormous had happened the night before.

"Come, sis. Let's talk. I know I'm usually not into having a heart to heart, but I know you are, so spill."

Bree walked back to her seat and dug in. After filling her empty stomach with a few bites of omelet, she cleared her throat.

"He scares me, Gwenn. I don't want to lose myself. Not anymore, I already have."

Her sister's eyes misted over, and she nodded. "Is this because of Mom?"

Bree shrugged and said, "Probably. Don't know."

"You know it's not only Mom's fault things went to shit with Rob."

Bree noticed how Gwenn never used 'Dad' to address their father. She always called him Rob. Being the youngest of the family, she had spent the least of time with him. Before he left their mom to deal with five girls between eighteen and six-years old on her own.

"I don't blame Mom."

Gwenn snorted and stood from her side of the kitchen counter to refill her coffee cup.

"I really don't, Gwenn."

"I get it. Mom lost herself. She took a lot of shit from Rob and we all know she's still not over him. And to make it worse, Rob never looked back. Never once did he call us on our birthdays. Or showed up for school plays or all that shit."

Bree blinked and the first tears fell down on her half eaten omelet. She pushed her plate to the side. "I can see myself in Mom. No matter how often they got into fights, she always worshipped the ground Dad walked on. I know I do that with Dec, too."

"You're in love with Dec, you're not some sicko trying to hold on to him."

They both waited a beat to let the importance of Gwenn's words fall between them.

"Never repeat this, please. I don't think Mom's a sicko."

Bree shook her head as she stabbed another few tears away. She giggled. "We're all fucked."

Gwenn stopped laughing and cleared her throat. "Whatever happened to Rob, anyway? Is he still here in Austin? Do you know?"

Bree shrugged. Their dad was a mystery to her. Supposedly, he left their family to be with the love of his life. Whoever that may be.

Their mother never went into details, other than that their

father was a bastard and needed to be castrated. Joan Ryan had brought the girls up on her own.

Caitlin had been eighteen and a rebellious teenager. Kera was fourteen, Fianna nine, Bree eight, and Gwenn only six years old.

Joan did everything to raise her girls into independent, strong women. Opposite of the needy girl Bree had been last night.

"Don't tell anyone about last night, okay?"

As if Bree's reasons suddenly dawned on her, Gwenn nodded and picked up their plates. Bree, by choice, would never speak of this night ever again.

9

DECLAN

"Tommy Aiden Mills. Get your butt down here," Keenan shouted. Declan's cousin leaned with one shoe on the lowest step and eyed the top of the stairs expectantly.

"Why do you always have to shout the boy's middle name when he's done stupid shit? Makes me jump too." Aiden grinned. Instead of cracking jokes, Declan wanted to be there for his cousin. He'd just entered the house behind his cousins and waited for Tommy next to Keenan.

"Shut the fuck up," Keenan said, not bothering to look over at Aidan, who walked past them into the living room.

The small feet padding the upstairs landing froze at Keenan's words.

"I know you're up there. Come down, son. And apologize to Miss Tully."

Tommy peeked around the corner on top of the landing, showing his honey blond hair.

"Miss Tully stinks!" Tommy shouted before he took a step back, making himself scarce again. Declan winced and gave an apologetic smile to Miss Tully. She didn't react as he'd hoped when she snubbed him. Tommy could be quite a handful, but Declan loved him with every fiber of his soul.

Keenan sighed and shook his head. His fatigue rolling off of him. Being a single dad for the past two years had been taking its toll on Keenan.

They had been having a few drinks at Lucky when Keenan's babysitter, Miss Tully, called. She needed him to come home immediately, and Aiden and Declan had tagged along. It was no inconvenience when Keenan lived directly across the street from Declan.

Miss Tully stood next to Keenan and pursed her lips. Just when Declan figured she would take the high road, she said, "Such a misbehaved, rude boy. And to think he's only five years old."

"Excuse me?" Keenan said as he whirled around to look Miss Tully in the eye. The sixty-something year old woman took a step back and cleared her throat.

"You should be more strict with him. He almost drowned my cat tonight!"

Keenan went red in the face. Declan had enough training to diffuse this situation, so he said in a gentle voice, "Miss Tully, I believe Tommy only wanted to wash your—"

"Pussy!" Aiden shouted. He just had to go there and derail Declan's attempt in peace making. It took Declan off guard and he quickly coughed to hide his laughter.

Miss Tully gasped and turned red. "That's what I mean. How despicable!"

"He gets it from me, just like his middle name," Aiden said, laughing loudly.

Keenan pulled in a large breath and slowly blew it out while staring up at the ceiling. He was probably counting till ten in his head before reacting.

"I can see that," Miss Tully said. She yanked her trench coat from its hook and walked over to the carrier where she'd stored her drenched cat. "Come, Missy. I'm taking you home. And we're never coming back!"

Without bothering to put on her coat, she grabbed the carrier in her arms and stomped out.

"I'm counting till three and your butt better be down here," Keenan boomed.

"One... Two..."

Tommy's angel face appeared on top of the landing. He ran down the stairs and jumped from the third lowest step into the waiting arms of Keenan. "I'm sorry, Dad."

Keenan snuggled his son into his arms, and Declan heard him sniff. Declan smiled at father and son.

"I know, son. But cats don't like water. I hate to think you were bullying the animal."

"I wasn't, Dad. I promise. I was in the tub and wanted to wash the cat. Why's that bad?"

"You were taking a bath? Where was Miss Tully?" Keenan searched Tommy's eyes for answers. Had something bad happened with him tonight? Declan shifted his stance and listened closely while observing Tommy. Nothing seemed out of the ordinary with the little boy.

"Downstairs. Talking on the phone. Miss Tully said I smelled."

Keenan bristled. "You are not to take a bath by yourself, she knows that! Anything could've happened to you."

Declan put his hand on Keenan's arm and tried to calm him down when Tommy flinched at his father's words. "Nothing happened, Keen. It's okay. Tommy is okay."

Keenan closed his eyes and nodded. He kissed the top of Tommy's hair and held on stronger.

"Damn old bat," Aiden said from the living room.

"Bats are cool," Tommy said. He looked over to Aiden. "Miss Tully is NOT cool!"

The Mills men all laughed. They settled into the living room, Tommy sitting on his father's lap. Tommy eyed Aiden and said, "Take it back. She's not a bat."

Aiden leaned in. "I take it back. But do you know what she is?"

"Aid...." Keenan said in a warning voice.

Aiden winked at his brother and looked down to his nephew. "She has the face of a blobfish."

Tommy giggled and said, "What's that?"

Aiden said, "Look it up. Here, I'll give you my phone."

As they searched blobfish on Aiden's phone, Keenan and Declan shared a look.

Thank God nothing happened with Tommy all alone in that bath upstairs while the old blobfish was yapping on her phone.

Declan nodded and busted out laughing the moment he saw a white gooey figure on Aiden's screen, with a protruded nose above turned down lips.

"The resemblance is striking, Cuz," Declan said.

Aiden laughed again. "Damn, your taste in nanny's is bad, Keen."

"Not as bad as yer taste in women," Keenan said.

"Yeah, I think you're right," Aiden said, before he held up his hand. "Although I like to see myself more the type for the 'blow-fish' kinda girls."

Declan snorted, and Keenan narrowed his eyes once again at his brother.

"What's a blowfish?" Tommy asked as he stretched out his arms to return Aiden's phone so he could scroll for a picture of the animal.

Aiden's upper lip turned up. "It's the best kind. They can hold their breath, even with their mouth stuffed."

Keenan growled. "Stop talking if ye know what's good for ye."

Aiden laughed it off. "It's actually a myth that they hold their breaths, Blondie."

"But they look like they're gonna explode!" Tommy said.

"They do that to scare off other fish," Aiden said.

"Why?"

"Because he doesn't like to get eaten, Blondie." Aiden tickled his nephew.

"Maybe you would like to get eaten? I'm feeling reeeal hungry..." Aiden said, aiming for his best cartoon villain tone. Declan laughed at his bulky cousin acting like a kid again.

Tommy shot off Keenan's lap and ran from the living room and up the stairs. "Come and get me, uncle Aiden. You'll never find me!"

"When you find him, take him to bed, will you?" Keenan shouted. "I'll be up in five."

Aiden didn't bother to answer his brother. He took the stairs two steps at a time and shouted, "Boe-ha-ha-haaaa!"

Declan and Keenan smiled at Tommy's high-pitched squeal, followed by spirited laughter by them both.

"Damn, he's a great kid," Declan said.

"He's the best. I can't believe I've let that woman babysit him. I knew in my gut something wasn't right with her. I always go with my gut. Shit, what do I do now?"

"Do you need help to find a replacement?"

"I know my sisters and Mom are happy to help. There's so much going on right now with me and Aiden finally taking over the business from Dad. I need to work. But he needs structure. I can't have him hopping between my sisters and Mom. Tommy needs someone who can pick him up from Kindergarten. Someone who can stay with him four workdays of the week. Take him to play dates and all that shit. He needs a stable home after all that's happened."

"You're such a great dad, Keen. I hope you don't beat yourself up about—"

Keenan scrunched his nose. "I don't want to talk about her. Let's talk about you. How are things?" Keenan asked.

Declan let his head fall back on the brown leather sofa and

stared at the ceiling. He sighed. "She's not returning any of my calls."

"Does anyone else know what happened between you?" Keenan asked.

"No. I've told no one. You know why I haven't told Ro any of this. He's *this* close at getting his nose punched if he makes one more wise crack about the Ryan girls."

"You haven't even told Bren?"

Declan closed his eyes and shook his head. Normally, he would tell his oldest brother everything. He'd talked multiple times with Brennan about his feelings for Bree.

"No. Bree texted me she wanted to keep it a secret. If you hadn't seen her sneaking out of my home this morning, I wouldn't have told you either."

Keenan snickered. "Yeah, it was quite the show. Tommy said, 'Why is Miss Bree running, Dad?' and then he asked me, 'What happened to her hair?'"

It vexed Declan that he'd missed the sight of her mussed up hair. He'd wanted to hold her in his arms this morning. To give her a kiss on the nose before he got out of bed and make them both breakfast.

An omelet with the sunny side up for Bree, scrambled eggs with crispy bacon for him. He knew what his girl liked for breakfast. And after last night, he also knew what she liked in bed. He had to shift his seat at the image of her shredded panties he'd kept in his underwear drawer.

"Still, what are you going to do about it?"

Declan leaned forward with his elbows resting on his knees. "I'm giving her some distance. I haven't texted her since this morning. But she's never going to reach out to me, Cuz. I just know it. She wants to forget it ever happened, and I have no clue why. It was the best night of my life. The best fucking sex of my life."

"Now we're talking!" Aiden said as he hopped down the stairs.

"I'm upstairs for one moment and you guys start the pillow talk. Who did you have sex with?" Aiden plopped down on the sofa.

"No one," Keenan and Declan said at the same time.

"Ooooh, now I *know* this is going to be juicy. Juicy as the pussy you were talking about, am I right?"

Declan cuffed the back of Aiden's head. "Shut ye damn face."

Aiden winced as realization dawned. "Sorry, Dec. Didn't mean to talk about Bree like that. I take it back."

Declan grunted and gave a brisk nod.

"So, how was it?" Aiden said.

"I'm not going to—"

"Ye were just telling me brother ye had the 'best fucking sex of ye life' and ye didn't want to tell me? And I'm supposed to be one of ye best mates?" He brought out his Irish brogue, so Declan was sure to know Aiden was pissed.

Aiden stood from the sofa to walk over to the kitchen. He was probably in search for something to drink. Or to grab an utensil to knock Declan on his arse.

Declan followed his cousin into the kitchen. "Bree wants to keep it a secret. She regrets it ever happened, and she doesn't want to talk to me."

Aiden searched for something in the fridge, his back to Declan. Declan rolled his neck back and forth and then took a deep breath.

"Keenan only knows because he saw Bree leaving my house this morning. She hightailed it out of there at the crack of dawn. Too damn afraid to stay and talk."

Aiden handed Dec a beer. "Okay. I get it."

"Thanks," Declan said as he accepted the beer and took a pull. He wiped his lips with the back of his hand and leaned against the kitchen table.

"Now that you finally made your move, it's time to work on closing the deal."

"I fucked up, Aid. I should have handled things differently. I never should have taken her home and—"

Keenan walked into the kitchen. "Let's work out a plan."

"Guys, I don't think—" Declan tried, but his cousins were like dogs without a bone.

"I hate seeing you this way, Dec," Keenan said as he accepted a beer from Aiden.

"Blondie's asleep?" Aiden said, and Keenan nodded.

"And I hate seeing *you* the way you are, Keen. You need to let us help you more with Blondie," Aiden said while closing the fridge again.

Keenan scratched his beard. "Aid... I'm doing the best I can. Evangeline—"

"And that's another thing. I hate seeing you still pining over her arse!" Aiden said while pointing his beer at his brother.

"It's because you've never been in love," Keenan said. "Once you've been there, you'll know. Until then, shut the fuck up."

"Guys..." Declan tried to stop the brothers from saying things they would regret later. He stepped closer to Aiden and placed a hand on his shoulder to stop him. But Aiden was on a roll now. A vein in his neck bulged as he clanged his bottle on the kitchen counter.

"She left you. And left that beautiful angel boy upstairs. He was only three years old," Aiden's voice hardened.

"I was there, Aid. You don't need to point it out every two weeks," Keenan bristled and widened his stance. Declan placed a hand on Keenan's chest. He wanted to remind Keenan he was there in case he'd forgotten and wanted to knock his brother on his arse.

"What kind of mom does that? He still cries about her in his sleep. I can never forgive her." Aiden let his words trail and wiped at the corner of his eye.

"Luckily, you're not a factor in this," Keenan said, his nostrils flaring as he tried to calm himself down by taking a deep breath.

"This isn't helping any of us," Declan said. "Keenan and Tommy are on their own now, and Keenan, you're doing a damn fine job at being a single dad." He slapped Keenan on his back. Keenan cleared his throat and looked down at the kitchen tiles in front of his feet.

"Evangeline is gone," Declan told Aiden. "She left and is probably never coming back. Aid, you know it's still painful. Not only for that sweet little boy upstairs in his dinosaur pajama's, but also for your brother. You don't need to be a dick about it, okay?"

"Okay. Sorry," Aiden held out his knuckles for Keenan. As their knuckles touched, Declan let out a sigh of relief. "Okay," he said, reluctantly. "Let's talk about a plan for me to work things out with Bree."

10

BREE

Bree jumped when the hot-blooded Arab kicked his long leg against his stable door. Fianna had just taken him out and guided the glossy brown animal with her hand on his rope halter. "Easy," Fianna said as she placed a hand on Bree's arm.

"If you make sudden moves, you'll scare him."

"I know. He just took me by surprise. I guess I was daydreaming."

"Hmm." Fianna pursed her lips.

Northstar clip clopped his hooves next to Fianna, echoing throughout the stable. Bree appreciated this regal beauty even more when Fi let it gallop into one of the enclosed fields at the Moore ranch.

Fianna watched her horse run after two other horses and smiled. She shifted her stance and her smile fell the moment her eyes found Bree's.

"Are you not even going to tell me what's been on your mind?"

"What?" Bree feigned to be clueless, but the fiery Ryan sister was back in Austin and wouldn't stand for being left in the dark any longer.

"Daydreaming, eh? Thinking about that yummy co-worker of yours?"

Fianna and Bree turned at the sound of Gwenn snorting behind them.

"What did I miss?" Fianna tilted her head to the side and narrowed her emerald eyes at Bree. "I'm always the last one to know... What haven't you told me?"

"It's nothing, sis."

Fianna didn't seem to believe Bree'd dismissal as she huffed and walked away into the field. Her sister stuck out against the greens with her bright red, long hair. Bree held up her hand when Gwenn opened her mouth.

"Before you say anything, you know how she gets about the Mills guys. She'll go on and on about how it's stupid that I'm still in love with Dec. I'm sorry, but not today...."

Bree placed a booted foot on a low wooden board and leaned her under arms over the top wooden board that made up for a makeshift fence.

She gazed around the Moore ranch. Bree waved at Declan's cousin Emmy, who sat a hundred feet away on her knees, planting something in her fall vegetable garden. She waved a dirt-covered hand back at Bree.

After months of scorching hot Texas weather, October offered cool nights and bearable days. Bree loved coming to the Moore ranch when they were kids. She didn't have a feel for horse riding, but loved to groom the horses. Whenever Bree was on the ranch, Emmy would take her under her wing to help farm the land.

"Well now, isn't that Gwenn Ryan standing on my land?"

The Ryan sisters looked over at a bundle of gray hair that sneaked up on them from behind. Before Gwenn could react, Shauni Mills-Moore had already taken her in for a bear hug. With a strong and weathered arm, Shauni engulfed Bree's shoulder to tug her into a three-way-hug.

"Shauni!" Gwenn said.

"I'm so glad you're safe and sound. We've missed you," Shauni said. And in a whisper she added, "Thank you for your service, darlin'."

Gwenn nodded and cleared her throat before she settled her gaze at something in the distance.

"I was so upset when we couldn't make it to your welcome home party! But unfortunately these farm animals give birth at the most unlucky times."

"It's okay, Shauni. I came to see you instead." Gwenn shrugged.

"And I'm so glad you did." Shauni turned her attention to Bree.

"Hey, darlin'. It's been so long since I've seen you." Pops' daughter Shauni gave Bree a kiss on top of her hair. "I'm so glad your sisters are back. Does this mean we'll be seeing more of you now too?"

Bree's cheeks flushed. It hadn't been her intention to stop coming over at the ranch. It was just that she knew how close Declan was with his Mills and Moore cousins, and she'd tried to avoid him after last March.

"I heard what happened, darlin'." Shauni gave Bree an understanding smile while she squeezed her hand in hers. "But from now on, you keep comin' back here to see me, okay? I've missed our talks."

Tears pricked Bree's eyes at the warm welcome of Declan's aunt. Bree was disappointed in herself for staying away so long.

"I've missed you too, Shauni."

"Good." Shauni turned them all around and walked in the house's direction with her arms over Bree and Gwenn's shoulders. Shauni had inherited Pops's physique, and she often made remarks about her size. She said there was simply more of her to love.

"Come to the house when you're done, Fianna," Shauni

called over her shoulder.

"I will," Fianna said.

"Let's give your sister some time with Northstar. I've got some pumpkin pie in the oven with your names on it."

"Hmm, there's not even smoke coming out of the house," Gwenn joked and stuck her tongue out to Shauni. Her straight, gray hair swished before Shauni's dark blue eyes when she turned her head to Gwenn.

She smirked and winked. "Oh, I see you haven't lost your sense of humor in the desert."

Bree smiled at the memory of the Mills brothers trying to sneak some of Shauni's food from their plates into napkins to feed the farm animals with later. Shauni's husband Roger often joked the pigs wouldn't be nearly as fat without Shauni's cooking.

With a chef-cook for a daughter, the entire family had been happy when Emmy volunteered to cook instead.

"We saw Emmy in her vegetable garden. How was the latest harvest?" Gwenn asked.

"It could have been better, I'm afraid. Emmy started working at Lucky and I told her I would take care of her garden. But you girls know the only thing I know about food is how to put it in my mouth. Not how to grow it and certainly not how to cook it." Shauni laughed the loudest.

They walked over to the ranch house with a wraparound porch. Shauni's dog Rudy came barreling down the porch. The mixed breed sniffed at Bree's outstretched hand and jumped with both paws against Bree's upper thigh.

"Sit, Rudy."

Bree passed the dog that instantly sat down at the command. Bree took a few steps to the man who'd called off the dog. Too bad she couldn't be attracted to Ryan Moore.

Ryan is the oldest child of Shauni and Roger, and their only son. Growing up in a household with five younger sisters made

Ryan even sexier in Bree's book. How protective he was of his sisters was a total turn-on. She cocked her head to the side and inspected Ryan some more.

Although he was tall, dark and very handsome, she didn't get that tingle she got from looking at Declan. He opened his arms and pulled Gwenn in for a hug. "Good to see ya again so soon. Your party was so much fun."

Gwenn hugged the big guy back and said, "It was fun. I hope you could get up the next morning?"

Bree's sister stepped out of Ryan's embrace, and he took Bree in for a quick hug. All the Moore cousins got the hug-bug from their mother Shauni.

"You know how our roosters cock-a-doodle-doo, darlin'. A party or not, Ryan still gets his butt in gear in the mornin'." Shauni smiled at her son before she entered the side entry of the house that lead directly into the kitchen.

Shauni kicked off her boots, leaving them next to the door. Bree followed her lead and almost tripped over Rudy when the dog came running back into the house.

"Rudy, out."

Shauni never looked over her shoulder to check if the dog obeyed. She stepped over to the oven and mumbled something under her breath about getting here just in time.

"Mom, have you seen my phone? I can't find it anywhere."

"Tara Moore, your phone is there where you left it." Shauni didn't make a move to help her daughter. Bree grinned. Tara always lost sight of her stuff and then asked others to help her find it.

Shauni opened the oven door and placed the tray with the pumpkin pie on her kitchen counter. Tara said nothing to her mother's wisecrack. Instead, she rolled her eyes at her mother's back and shook her head. "Emmy said to leave the pie in the oven."

"Well, Emmy's not here to keep an eye out. So I'm checkin'

the pie."

Tara walked over to her mother and leaned in. "See. The filling is cracking already."

Shauni narrowed her eyes at the offending pie before her. "Why does this always happen to me?"

"Because you don't follow instructions, Mom. You never listen." Tara had the decency to hide her smile behind her fist.

"Cracked or not, we're eatin' this pie." Shauni slid the pie on a plate and placed it on the kitchen table where Gwenn and Bree already took a seat. "I see you all later," Ryan said while turning back around for the kitchen door.

"You don't want to take a piece with you?" Shauni started slicing the pie that not only cracked, the bottom also appeared undercooked. Shauni cleared her throat the moment the soggy filling seemed soupier than anything else.

"Right. Well, you don't know what you're missin', son."

"I'll take my chances." Ryan winked at Bree and then stepped out.

"Damn ungrateful. Like he could bake a pie." Shauni and Tara locked eyes over the kitchen table and bust out laughing.

"If it has nothing to do with horses, count him out," Tara said and then hugged her mother.

"I'm going to look for my phone upstairs. I have to go in five minutes if I don't want to be late. Good to have you back, Gwenn. You too, Bree."

"Thanks," Bree and Gwenn simultaneously said.

"Take my car, Tara. I don't want you drivin' to that part of town in a car that's about to fall apart if you so much as fart inside."

Bree and Gwenn laughed while Tara groaned. With her blonde hair parted in two braids, she almost appeared sweet. "Mom, you're so embarrassing." Tara walked out of the kitchen.

"It's a gift that keeps on givin', darlin'." Shauni smirked and winked at Bree and her sister.

"They grow up so fast. Tara is an apprentice at a tattoo parlor, did you know?" Shauni licked a piece of pumpkin slosh from her thumb.

Bree nodded as she'd heard it from Tara's sister Emmy a few months ago. With her own chest tatted up with angel wings and a big heart with a 'Freedom' banner, Tara would fit right in at a tattoo parlor.

Tara walked back into the kitchen with her phone clutched to her chest. She personalized the phone case with the same image of her heart tattoo.

"So cool that you're working in a tattoo parlor, Tara."

"Thanks, Gwenn. If you'd like one for free, I can practice on you."

"No, thanks."

"Maybe you should see one of my pieces before you—"

"Nah, I'm good." Gwenn put her foot down, and nobody was going to change her mind. "But if I would ever let someone paint my body, it would be you, Tara."

"Okay, it's a deal." The teal eyes of Tara sparkled with mischief, like she already imagined a piece for Gwenn.

Tara kissed her mother's cheek and waved the Ryan sisters goodbye.

Shauni took a bite from her pie and winced. She kept on chewing and chewing and waved her hand at Bree for her to fill the glass in front of her with water. Bree handed the newly filled glass over and Shauni swallowed her food down.

"Okay, probably best to only eat the upper crust, girls."

Gwenn gave Bree a look while she hesitantly forked a piece.

"So, Bree. Tell me about Declan. What's going on between you two? My dad said you two are not even speaking?"

Bree's face heated, and she quickly eyed her piece of pie in front of her, in the hopes Shauni couldn't read her. They'd done so much more than speaking a few nights ago. Bree startled when Shauni placed her hand on top of Bree's hand.

"It's okay if you don't want to talk about it, darlin'."

"No, it's fine. Gwenn knows everything."

Gwenn murmured with her mouth full, "Yep. It's MIND-blowing..."

Bree groaned at Gwenn's reference to Bree's remark about having MIND-blowing sex with Shauni's nephew. Talking about sex in front of Shauni didn't sit right with Bree.

Shauni and Bree grew close over the years. The warmth of Shauni had been exactly what she'd missed at home. Bree could talk about her hopes and dreams without the need to defend herself for wanting to become a Kindergarten teacher. Something her mother didn't approve of.

"Shauni.... It's complicated."

Shauni took another piece of pie in her mouth and waved at Bree to carry on.

"We.... Uhm... I dated a colleague last Friday and the next day.... Declan decided he wanted me. He said he couldn't stand me moving on with someone else."

Gwenn clanked her fork at her plate. "He said 'thinking about you with another man made him crazy.' Don't know why that's so bad? You're being difficult and looking for faults. Just when you two finally can be together, you're pulling away from him. Life's too short, sis. This is exhausting."

Shauni eyed the Ryan sisters sitting at her kitchen table. She picked up her napkin and wiped at the corner of her mouth. "I agree with Gwenn; life's too short. But Bree being difficult? That's news to me. Now I haven't seen you in a while, so maybe things have changed..." Shauni smiled and reassured Bree she didn't think she was looking for faults in her nephew.

"She's been in love with Dec for ages. And I mean *ages*..." Gwenn said while fisting her straight brown hair to put it in a ponytail.

"I mean, sure. His timing is off. But come on. What else do you need him to do? Sign an agreement that—"

Bree leaned in across the table with her palms flat on the table. "What I need is to be able to trust him. To know that his intentions are true. I need him to love me like I love him!" Bree almost shouted the last words at her sister.

She closed her eyes and winced at her pounding head. A warm hand patted her arm. "Shh, it's okay, Bree."

Bree opened her eyes and returned Shauni's smile with a watery smile of her own.

"Sorry. Didn't mean to shout in your home."

Shauni busted out laughing and slapped the table with her palm like it was the funniest thing she'd heard in a long time.

"Darlin', the day nobody shouts in my home is yet to come. You know my kids, right? And if they're silent for once, Pops shows up and makes a ruckus."

Gwenn laughed , and Bree giggled along. She wiped an escaped tear away. All the pent up frustration came out now. Just Bree's luck that it happened at Shauni's kitchen table.

"Shauni, can you please tell me what to do? I'm stuck. I love Dec. I... I've always loved him. But he hurt me so bad when he said he didn't love me. My heart turned into stone after that night. The moments we saw each other, he seemed happy while I was withering away. Now suddenly, he wants to have his best friend back. He came over *once* in all of those months, and that was after having a bad date. I can't have him toying with my emotions...."

"Darlin', if it were up to me, I would drag you with me into Tara's rattling junk of a car and drop you off at Dec's immediately. But life doesn't work that way, honey. You need to know in your heart that you're Declan's choice. That he loves you for you and nothing else. Not because he misses a friend, or he hates the idea of you being with someone else. And quite frankly... I'm proud of you, darlin'."

Shauni held up a hand when Gwenn shifted in her seat, probably to give her opinion. "I know, Gwenn. We both know my nephew is head over heels. I see it as clear as you do. But what's important here is that Dec has his work cut out for him to get Bree to see and feel it. Dec has this thing that he always wants to do the right thing. But in this case, he messed up because of it."

"Thanks, Shauni."

Hearing from Dec's aunt he loved her felt good. Bree suddenly stood from her seat and hugged Shauni, who gave Bree a playful swat for causing the surprise.

"I want to get one last thing off my chest, if you'd let me."

Bree stood still in Shauni's arms. The dark blue eyes of Shauni misted over and she cleared her throat. "I heard your mother hasn't been around much lately, but I want you to know that you can always come to me."

She looked over Bree's shoulder and nodded at Gwenn. "All of you, Ryan girls. I respect Joan, because I know your mother didn't have it easy on her own. But deep down, Bree," Shauni looked Bree straight into her eyes again, "I know all your doubts are coming from something deep inside of you. Something that happened a long time ago to your family that has made you girls the way you are."

Of course, Shauni knew about Bree's father walking out on them when Bree had been only eight years old. Bree could have argued with Shauni that her past or her mother had nothing to do with Bree being so hesitant to trust Declan. But they would both know that would be a lie.

Shauni nodded. "I know we can't change the past. But you are in charge of your future, girls. Think about how you see yourself in twenty years from now. And if things need to change to reach that goal; go for it."

Bree hugged Shauni once more and held on even stronger. Bree wanted to be with Declan. It has always been him. But could she give him another chance while he held her fragile heart in his hands?

11

DECLAN

"Come on, man. You'll have to do better than that!" Ronan said before he put his black mouth guard back into his mouth.

"Fuck you," Declan said, and he turned his back on his brother. Declan walked over to his gym bag and threw his mouth guard inside. He slowly unwrapped the tape from his knuckles.

"If you can't stand the heat..." Ro bounced on his feet and added, "Come on, brothers. Who's next?"

It was Monday night, and he'd been at Duncan's dojo for their traditional Mills brothers fight night. Only his brother Donovan was at home with his Kate. They had just been together for a few weeks now, and Declan guessed it would take another more weeks for his brother to come up for air.

Luckily his brother Duncan, the former MMA-fighter and champion, got in between the ropes and took Declan's spot. Duncan matched Ro's physique the most out of all Mills brothers. And as his coach, Duncan could still give Ronan an ass whooping.

"Go knock him on his arse, Dunc," Declan said.

Declan acted like a moody bastard ever since Bree crept out

of his home. He couldn't talk with his brothers about it. Bree wanted to keep things a secret. Like she was ashamed of their night together. Ashamed of him.

He looked over at Duncan, who grunted and shifted his weight backward onto his rear leg. With his leading leg, he reacted to an incoming blow from Ro, who gave Dunc a round kick.

Declan wanted to cheer Duncan on, but the sound of an incoming text distracted him. His already rapidly beating heart pounded even harder against his chest.

He rummaged around his gym bag for his phone.

BREE: Want to come over?

Four words.

And it made all the difference in the world.

"I'm outta here." That's all he said before he speed walked to the dressing room. He made quick work of showering and got dressed. He passed his brothers on his way to the exit.

"Where ye going?" Ronan said with a busted lip. Declan smiled at Duncan's work. Served Ro's arrogant arse right.

"Home. See you later."

Giving Bree some time had been the right thing to do. He'd talked about a game plan with Keenan and Aiden. But after an entire night discussing every angle to work on Bree, he gave her some more time to work things out in her head.

On his way to his truck, he texted Bree.

DECLAN: Hi. Was at the dojo. Stepping into my truck now. Be there in ten.

He rang Bree's doorbell and took a deep breath through his nose. He exhaled slowly and counted to ten in his head. The weight of this moment suddenly dawned on him. She wanted to see him. At her place. Alone.

Bree's door cracked and his eyes instantly found Bree's. She blushed and opened the door further.

"Hi," she softly said.

Declan stepped inside and locked the door behind him. When he turned, he immediately pulled Bree into a hug. Stiff at first, she sighed and then relaxed in his arms.

"So glad you texted me."

"Me too," she whispered.

He leaned in and brushed her lips with his. Just a peck on the lips. But she'd let him, and this first step gave him hope.

She walked out of his arms and said over her shoulder, "I've got a new horror series waiting on us. Hope you haven't seen it."

He couldn't care less if he'd had. He was here, and that's all that mattered. He took a seat next to Bree on her sofa. He glanced at the television and said, "Haven't seen this one. Heard it was real bad."

Bree giggled. "I know. But it's one of the few things we haven't already seen together." Bree grabbed the remote and started the first episode. She'd already filled a bowl with popcorn and two glasses with soda.

Bree settled her back against the sofa, and Declan placed her throw blanket over their laps. She pulled at her end.

"I see you haven't changed a bit. You're still hoarding the blanket." Declan grinned when Bree attempted to act outraged by his accusation.

"You're the one who keeps wiggling and pulling. I'm just sitting still." She gave her next tug some grit, and he laughed.

They'd settled in on her sofa like the past eight months didn't happen. Although it wasn't quite the same. No. He was so much more aware of her thigh brushing against his when she leaned forward to grab her glass.

He was also very aware of Bree wearing a dress. It would have been so easy to slide his hand under the blanket and under her dress. Feel her up like a teenager.

He closed his eyes and waited for the urge to kiss her stupid to pass. He knew she wanted to take things slow, and he really wanted to follow her lead.

But after she'd set her drink back on the coffee table, he tugged her into his chest with his hand over her shoulder. He smelled her hair and welcomed the clean smell of coconut. Bree snuggled close and placed her hand on his abdomen.

"Why scream while you run up to kill him? Now he knows she's behind him."

Declan smiled. "It's because he has to survive so he can kill off her friends, duh."

"It's stupid," Bree said.

"This entire series is stupid."

He laughed when she leaned from his chest and narrowed her eyes at him. "Are you complaining about my choice? You pick something next time. Let's see if you can do better."

Next time.

Bree was thinking about next time.

"Why do you have that goofy smile on your face?"

"Because you make me smile, Bree. You always have."

Her face turned red and he reluctantly let her go when she sat up straight again and eyed him warily.

"It's true. You make me happy."

Bree finally nodded and said, "Ditto."

He palmed her cheeks and leaned in. Their noses almost brushed.

"I've missed you. And not only as a friend."

Bree bit her bottom lip, and he fought the urge to run his thumb over her plump lip.

"Let's do this, Bree. I know I've been a stupid fuck. But I'm ready now." His throat went dry while waiting on her response. This was it.

Bree sighed and let go of her lip. "I want to try, Dec. I really do. It's why I texted you tonight. But we need to go slow. I'm still scared that in a few months from now, you'll change your mind."

He cocked his head and furrowed his brows. "Why would I do that?"

"Because it took you this long... I don't know why you're suddenly interested now."

The wobble in her voice stabbed his heart. He'd caused her pain by rejecting her earlier. He needed to earn back her trust. How he would do that, he didn't know just yet. But he'd get there.

"I know we need to take this slow. But I promise you; you're it for me, Bree. I'll never let anything come between us ever again."

Bree nodded and said, "I'm going to refill our drinks. Can you hit pause?"

"Sure."

As he locked his eyes on her fine swaying arse, it hit him she hadn't respond to his last words. He walked into the kitchen and took his time checking Bree out. Hmmm, her curves were only getting better and better. Seeing her large tits sway in her black dress as she reached for a cabinet made him adjust his pants.

Bree caught his movement and giggled. "That's a first."

His upper lip tugged up, "Nah, it's only the first time I've let you caught me."

Her eyes went wide, and she swiftly turned and pulled the fridge open.

He took the soda out of her hand, and she closed the door. He placed the drink on the counter and took her hand in his. He brought her open palm against his erection.

"This... you feel this?"

Bree swallowed and nodded. Her wide azure eyes locked on his.

"Only because of you. I feel like a damn teenager again."

She squeezed him, and he groaned.

"Remember that summer when your mom was a week away for a new job? And you stayed over at our house with Gwenn and Fi? I jerked myself almost raw during that summer. You were sunbathing in our backyard in those skimpy bikini's every day."

She giggled. "I remember that... I did that on purpose."

He closed his eyes and took a deep breath through his nose, while she held a tight grip of his hard length.

"Damn, you were so hot. And my hormones were raging back then. I was fighting so hard to keep my distance. I was so confused. You were my best friend and all my fantasies were about how I would fuck you in that damn red bikini."

Bree opened his jeans and slipped her hand inside his boxer briefs. His breath caught when her chilly hand, from holding the drinks, surrounded his warm flesh. Goosebumps traveled his spine. She tugged playfully at first, but when he pushed his hips, she moved her hand up and down.

He helped Bree when he pushed his jeans and boxer briefs from his hips. She took him out and kept a steady rhythm of pumping.

"Tell me more..." she whispered.

"I never stopped lusting over you. It's always been you... Aaah, I'm almost there..." His toes curled in his shoes. He couldn't believe they were standing in Bree's kitchen and she was about to give him one of the most intense orgasms of his life. Again.

"And now we're here. And you're more beautiful than ever.... aaaaargh!"

He held himself up by placing a hand on the counter. He almost buckled while shooting out his release over Bree's hand.

"That was so hot," she smiled like she knew exactly how she'd just blown his mind.

"You're the one that's hot, Bree." He kissed her nose. He tugged himself back in.

She walked over to the faucet and washed her hands with soap.

"Nah, just sticky." She watched him over her shoulder and laughed.

He caged her in from behind while she washed her hands.

He rested his chin on her shoulder and whispered. "I can't believe I just came like some sixteen-year-old. It only took a few jerks."

Bree swayed her arse against his front. His flaccid cock got her message loud and clear, and turned half-mast in a heartbeat.

He kissed her behind her ear, and she turned off the faucet. Bree gripped the counter and leaned her head back against his shoulder. He had several options to go from here, taking this into the bedroom was one option. But he smirked because the opportunity presented to him was just too good to be true.

He positioned Bree so he could kiss the side of her throat.

With his arm completely extended, he took the pullout kitchen faucet. After taking aim, he yanked the tap to cover the front of his girl with water.

"Aaaah! I can't believe you!"

Bree tried to wriggle free from his firm hold while her signature hearty laugh traveled through the kitchen. "Don't tell me this is payback for the time I tripped you into the kiddy pool, ages ago?"

"Yep."

She giggled while she tried another halfhearted attempt to break free. "I can't believe your level of pettiness."

He busted out laughing. "I know."

Only with Bree, he acted like a fool. Never at work. Not around his arsehole twin, who needed Declan to guide him to the straight and narrow. It had been too damn long since he'd acted this carefree.

Bree got a hold of the tap and shut down the spray. She turned around and his eyes zeroed in on her heaving chest. The wet material of her dress clung to her heavy breasts, and he instantly knelt down in front of her.

He sucked the damp material with her hard peak underneath into his mouth.

"Ooh, Dec."

Bree wobbled at first but steadied herself with one hand upon his shoulder and the other at the back of his head, holding him close to her breast. He made work of her top button and leaned back.

He just then noticed the buttons went all the way down to the hem of her dress. He eyed his handy work while unbuttoning one after the other.

He revealed a black lacy bra and tugged the cup down. His tongue swirled over her nipple and when he nibbled the peak, Bree fisted his hair. He watched Bree as she closed her eyes, fully enjoying the sensation. He kissed her nipple before he let go.

Water droplets followed his hands downwards. He caught a droplet on its path over her belly button with his tongue and she giggled. It brought him out of his daze and he looked up to see Bree smiling down at him.

He stood from the kitchen floor and grabbed Bree behind the back of her thighs. She let out a squeal and crossed her arms around his neck. "What are you doing?"

"I'm taking you to bed. Fuck that horrible TV-show. Forget about the mess we made in the kitchen. I'll take care of it. But first, let me take care of you."

Her one-bedroom apartment was a labyrinth, with furniture standing in his way as he walked them over to her bedroom. Something unrelenting connected with his shin, and he grabbed a stronger hold of Bree.

"Ouch! Damn table."

She giggled against his lips.

"Almost there," she whispered.

When he finally laid her down in the middle of her bed, his eyes grew wide when she hurried out of her dress. She made work of her bra and shimmied out of her boy shorts. Giving a full view of her shaved pussy lips.

"Hot damn."

He would never get enough of the sight of her lying naked, seducing him with her curves to make his move.

He rid himself from his shirt and jeans and picked up the condom he'd put earlier in his back pocket. Bree hoisted herself higher upon the matrass. Giving him more room to work with.

She looked up at him under those long lashes, suddenly trying to read him. Gauge him.

As he entered her, she whispered against his ear, "I promised myself to never get caught up with you again,"

He stopped moving. "Why would you promise yourself something like that?"

"You scare me, Dec."

He jerked back his head and gazed into her misty eyes. "You know me, Bree. I'm still me. Even after everything that happened between us."

She nodded, but seemed still unsure.

"If you want me to stop, say it," he said. He sure hoped she wouldn't stop him now, his painfully hard dick held still inside of her on his last will power.

"I was so angry with you," Bree said. Her frolic mood from just moments ago evaporated.

"Are you still angry with me?" He couldn't believe they were finally having this long overdue conversation while he had his dick inside of her.

Bree shook her head while she closed her eyes. He kissed her nose, and she sighed.

"I just... need to take things slow."

"*Now* you're telling me?" He made a show out of looking down at the spot between them, where they connected. He arched his brow and smirked. Her entire body shook beneath him as she laughed.

"No, I don't want you to stop. But... Let's keep this to ourselves—just for a little while. I don't want to ruin what we have with everyone butting in."

He could see where she was coming from. But he didn't want to be anyone's dirty little secret. It just wasn't his style to sneak around. He always stood for his actions.

"Okay. I'll give you two weeks. And then I'm making you mine. Officially, because I already think of you as mine."

She clamped down on him, and he groaned. "Oh, you like that idea, eh?"

He moaned as she crossed her ankles behind his back, pulling him further in.

"Tell me," he whispered against her throat before he nipped her.

"Ooh, Dec..."

"Tell me you're mine, Bree..." He moved in and out of her with a leisurely pace. Enjoying the thrusts and pulls. He took the time to reward himself with every sigh and moan he coaxed from Bree. Every shudder she offered as he fingered her bundle of nerves.

He picked up his pace and bottomed out.

Bree bucked and thrashed as she came for him.

"Yes!"

Whether she'd agreed to be his or if it had been her orgasm talking, he took it. He was a patient man. Two weeks was nothing when it meant he could have Bree for the rest of their lives.

12

BREE

"I feel your chest shaking with laughter, you know. You can't hide it." Bree fake grumbled.

She pulled her head from her clasped hands on top of Dec's chest. Declan turned his smiling face away, and she inwardly sighed. Joking around with Declan in bed was everything she'd ever wanted.

How long had she been lusting over him, anyway? All those casual late night calls that ended up in Bree taking care of her sexual frustration in her bathroom after hanging up with Dec. She finally had the real deal beneath her. Hmm. The realization gave her flutters.

She leaned in and gave his bare chest an open-mouthed kiss. She got on her knees in between his parted legs and worked her way down. She traced a path down to his dusky trail of hair with her tongue.

Having slept naked together in each other's arms proved very useful in the morning. She grinned when his dick twitched the moment she blew on the head.

Playing with Dec was fun. It always had been fun between them. He didn't show his goofy side to just anyone.

Bree had to work really hard to coax that first smile from of him when they were kids. She'd wanted to make the sad boy next door smile, and she didn't stop nagging him with silly jokes until he cracked. But nowadays, she knew exactly which buttons to push.

Although, having fun in the bedroom was an entirely fresh setting. Finally, she could enjoy all of him.

She kissed the head of his hard length, and he groaned. He fisted her long curls with both hands into a ponytail. She looked over at his closed eyes and realized her teasing had been almost painful for him. His flushed cheeks made Bree smile.

She licked her lips and said, "Mmm."

She took him into her hot mouth and Dec's grip on her hair fastened.

"Oh, shit. I... oh shit..." he said.

She sucked at the tip and then swirled her tongue around him.

"Oh, yes. Just like that. Fuck."

He bucked once, almost gagging her. That had been the exact reason she hadn't tried this before. He quickly held still. "Sorry. It's so good. I try to keep still, baby."

She hummed around him, and he moaned again. The vibrations were probably too much. She pulled him out of her mouth and licked from the base to the tip. She glanced up at him and his eyes blazed with fire. "Fuck. I don't even want to know how or who..." He closed his eyes and shook his head before letting it fall back onto his pillow.

"Just you. Only you." She whispered, and she felt him getting even harder underneath her fingers.

"Fuuuck...."

She leaned in to pull him into her mouth again, when he suddenly hoisted her up by her armpits.

"Dec!"

"I want you riding me, Bree. Have your tits sway in my face."

She giggled. She was sure he had an obsession with her breasts. She'd woken up with a hand between her legs and one engulfing her breast.

He placed her so; she could easily guide him inside of her. The way he pierced her, stretched her, was almost painful. She bit her lip and tentatively lowered herself a few inches more.

Declan took both breasts into his hands and pushed them together. He rolled her nipples between his thumb and index finger. Bree got wetter by the second. "Yes, Dec."

"You like that? Like me playing with your nipples?"

He said in a low voice and when she locked eyes with him, their connection made her clamp down on him.

"Fuck, yeah." He bucked up and couldn't go any deeper.

A fine sheen of sweat covered Bree's back by the time she rode him. His hips shot off the bed at the same moment Bree came down—hard.

"Yes!"

Over and over again, he kept pumping his hips up. He held her down against him, and she stared between their bodies, watching him push and pull.

"I'm so close…"

"I know, Love. I can feel it. Come for me."

She leaned her upper body over his and kissed him. Her heart lay on top of his, beating its own erratic drum. He palmed her cheeks, and they stared in each other's eyes. His hot breath touched her lips after they broke free from their kiss.

"I'm coming…." She moaned. Goosebumps traveled her skin and her head felt light. She raced him to orgasm. His hands fell down and grabbed her hips again.

"Yes…" Declan groaned his release.

His thrusts slowed down and Bree came down from her high.

He kissed her nose, and she smiled.

"Wow." They both said.

Bree giggled and Dec almost slipped from inside her.

"I'm going to the bathroom."

He let go of her hips and gave her butt a playful slap when she got out of the bed. She smiled over her shoulder and her heart skipped a beat at the sight of him.

Like a male model, he laid in her bed with his arm behind his head. She took her fill of his mussed raven hair, his strong pecs and hard abs. When she trailed her eyes back up to his gray eyes, he winked at her. She shook her head, smiling and closed the bathroom door so she could clean herself up.

"Shall I make us some breakfast?" He called out from the bedroom.

"Sure. What time is it?" She turned to her mirror and smiled at her reflection. Messy hair and pink cheeks. Waking up with Dec did wonders for her complexion.

"Almost seven. Shall I drop you off at work?"

Bree cracked the bathroom door and found Declan smirking at her.

"Why are you so shy? Let me see your beautiful body, Bree."

Her heart rate picked up, and she almost caved. But then she remembered the time. "Shit. I need to hurry. It's my turn to pick up Kate today."

She turned and jumped into her shower stall. She waited for the water to warm and made quick work of showering. She'd left her hair dry. No time.

When she walked back into her bedroom, she spotted her phone lighting up with a message.

GWENN: And?

Her sister had urged Bree to reach out to Dec last night since she was staying the night at Cait's apartment. Bree smiled and shot Gwenn a quick text.

BREE: You should consider a new profession ;-)

Bree laughed when her sister immediately replied.

GWENN: Dentist?

She let out a snort giggle.

BREE: Eh, I was thinking of matchmaker... Why dentist?

GWENN: Because it's like pulling teeth with you. Did he come over last night or not?

Bree put on her underwear and pulled on one of her favorite dresses. She picked up her phone again and replied,

BREE: Yes. And I'll tell you all about it tonight. LY.

GWENN: FINALLY

GWENN: LY

The aroma of omelets wafted into the bedroom. She'd always been happy with her snug apartment, but at times like this, she hated how everything was so compact. Every cooked meal dominated her entire place. She walked out on her black pumps and turned her back to Declan behind the kitchen counter.

"Can you zip me up?" She brought her hair down over one shoulder and glanced over the other at Declan.

"Sure." He placed a hand on her hip and she felt her dress tightening where the zipper of her moss green dress went up.

"It's good to have me around, eh?" She heard the smile in his voice.

She nodded. "Yes. I can never reach this one properly."

The zipper got stuck, and he brought the zipper down a bit before pulling it back up.

"I hope you never wear this one to work then," he chuckled.

"Normally, I'd ask Gwenn. Or before that, I'd ask someone at work for help." Bree shrugged. He froze for a moment.

"Not that guy, I hope."

Bree bit her lip. Maybe she shouldn't enjoy his jealousy as much as she did. But it felt good to have the tables turned for once. She said, "Oh, yes. Almost every other week."

He gave her zipper a brisk tug, and the motion unbalanced

her. She gripped the counter and did her best to keep from laughing.

"Last week, I asked him to fasten my bra. I was on the playground and my bra hook suddenly broke. Poof!" She emphasized with her hands mimicking a bomb explosion.

He turned her around by her shoulders and she said through her giggles, "And the week before, I had these stockings…"

Declan's scowl made room for a smirk when it dawned she was messing with him. "That's so, eh?"

Bree nodded. He cocked his head and studied her. His ocean gray eyes seemed darker somehow. "It's ridiculous how much I want to punch that guy in the face."

"No need. He's sweet but—"

"Sweet?" He let go of her shoulders and she immediately missed his warm hands on her body. Bree blinked a couple times.

"Are you serious? Come, give me a kiss." She stepped closer and placed a hand on his cheek.

He held his lips stiff against hers. She pinched his side to snap him out of his stupid mood. "Ouch!"

He furrowed his brows, and she had to work hard not to laugh at his boyish look.

"I remember you double dating some bimbo, you know. If we do this, we'd better forget the past. I used to have a Susanna in my class… I hated the little girl at first sight. Just because you dated a Susanna ages ago."

Declan chuckled and shook his head. "Poor girl."

"It's irrational. I know," she said.

He pulled her in his arms, and he sniffed her hair.

"I'll try to forget about him. I'm sorry. I didn't mean to go all caveman on you."

One hand went to the nape and goosebumps traveled her skin.

She rested her head on his chest and closed her eyes.
"It's okay. It's all a bit new."
His other hand trailed down to her butt, and he squeezed.
"I can't wait to tell everyone you're mine."
"Hello.... caveman much?"

13

DECLAN

After calling in with dispatch, Declan closed his door and walked up to Caitlin, who'd already exited the patrol car.

"Let's do this," she said.

They walked up to the second apartment building in a row of three. Their shift would end in half an hour and Dec couldn't wait to go home and shower. It's been a long day. A day where one call after the next came in.

Normally he'd liked the fast pace of his job. But he glanced over his shoulder to Cait, from the peaks of hair sticking out of her bun, to the bags under her eyes.

It seemed like his seven-year-older partner had enough of walking the beat. She'd been up for a promotion this year. But unfortunately, after killing Kayla's stalker, Cait hadn't been the same and someone else at the precinct earned her spot as a detective.

"I can't believe I promised my mother I would come over tonight." Cait said.

"Yeah, Bree told me about tonight."

Cait held her step and said, "Oh? You're talking to my sister again?"

At least that put a smile on her face. He nodded and said, "You'll have to ask your sister about that. Not my place to tell."

She rubbed her chin.

"Hmm. Okay. I'll do that."

Declan walked into the apartment building, close after a man that had used his key to open the central door.

"Can you point me the direction to the stairwell?"

The man narrowed his eyes at the two police officers walking into his building without first ringing the bell. He had no time to discuss ringing the bell first. They needed to check out the scene.

"Thank you." He took off into the direction the man pointed at.

They'd received a call about a commotion in the stairwell of this apartment building. The old woman that called it in said she heard strange noises coming from the stairs.

He opened the door to the stairwell and Cait followed him inside. They took several flights of stairs before he heard a man groaning. He held his hand on his hip where his gun rests.

"Aaaah," a low male voice said.

Taking two steps at a time, he walked into a sight so absurd; he needed to bit his lip to hold his laughter.

"Ma'am. Can you please unleash this man?" Cait asked the woman dressed from top to bottom in neon fire red leather. The naked middle-aged man sitting on his knees held his lips against the woman's pumps. He didn't stir.

Except for his manhood. The moment Cait raised her voice; Declan became painfully aware the man got aroused.

"Oh, this is rich." Cait said. She narrowed her eyes while looking at the man. "I don't even want to cuff you. That would only be a reward for you." Cait turned her back to walk down the stairs.

She said over her shoulder, "I'm getting some fresh air. I can't believe this shit."

"Cait. Wait. We have to—"

Bree's oldest sister whirled around and pointed her finger in the couple's direction that finally had the decency to blush.

"You're wasting everyone's time here. I can't believe it. You probably got off on the idea of people calling the cops on you. Well, fuck that. And fuck you."

Declan held up his hand before the woman in leather could respond. The man blinked a few times but held his head down. He clearly waited for permission from that woman to move his ugly, rumpled arse.

Declan nodded at the clothes lying next to them. "Put your stuff back on. And never do this shit again."

He left the couple without hearing their sorry ass excuses. He went outside to search for his partner. He was worried for Cait and not interested in writing the weird couple up for indecent exposure.

He found her at the park in front of the apartment building. Cait sat on the concrete bench with her head hanging down. She looked up when he sat down next to her.

"I've had enough. Every day, we put our lives on the line. And for what? I mean... I'm just so mad!"

Declan took a moment to let Cait rant.

"I know you're not doing this as long as I have, but come on, Dec. Aren't you sick and tired of it all?"

He stretched his legs and crossed his ankles. He looked up into the dark sky before he watched people walking in and out of the three apartment buildings. He could envision a background story for every person passing by.

The girl with a stack of books was probably studying for exams. The guy running around with the too tight spandex, hoped to get noticed by the woman stretching over there against a tree. People still fascinated him.

After years of walking the beat, people still surprised him. And as long as he could help people, he still found meaning in his work. All the other shit that happened on duty hadn't jaded him. Not yet.

But he got his criminal justice degree for a reason. He wanted to conduct investigations and knew the dynamics of his job would change if he'd got a promotion to be a detective.

"Sometimes, I just want to scream at them. Or punch their lights out."

He'd hoped she had calmed down by now, but since she was still so angry, he said, "When was the last time you talked to that guy?"

Cait had mandatory sessions with a professional at their precinct, ever since she killed Kayla's stalker. They all witnessed Cait's transformation from a devoted LEO to a colleague who could fly off the hook in a heartbeat. Not only at the notorious assholes at their precinct. Even Shelly, who worked the desk and asked Cait how her day went got an ear full.

Cait scoffed. "Yeah, right. I'm done talking. Apparently, I'm messed up in the head because of my dad walking out on us. Boehoe. Like I'm the only one raised by a single parent."

Declan turned in his seat. He had enough. "Exactly. Boe-fucking-hoe."

Cait righted her shoulders and narrowed her light blue eyes at him.

"You don't want to do this with me, Dec. I mean it."

"Well, just sayin'. Stop feeling so damn sorry for yourself. If you hate this job, go find yourself a new one. If you want to stay in this line of work, go work out your problems. Fix whatever needs to be fixed so I can have my partner back. Because this," he waved his hand between them, "Is exhausting."

She stared back at the apartment building they'd visited tonight. "Well, if it only were that easy..."

He leaned forward with his elbow on his thigh. "You're stuck, Cait. Whenever I see you outside of work, I see you smiling. I hear you joking around with my brothers and I miss that on the job. Last year, we would've cracked up if we'd found those idiots in the stairwell."

Cait chuckled as she probably envisioned those two again. She stabbed a tear from her cheek. "What a fuckin' disaster, those two. Can you imagine that? Only the thought of getting arrested got his little wiener up."

He laughed and bumped her with his shoulder.

She waved her fist in the air and extended her pinky. "That's what he's working with. Poor guy."

The moment their eyes met, they busted out laughing again.

After a few moments of comfortable silence, Cait asked, "So, you're talking to my sis again?"

"You can never let go of anything, eh? At least that's still the same."

Cait huffed. "Maybe."

She smirked and said, "But you're still bad at deflecting."

He shook his head and smiled.

"Yeah, okay. Talk with your sis. I'm going back to the car."

He stood from the bench and walked into the direction of their patrol car.

"Maybe it's time for a change."

Halting his steps, he watched Cait walking up next to him.

"A change?" He asked and arched his brow.

"Yeah, I mean. You and Bree are finally together. Maybe it's time for a change for me too. Maybe a change of scenery? You know, spice things up."

He followed her lead as she'd passed him. He said against her back, "Oh, you mean you want someone to take the stairs with."

She turned and walked backwards while smiling at him.

"I see what you did there, Dec. But I also noticed you didn't deny being with my sister."

He walked around the patrol car and stepped in. He buckled up and waited for Cait to do the same. He started the vehicle while Cait called them back in. After parking the car, they walked up to the station. He put his arm over Cait's shoulders.

"Good luck, tonight, Ryan."

As usual, she narrowed her light blue eyes at him for calling her by her last name.

He bumped his hip to her, and she knocked her fist against his bicep after she stepped out from under his arm.

"Sometimes I forget you were the pimpled boy next door to us. And that you know all about my family."

He chuckled. "Why else would I wish you good luck?"

14

BREE

Bree's mother droned on and on about how she found the perfect statue for her boss. Bree took a sip from her tea to hide her yawn. Declan had kept her up all night.

Bree squirmed her thighs together at the thought of bringing Declan to orgasm with her hand. She'd never been so bold in her life.

"What's up with you, Bree?"

Bree jerked her head in her mother's direction. Joan Ryan peered over her coffee and narrowed her eyes.

"You're acting different."

Before she could dismiss her mother's observation, her sister Fi added, "I know. You've got some color back on your cheeks. It's almost like you're no longer heartbroken."

"There's nothing to tell." Bree shot up from her mother's red sofa and excused herself to go to the bathroom. She needed to get out from under her mother's scrutinizing stare.

Her mother had finally returned from Brazil. She worked as a PA for a billionaire and often lived abroad for months on end. Bree was proud of her achievements. It hadn't been easy for Joan as a single mom of five daughters.

Bree washed her hands and walked out of the bathroom. She

stopped dead in her tracks in the hallway when she overheard her mother.

"I'm glad she's finally moving on with her life. It's painful how she always followed him around all the time. Declan Mills will never love her like she loves him."

Tears pricked Bree's eyes and her ears drummed. But she didn't miss Fi's response.

"I know. I feel sorry for her. Just look at Ronan, I—"

Caitlin interrupted Fianna and said, "There's nothing wrong with the Mills family. You had a bad experience with Ronan. We get it. Now, get over it. Declan has nothing to do with his twin stepping out on you. He's a good man and a good fit for Bree. It's time to let it go, Fi."

"I don't hate all Mills men. I work for Duncan at his dojo, and he's great. And I love Pops. But Ronan? I still hate him," Fianna said.

"Shocking. Never would've guessed," Gwenn said.

Bree couldn't believe that's the way people talked about her when she left the room. She felt like a fool. But Dec rejected her last March. So to a point, her family was right to question his love for her.

She'd wanted to tell her mother and sisters tonight she was trying to work things out with Declan. But as she stood there, hiding in the hallway from her family's judgmental remarks like a scared little kid, she knew she'd done the right thing to take things slow.

She just needed a few more weeks to be absolutely certain of his love for her. And then she would tell her family.

She entered the living room and Cait gave Bree an apologetic smile. Bree returned her smile and sat down next to Gwenn. Gwenn bumped her shoulder to Bree's arm and whispered in her ear, "Just another hour. We're almost halfway through."

Bree couldn't suppress her giggle quick enough and Joan cleared her throat.

"Gwenn. How's sleeping on Bree's couch working out for you?"

"It's fine, Mom."

Bree wondered how Gwenn's night had been last night at Cait's apartment. Gwenn often woke up in the middle of the night because of her nightmares. It's the reason why she wanted to take the couch. So she wouldn't wake Bree.

Joan tapped a long, red fingernail against her chin. "Hmm. And work?"

"What about work?" Bree felt Gwenn stiffen next to her.

"Well, how about finding a job so you can support yourself? I didn't raise you to profit from your sister's hospitality."

Bree didn't stand up to her mother as often as she'd liked, but considering it was Bree's hospitality she'd mentioned, Bree said, "Gwenn can live with me until we're both ninety and senile."

Kera laughed and shook her head. Bree jutted her chin to her mother to come with another spiteful remark.

Normally, Bree would swallow her pride because she knew her mother meant well, and she had their best interest at heart.

But when Joan opened her mouth, Bree quickly added, "I love having Gwenn at my place. She's my sister. I'd like to think you would be happy to see your daughters taking care of each other."

Joan waved a hand in the air. "Pff. I'd rather see Gwenn grow up. She may be the youngest, but she can't stay forever with you and hide out for the rest of the world."

"I'm right here, Mom. Stop talking like I have no say in this."

"Well, it's your sister's couch. So, it's up to Bree to give you a kick under your butt, isn't it?"

Bree glanced over at Gwenn, who pulled her long, brown hair into a ponytail. It was Gwenn's tell she was fed up. Her eyes shot daggers at Joan. Gwenn was about to say her piece, but Joan missed these signs and continued her rant.

"Didn't I teach you girls to never rely on anyone? To be self-sufficient? Have you even looked for a job, Gwenn?"

Gwenn stood from the sofa and flung her arms wildly in the air. "I may be fucked in the head, but looking at you, I realize my deployment is only half to blame. You're toxic. And I'm leaving."

Gwenn pulled Bree from the couch. "And Bree's coming with me." Gwenn tugged Bree on her way to the door. A bit stunned at being manhandled, Bree waved her sisters goodbye over her shoulder.

"Think about how you treat your daughters next time you're home for the first time in months. Welcome home, Joan." Gwenn said.

Joan winced when Gwenn didn't call her Mom. Gwenn had just put Joan into the same category as Rob, their absent father. Joan stood from her seat and strode over to the front door where Gwenn and Bree pulled on their coats.

"I'm sorry, girls. I just want what's best for you. I hate that you're wasting away on your sister's couch. You've got so much potential." Joan stroked Gwenn's cheek and Gwenn's shoulders tensed.

Bree buttoned her coat, ready to go home. She was glad Gwenn made the decision for her to leave. Bree had been done with this visit the moment her mother talked behind her back over how stupid she'd been in following Dec around all these years.

"Then why don't you say so like a normal person? I always feel like I'm letting you down. First with my deployment. Now this. I can't win with you."

Joan sighed. "I'm sorry. I've done everything I could to show you girls you can achieve anything you set your minds to. I don't want you to end up in a situation like I did when your father left us. Now that I'm away a lot, I feel like the time we do have together, I should guide you."

Gwenn hugged Joan. "We just need you to love and support

us. Believe me, I know I need to step up my game. But just... give me some time. It's only been a few weeks since I'm back. You have no idea what I've been through."

They ended their hug and before Joan could say anything, Gwenn said, "I'm not ready. Maybe I'll never be ready to talk about it."

Joan nodded and kissed Gwenn's cheek. "Okay. I'll take a step back. But just a small one."

Gwenn rolled her eyes, smiling. "Thanks."

Joan turned to Bree to pull her in for a hug.

"I'm glad to see you're moving on from your crush. You deserve so much more, Bree."

Bree closed her eyes and held her tongue. Not willing to get into another argument, Bree nodded. She needed to have another talk with Dec after this night.

It only took one remark from her mother for the doubt to settle in again. Declan hadn't said he loved her yet. Maybe she was pushing it. But she knew she wasn't able to give him the ultimate piece of her heart without those words from him.

The sisters got into Bree's car and they took off to Bree's apartment. Gwenn pulled down the visor and wiped some smudged mascara from under her eye.

Bree glanced at Gwenn and before she could even ask, Gwenn said, "No. Not doing this. I'm fine."

"Okay. Just know that I'm here for you, okay?"

Bree watched the road and almost enjoyed the moment of silence. What a night. Joan Ryan sure knew how to let everyone know she was back in town.

"What? Why are you smiling?" Gwenn asked.

"It's nothing, really. Just thinking about how we finally got Mom to say she's sorry."

Gwenn huffed. "Took her long enough. It's that we love her.... But damn, I really hate her lack of filter."

Bree switched lanes and said, "I know. I heard her talk about me and Dec. Do you think—"

Gwenn turned in her seat and said, "No. Stop it. Declan loves you, sis. Mom has some serious issues. It doesn't matter who we end up falling in love with, Mom's always going to find faults in them."

"Just like she does with us…" Gwenn added in a whisper.

"I'm sorry."

Gwenn let out a sardonic laugh. "You don't have to be sorry."

"I know. But I hate seeing you like this. I just wished I could do something for you." Bree parked in front of her apartment building and shifted in her seat. They both sat still in the car.

"There is one thing you can do for me."

Bree perked up and tilted her body toward Gwenn.

"Oh? Tell me."

"Give Dec a real shot." Gwenn leaned in and placed her hand on Bree's arm.

"I know Dec fucked things up between you two. And I know you're scared to trust him."

Bree let out a long, low sigh.

Gwenn continued, "Rob fucked us all up the day he walked out on us. I sure as hell thought I would never trust a man. Shit. I've just spent months in the desert, counting on the guys on my team to have my back. Do you know how hard it's been to trust those macho assholes?"

Bree offered a flash of a smile that didn't reach her eyes. "I don't know how you did it. I would've been scared out of my mind."

Gwenn unfastened her seatbelt and redid her ponytail. "I was, sis. Fuck. I'm still scared of waking up in the middle of the night, reliving those same nightmares, over and over again."

Bree unfastened her seatbelt and leaned in to hug her sister. "I'm here for you."

"I know. You're already doing so much for me. And I'm here for you, too. That's why I'm telling you to ignore our mother."

Gwenn placed a hand over Bree's heart.

"Listen to your heart. I know you still love G.I. Joe."

Bree giggled, and Gwenn let her hand fall down.

"I do," Bree said.

"Well, there you go. Come on, sis. Show the rest of us Ryan girls how it's done."

Bree nodded. "I'll give it a shot."

15

DECLAN

"Okay, so I need to put this in the oven for how long?" Declan slid a lamb shoulder dish into his oven and closed the door.

"About an hour. Just check it after forty-five minutes, see how it goes. And when it's done, let it rest for fifteen minutes and remove the twine. Did you toss the potatoes around the garlic and rosemary? Oh, and thyme?"

Declan smiled. He held the phone between his shoulder and ear while he rasped the carrots. "Yes, Emm. I've done exactly what you've told me to do. Was just checking for the time. I don't want to ruin it now."

"I wonder who you're making this for. It better be for a certain Kindergarten teacher I know."

Bree's always been close with his Moore cousins and especially his aunt Shauni. It was no surprise Emmy rooted for Bree. He wanted to shout it from the rooftops, but Bree still kept her distance out of fear of having her heart broken again. But eventually, she would give in.

"I can't tell you anything, Emm. But let's hope that after tonight, I can reveal who my mystery guest is."

"Okay," Emmy said,, and she quickly added, "I would never

blab about you or Bree, Cuz. Take your time. Your secret is safe with me."

Emmy was making it damn hard for him to not just tell her.

"Goodbye, Emm. And... thank you."

"Have fun!" Emmy singsonged before the line disconnected.

Declan whistled some tune while washing his hands in the sink. He smiled at the memory of a soaking wet Bree last week in her kitchen. They vibed like it had always been this way.

He jolted when his doorbell rang. After drying his hands, he walked over to his front door.

"Hey, Dec. I'll be out of your hair in a minute, just wanted to bring this over to you."

Declan took a step back to open the door further for his cousin Keenan, who carried a cheese platter with a stylish bell jar on top. In the kitchen, Declan peered inside and spotted a colorful array of meat, cheeses, nuts and grapes.

"I know Bree's coming over, and I wanted to give you some small bites to share. There's some prosciutto and salami in there. Also, a slice of Brie, a bit of goat cheese and my favorite, bleu cheese. It's strong, but when you both grab a bite, at least you'll both stink."

Declan clasped his hand around Keenan's shoulder and squeezed. "Thanks, Cuz. You didn't have to do this."

Keenan shrugged. "I know. But I wanted to help. I know how busy you are. You never cook whenever you're home alone. Tommy's mom always loved this shit. So I figured, if dinner would suck, at least you got this covered."

Declan chuckled. "Thanks for your vote of confidence."

Keenan turned and shot a glance at the oven. "Ah, I see you're taking this to the next level. Good."

Keenan arched a brow. "Emmy?"

"Yep."

Keenan smirked and walked into the direction of the front door again. "Good thinking, Dec."

"You know me. Always prepared."

Declan knew his reputation with his family. He wasn't a go with the flow kinda guy. Freewheeling wasn't in his dictionary. He could adapt easily, sure. He had to in his line of work. But if he could help it, he would have as much control over this night as possible.

"Have fun, Dec. You deserve it."

"Thanks, Keen. I'll bring the dish back to you tomorrow."

"Nah, you enjoy yourself and stay inside. I hope to think she'll not run out on yer arse again in the morning."

"Later, man," Declan said. He hated the reminder of Bree sneaking out of his home that first time weeks ago.

After finishing up the rasping of the carrots, he placed them in a separate dish into the oven. His heart rate picked up when his doorbell rang again. He wondered if this nervousness would ever go away.

He opened his door and his breath caught in his throat. Bree smiled up at him and blushed. Her long curls were down and fell over her breasts. A tight fitted white shirt above an even tighter pair of jeans made him clench his fists. He almost yanked her from his porch to haul her over his shoulder and up the stairs.

But he didn't.

"Hey, Squirt."

Bree narrowed her eyes at him. Not what he expected.

"What?"

"You know, I've always hated that stupid nickname. Can't you come up with something else? It reminds me of how you still see me as a little girl, bugging you all the time." She didn't kiss him and strode inside.

"Well, okay. Hi, Grumpy. Welcome?"

He bit his lip so he wouldn't bust out laughing. Bree had practically steam coming out of her ears.

"Grumpy?" Bree clanked the bottle of wine in her hand on his kitchen counter.

"That's what you come up with?... Grumpy?"

He stepped up to her and halted his steps when she held a hand in the air.

"You're telling me I look like one of the seven dwarfs? Do I need to pluck my eyebrows? Maybe shave my beard?"

He couldn't hold it in any longer and laughed. "No, but maybe you can smile? If you'll stop pouting, you're so much cuter."

He closed the distance and kissed her scowl off her face. After only a few seconds, she leaned into him and giggled against his lips.

"I can't believe you," she said.

"And I can't believe how one word can sour your mood like that. If you really hate me calling you Squirt, all you need to do is tell me. I'll find you a new nickname."

"No, thanks." Bree scrunched her nose. "If your next best thing is Grumpy, I'll take a pass."

He leaned in and whispered in her ear, "What about Sugar Plump? Or Butter Butt?"

She giggled, and he tugged her earlobe with his teeth. She moaned and fisted his shirt. He kissed her lips, and she opened up for him. Their tongues played with each other. He grabbed her arse and squeezed. Just when he was about to take her upstairs to his bedroom, the oven beeped.

"Shit. I need to—"

Bree cleared her throat and took a small step back. She glanced around the room and said, "Sure. Erm, shall I open the wine?"

"That would be great."

He grabbed the wine opener and handed it over. "The glasses are already on the table."

"Oh, okay."

He took Keenan's appetizers and walked up to his kitchen table. Bree looked over her shoulder and her blue eyes widened.

"Oh, wow. That looks so good."

Declan placed the cheese board on the table. "I can't take any credit. Keen dropped this off."

"Keenan? But we've talked about—"

"I know, but he saw you that morning when you bolted at the break of dawn." He grimaced and said, "And Aid overheard me and Keenan talk. But Keen and Aid are the only ones, I swear, Sq—Bree."

Bree's groans made her feelings loud and clear. She was not happy with him.

"I respect your wishes. Please, don't be mad, Grumpy."

He tried to make light of the situation by calling her Grumpy again. He crossed his fingers, hoping she wouldn't make an issue out of his cousins knowing. Although he could see why she would be mad.

"Gwenn knows about us too. I guess it's good to have someone to talk to. It's kind of a rare situation we have on our hands here."

"Nothing rare about us, Bree. We're just us."

Bree cocked her head like she wanted him to say something else. He paused a moment but let it go. He pulled the glass from the cheese platter. Bree instantly pushed back her chair and covered her nose with her hand.

"Oh, my God. What's that smell?"

Declan grinned. "Uh, cheese?"

"When did Keenan bring this over? Three years ago?"

Declan laughed with his head back.

"No, Grumpy. Just before you got here."

Bree shook her head and muffled her words. "I can't... I think I'm going to be sick."

"Aren't you being a bit dramatic? I mean, it's blue cheese. Normally, you'd eat that shit for breakfast if we'd let you."

He quickly placed the glass back over the cheese when Bree turned green in the face. "Shit. I'm sorry. I'm going to get you some water. Sit tight."

He took the untouched board of cheese with him into the kitchen and placed it on the counter. After filling a glass with water, he walked back to the table where Bree loudly inhaled a breath of fresh air her through her nose.

"That's it. Deep breaths. Here, take a sip."

Her shaky hand reached out for the glass. He ignored her hand and brought the glass to her lips. He helped so she wouldn't spill.

She swallowed a few sips and cleared her throat. "Thanks. I've been feeling a little off these past days. I'm sorry I was cranky with you. I'm totally ruining this night, aren't I?" Bree held her head with her hand.

"Nah. I get to be with you, so I'm good."

Bree pulled down the hem of her shirt. "Sure?"

What did he need to do to prove himself? He wanted to shake some sense in her. Obviously, that wasn't an option.

She avoided eye contact and said in a soft-spoken voice. "Okay. Let's eat."

"You sure? I can get you some buttered toast if your stomach's upset?"

She lightly shook her head and smiled. "That's unnecessary. But maybe we could skip the cheese?"

He squeezed her shoulder on his way to the kitchen. "Yeah. That's probably a good idea." While pulling the twine from the lamb, he shot a glance at Bree's sitting with hunched shoulders at his kitchen table.

He knew Bree. She was probably sitting this night out because she didn't want to hurt his feelings. He picked up the dish with the lamb and placed it back into the turned-off oven.

He rummaged around his cabinets. Bingo. He walked over to

Bree with his hands full and gave her a kiss on top of her head before sitting down next to her.

"Here, I think this will do the trick."

After stacking his plate with slices of white bread, he placed the peanut butter and jam on the table. Bree chewed the inside of her cheek. "But... you've put so much work into dinner."

"I'll bring it over to Keenan tomorrow. Let him enjoy it. You know how I like my peanut butter and jelly. It's no hardship for me. In fact... you're doing me a favor."

He winked and smeared a heavy amount of jelly on his bread.

Bree snorted and fell against him with her shoulder to his. "You're crazy."

"Damn right I am. About you."

She gave him a blinding smile, although her chin wobbled. He kissed her nose and placed a slice of bread on her plate.

"So, are you in?"

Bree pulled softly at her earring and gave it a moment before answering, "Yeah. I'm in."

16

BREE

Bree woke up in a cold sweat. Her hair stuck to her head. She tried to roll to her side but instantly stopped moving as a wave of nausea came crashing over her.

Another gag reflex followed, and she shot off the bed, not caring about the drumming in her ears. Just in time, she knelt in front of the toilet.

"Yowza!" Gwenn said behind her as she grabbed Bree's curls and fisted them in a ponytail.

"Dec told me last night to check up on you. He said it could be bad... he wasn't kidding."

Between her second and third round, she asked, "When did he do that?"

"When he brought you here. After he'd tucked you in."

Gwenn rubbed her back, and Bree took a deep breath. Yuck, she smelled sour jelly. She gagged again and after another two rounds she said, "I'm going to wash up. Thanks, Gwenn..."

"I thought you were feeling better? Didn't you puke earlier this week?"

Bree groaned, as she couldn't get into it now. "Please..." she whispered while she grabbed the sink to pull herself from the cold bathroom tiles. She needed to clean them. Perhaps she could do that first before taking a shower?

"No, no. Don't even think about it. I'm taking care of it. You go on, now." Gwenn motioned for Bree to get under the spray that she'd just turned on.

"Nothing I haven't seen before. I have the same tits and ass. Now, go!" Gwenn pushed the shower door further open. She pulled Bree's camisole over her head and fisted it in a ball. She dunked it in the bin and made a work of Bree's underwear.

"Okay, easy... the moment you feel dizzy or sick, and you can't call out, you tap on the glass of the shower door, okay?"

Bree nodded, and when Gwenn looked over from wetting a towel in the sink, she said, "Thanks, Gwennie."

"No problem."

After her shower, Bree dressed herself into her favorite pajamas and climbed into bed. Gwenn brought her some ginger tea and gave her salty crackers.

"Hmm, these actually work," Bree held one cracker up into the air. Gwenn walked past her with a pile of dirty laundry and said, "Oh, you're so fucked, sis."

"No, they work. I feel better already."

Gwenn walked out of the room and shouted over her shoulder, "I'm calling Kera."

"What for?" Bree winced at her own shouts.

Gwenn walked back into Bree's bedroom with her phone against her ear. "Hmm-mm, yeah. And while you're there, can you grab me some tampons? Yeah, one box is enough. My guess is I don't have to share them in a loooong time."

"What is that all about?" Bree said while perching herself on the bed. She rested her head against the headrest of her bed. She'd always liked this type of hotel beds with their padded headrest. It was the first thing she bought when she'd had saved up enough from her first paychecks. Never once regretted it.

"How long have you been feeling sick?" Gwenn said and

eyed her sister peculiarly. She looked from Bree's eyes over to her stomach and up again. Bree shifted on the bed.

"I... um, on and off a couple of days? A week maybe? It's just a bug..."

"Exactly!" Gwenn waved her hand in the air with the phone clenched between her fingers.

Bree's head pounded. "I don't know why it's so special now. So I got sick again. It's not like you haven't been sick before?"

"Geeez... Okay, if that's how you want to play it."

Bree narrowed her eyes at her sister, "What in the world are you talking about? Here I was thinking you were so sweet in helping me. Why are you badgering me?"

Gwenn stalked out of the bedroom and said, "I'm so happy I called in reinforcement."

Bree placed her hands next to her thighs, leaned over her legs and shouted in the doorway's direction, "Stop talking army. You are not on a mission here!"

"Take some rest. Kera will be here shortly."

"Whatever," Bree muttered. "Just my luck, *she* had to stay with me. I get sick for a few days and she sends in the cavalry. Pff."

And then it clicked. She gasped and held her hand before her mouth. The thoughts running through her head made her nauseous again. This time she didn't spill. After going at it for two rounds, she brushed her teeth again. She slumped over to her bed and waited for her sisters to join her.

She'd heard their whispers in the living room. After a few more minutes, Kera walked in first into her bedroom. She had brought a white paper bag. The kind you'd get at the drugstore.

"Nooo..." She shook her head and pulled her knees up to her chest. She linked her fingers as she folded her hands against her shins.

"Sweetheart, just to be sure," Kera said, and she held out the paper bag. She cocked her head and her coppery bob swished.

"But I'm on the pill..."

"I know, sis. But it hasn't been that long ago since I referred you to someone for a prescription for birth control. If you didn't begin your pill until after your period started, you had to wait seven days before having unprotected sex. Didn't the doctor explain this to you?"

"I thought it immediately protected me was immediately protecte...." Bree sobbed, feeling trapped like a caged animal. What was she to do now? How could she ever tell Declan she's pregnant after promising him she had been protected?

Kera joined Bree on one side of the bed and Gwenn on the other. Bree leaned with her head against Kera's shoulder, and Gwenn laid her hand on top of Bree's hand and squeezed.

"Take the test, Bree. Just to rule it out," Kera said.

"Okay..."

Bree got up from the bed and grabbed the paper bag from the nightstand. She sat down on the closed toilet lid and peered into the bag. Her sister had gotten her two different pregnancy tests. Bree took a deep breath and went ahead.

"What's taking you so long?" Gwenn shouted.

"I couldn't pee, okay?" Bree raised her voice. "And I had to do both."

She just knew that her sisters were rolling their eyes behind the closed doors.

"I'm coming in. Stand back," Gwenn said.

"What did I say about treating this like a mission?" Bree said the moment Gwenn pushed the bathroom door open.

"Fuck that. This is a mission. You might not know it, but getting us all ready to be a mom and aunts is one hell of a mission," Gwenn said.

"Don't jump to conclusions. You don't know if—"

Bree whirled around when Gwenn reached behind Bree to pick up the two sticks. She waved the sticks in front of Bree's face.

"See!"

One white stick read 'pregnant' and the other showed a definite blue cross. Her heart skipped a beat and her chest tightened.

"I think I need to lay down," Bree whispered. She wiped the new sheen of sweat from her forehead.

"Come, let's get you back into bed." Kera placed her arm around Bree's shoulders and guided her back into the bedroom.

"Can you give us a moment, Gwenn?" Kera asked.

Their youngest sister nodded. "I'll be in the kitchen, making us brunch." At Bree's scowl, Gwenn winced and said, "I'll just make something for Kera then. Sorry."

Bree settled in under the covers. She couldn't believe there was a baby growing inside of her. A small child. With Declan's DNA. Would the baby look like him?

Kera sat down upon the covers next to Bree and patted her thigh. "I'm sorry, Bree. I've been so busy with making things work at the hospital... this comes a bit out of left field. You know you can talk to me about anything, right?"

"I know you're still finding your way in the ER. And I'm so proud of you, sis. I would never resent you for it. You know that."

Bree sighed and pulled on a loose thread on top of her cover. "You must wonder what I've been up to..."

Kera giggled, and Bree jerked her head in her sister's direction. Kera's green eyes sparkled.

"Oh, I know all about the birds and the bees, sis. I'm pretty sure what you've been up to." Kera winked.

Bree shifted on the bed and crossed her arms. "I mean with whom."

"I have my suspicions. I'll just let you talk whenever you're ready." Kera raked her hand through her strands of russet hair.

The person sitting next to Bree wasn't her sister Kera. No, this was the professional field medic turned EMT talking. And because Kera reacted so cautiously, with an almost occupational distance, Bree blurted, "It's Dec's."

Kera gave Bree a watery smile. "Oh, sis. I know this is far from an ideal situation. But I'm happy he's the baby's father." Bree had a fluttery, empty feeling in her stomach. True, the good news is that Craig couldn't be the father since they never had sex. That would have been even worse.

"I don't know, Ker. We're not even together, like... we've talked about seeing how things would go. And I made him promise to keep things a secret because I still wasn't sure about him. About us."

She pressed her trembling lips together.

"I'm screwed," Bree said as she rested her head against the headrest.

"Yep. In a few months' time we'll all see the proof of that." Gwenn snickered. She stepped back into the bedroom and Bree glared at her sister.

Gwenn dipped her chin. "Sorry, I know I'm not helping. But this is how I cope with stressful situations."

Bree waved her hands in the air and said, "It must have been all shits and giggles in Afghanistan, then."

"Stop it. Both of you." Kera said, and she narrowed her eyes.

"Let's stop this bickering and think about your baby. Of course, Dec is also a factor in this. But since you're just finding out, today is all about you and what you make of this huge bomb that fell into your lap."

A sob escaped Bree's lips and Kera held Bree close. She slid her arm over Bree's shoulder, and Bree shifted so she could lean her head against Kera's shoulder.

"I'm so stupid..."

Kera patted Bree's back. "No sis. Don't beat yourself up about it."

"I feel like I've let myself down by getting pregnant with Declan's child. He's never going to love me for me now. The moment he hears I'm carrying his child, he's going to chase me for the sake of this baby. But being with Declan would be on false grounds. Not because of his love for ME."

"Damn, sis. You're fucked in the head."

"Gwenn!" Kera chastised.

"I'm right, though. She's thinking about Mom and Rob's shitastic relationship, and it ruins all her chances to be happy."

Gwenn turned to Bree. "I know you love him. And even though he hadn't said the words, that man is in love with you. With YOU and sure, the moment he hears you're pregnant, he's going full throttle. Because we all know that's who Declan is. But don't for a moment think he doesn't love you. Because he does." Gwenn stood a little taller and crossed her arms.

"Although Gwenn could work on her timing and deliverance," Kera gave Gwenn a pointed look before she turned her eyes on Bree again, "She's right, you know."

"I'm still in shock... I'm going to be somebody's mom. I don't think I'm ready."

"Bullshit." Gwenn said and fisted her sides. Bree was about to pull the covers over her head to cut herself off from her sister. That, or she could evict Gwenn from her couch. At least then Joan would be happy.

"You take care of a class full of kids. Now if I'd said I'm not ready for a baby, everyone would agree with me. But not you, Bree. You were born ready to care for others. In a sick way, I'm secretly glad you're preggers. Gives us a chance to see how it's done by one of the best."

Bree barely held in her laughter. "I'll take that as a compliment."

"As you should, sis. Now, scoot your ass over. Let aunti Gwenn snuggle with her niece or nephew."

They watched a marathon of *Friends* episodes together and Bree tried her best for the rest of the day not to break down and cry. Her sisters might have taken this news rather well; she was dreading her upcoming talk with Dec.

Because if Dec couldn't love her like she needed him to, they would have to end things. Romantically, that is, because this baby would bind them together forever.

She couldn't be with him if Dec only stayed with her out of obligation. There was no 'taking things slow' now. The moment of truth was coming, and she had to face the music.

DECLAN

"I take it you haven't had a talk with Bree yet?" Brennan said.

"Shit, man. We've talked all right. We..."

Declan moved in closer and he lowered his voice since they stood in Thomas Tavern, surrounded by family and friends. It was Errin's farewell party, and he was there to say goodbye to Errin, but mostly to support his oldest brother.

Brennan was head over heels for the Walsh sister, but she was moving back to Jersey to follow her dream of becoming a famous dancer.

Although Brennan had enough on his plate with the love of his life leaving him after tonight, he still found the time to check up on his brother.

Growing up, Brennan had been there for all the Mills brothers. Their mother had died of breast cancer when Ronan and Declan were only six-years-old.

The fourteen-year-old Brennan had been the rock they all could depend on. Not their dad, Sean Jr., because he'd checked out, overwhelmed with grief.

Brennan never got to have the childhood like the rest of them. He was the young boy, acting like the man of the house.

The tension between Sean Jr. and Brennan had been like another cancer, spreading its ugliness throughout their family.

Declan looked up to his big brother. Brennan was the one who'd successfully steered Declan's twin Ronan in the right direction. Each Mills brother had dealt differently with the loss of his mother. Declan wanted to make his family proud. And help Brennan wherever he could.

His twin had always been the polar opposite. Ronan fought in school. And out of school. Wherever Ronan was, followed trouble. He picked on other kids. Knocked a boy's tooth out for looking funny at him. Declan was certain it was solely because of Brennan's guidance that Ronan finally turned away from the dark path he'd started.

Even though Bree wished to keep their hook-ups a secret, Declan felt like his big brother deserved to know the truth. Brennan stood by him when Declan was heartbroken because of the Bree situation. He'd talked with Declan about regretting letting Bree go. They had talked about the loss of Bree's friendship. The least he could do was give Brennan a heads up about the recent developments.

Declan said, "We spend one night together at my place, and then again two weeks ago. Fuck, Bren. That first night was everything, man. But every time I think we can finally be together, she freaks out. She's been ignoring me for the past weeks."

"Why didn't ye tell me something had happened between yous earlier?" Brennan said. He widened his stance and crossed his arms. His sudden Irish brogue let Dec know how upset he was with him.

"She's spooked, and she wants to keep it between us. She doubts my feelings, but I'm going after what's mine. Ever since I've first laid eyes on her dark curly head..." Dec shook his head, smiling.

"Damn, is it even possible to find the love of your life when you're just eight?" Declan asked.

Brennan slapped Dec's back. "I'm rooting for you, bro."

"Thanks," Declan said as they walked over to the booths where the rest of the Mills brothers and cousins sat. Errin's sisters Kate and Kayla were there, and the three Ryan sisters: Fianna, Caitlin, and Bree.

He'd brought Bree home after she'd gotten sick at his place. At first, she'd told him she didn't want to give him the same bug, so she didn't want him to come over. Although a bit bummed out she wouldn't let him in to take care of her, he gave her some space for a few days.

Of course he'd kept in touch with Gwenn. But it wasn't the same. He wanted to be there for her. But Bree refused.

She had shot even his offer to drive her tonight down. He leaned in over the table and watched how Bree laughed at some joke from Errin. Bree turned her head from him the moment their eyes met.

He scooted from the booth and walked over to the bar. After ordering himself a beer, Declan had the feeling he was being watched. Goosebumps traveled over his spine. He looked up and in the mirror's reflection behind the bartender; he held Bree's eyes.

He saluted Bree with his beer bottle, and she gave him a half smile. Not wanting to look too eager and talk to her in front of all their family and friends, he stayed put. He looked down to his beer bottle and peeled on the label.

"Hi," Bree said as she placed her hand on Dec's shoulder.

"Hey, Love."

"Since when do you call me that?" Bree asked as she took the stool next to Declan.

He turned on his stool. "Since you told me to never call you Squirt ever again," he said. "So I won't." He peered into her eyes and she blushed.

"Dec, I know I've come off like a crazy person these last couple months. Gwenn said it's been unfair of me to not return any of your calls. And she's right. I know she is. It's just that—"

"Well, if it isn't G.I. Joe and his Squirt. Are we finally getting to see some action, G.I. Joe?" Ronan said in his loud voice. Bree winced before she narrowed her eyes at Declan's twin. He knew she could handle Ro. But Declan wouldn't let things slide.

"We're in the middle of something here, Ro."

Ronan bumped his shoulder to Dec's as he wormed himself in between Declan and Bree. He turned his back to Dec. "So, Bree. Are ye still in love with my brother?"

Before Bree could answer him, Declan stood from his stool and pushed his twin out of Bree's way.

"Back the fuck off, Ro."

Ronan whirled around and held himself steady by gripping the bar. He almost accidently pushed Bree from her stool, but she'd jumped before he could do so. She stood with a hand on her stomach and one against her chest.

Before Declan could ask her if she was okay, Ronan spat at him, "Always letting her come between us. I'm sick of it, bro."

Never once had Ronan hinted about his feelings. His sneer blindsided Declan. When they were kids, it had always been Ro, Dec and Bree hanging out.

Sure, when they got older, they hadn't been the three Musketeers anymore. Ro hung out with a different crowd. He was on a warpath all the time. Fighting, smoking, and underage drinking. Not the people Dec wanted to sniff around Bree.

So they kept their distance whenever Ro was with those other people. Declan always thought that Ro hadn't mind. That he broke up the three Musketeers because they hadn't been cool enough, anyway.

After Ro's dark period, he grew closer again with his twin. But Dec never knew about Ro's feelings. He wished Ro had said something to him.

Bree laid a hand on Ro's arm. "I'm sorry you feel this way, Ro.

I really am. We could have all been friends. You and I were friends for a long time."

Ro swallowed his first response.

"Yes," he said, after a beat. "Before the whole Fi situation."

"Well, she's my sister, Ro. I don't expect you to choose me over your brother. Not if I ever hurt your brother. I'm sorry, but you hurt our friendship by cheating on Fi. I was so damn angry with you."

Ronan's shoulders slumped, and he looked over at Declan. They shared a long look, and it let Ro know he was in the wrong.

"Shit. I'm sorry, Bree. I'm an arsehole."

"Yes, you are," Bree said as she grinned from ear to ear.

"Couldn't you at least pretend to think about me being an arsehole? You just throw me under the bus like that?"

He gave her shoulder a soft bump with his bicep and again, Bree held her abdomen. She smiled at Ronan but took a tentative step back.

"I really am sorry, Squirt. Seeing you two together at the bar took me down memory lane. Thinking about yer sister always rattles my cage."

Declan felt for Ro. He really did. But Ro had to deal with his feelings and not lash out like this.

"It's okay," Bree said.

"It's not okay," Declan said. "But we'll let ye off the hook if ye let me and Bree be. You get what I'm throwing down here?"

Ronan smirked. "Loud and clear. Go get her, G.I. Joe." He saluted Declan and turned on his heel.

Declan took Bree by the hand and steered her in between his thighs as he sat down again on his stool. She placed her hands on his shoulders and he tugged her even closer by bringing his hands upon her arse.

"Why are you running from me, Love? Why are you still fighting this?" Declan asked.

He squeezed her to him a little tighter.

"We need to talk, Dec."

His heart lodged in his throat as he stared into Bree's eyes. There was an uncertainty there, a feeling in her eyes he wished he could take from her. He would do anything to get the chance to do so.

Declan leaned in and let her scent of fresh flowers roll into his senses. He couldn't stop himself as he kissed her. She parted her lips on a gasp. His tongue invaded her mouth while his fingers dug into her warm flesh through her black dress. He could spend a lifetime kissing Bree.

"Dec..."

Bree nipped at his bottom lip, bringing him back to the bar at Thomas Tavern. He was suddenly reminded she'd wanted to keep their relationship—or whatever it was, a secret and they had just kissed in front of everyone.

"You sweep me off my feet every time we see each other, Dec."

"Is this why you're ignoring me? Why do you need distance between us, Love?" Why would she want to back out now that they could finally be together?

Bree took a small step from him, and he let her. She scooted her barstool closer to Dec and sat down.

"Can I order something for you?" Dec said after he flagged the bartender.

"Yes, water, please."

The bartender nodded. Dec scrutinized Bree. She seemed different somehow. Had she lost weight? She seemed tired.

"Are you still feeling sick?" he asked and placed his hand on her under arm that rested on top of the bar.

She jumped at his question and couldn't meet his eye. Alarm bells went off in his head and he took back his hand. He let the silence turn awkward on purpose. He figured he'd asked enough questions, and it was time for Bree to do the talking.

Bree drank a few gulps from her glass of water. She cleared her throat and swiveled on her stool.

"So...."

Declan crossed his arms and couldn't stop his one eyebrow from pulling. He knew he did it whenever he questioned someone on the job.

"Dec... I..."

Declan looked over Bree's shoulder at a pair of college jocks getting into a heated argument about being first in line to order drinks.

"Love," he said as he took her by the arm, "I need you to get behind me. Now."

He tugged her behind him just before the bigger dude punched the lanky guy at the bar. Glass flew all over the place. He needed to get a handle on this situation and separate those stupid fucks.

"Ro!" Declan shouted. "Take care of Bree!"

But Ro had an entirely other idea. He flew right at the bigger guy who threw the punch. "Oh, no ye don't! Here's someone of yer own size. Think ye can handle me, fuckface?"

Declan tried to hold Ronan off, but he didn't want to leave Bree vulnerable behind his back. Being a professional MMA fighter, Ro could handle himself. So Dec brought Bree to safety.

"I'm all right, go help Ro," she said.

He didn't respond to her protests as he dragged her outside. Fianna was standing on the sidewalk and called out to them.

"I can't believe he's at it again. Some things never change," Fianna muttered before she put her arms around Bree. The sisters hugged. Fianna looked over Bree's shoulder and mouthed 'thank you' to Declan.

He nodded and turned around to go help his twin. Again.

18

BREE

"You can't blame everything on hormones, sis. That's ridiculous." Gwenn chastised Bree while they searched the aisle for cranberry sauce.

"These hormones are the ones being ridiculous!" Bree walked around with her hands flying above her head.

"One look in his ocean gray eyes and I was putty in his hands. I couldn't even remember my name, let alone tell Declan he's about to become a Daddy!"

A gasp from behind Bree's back made both sisters jump. Bree whirled around and stood face to face with her best friend, Kate.

These past months without Dec in her life, Kate had been her rock. But lately, Bree dodged Kate because she didn't know how to tell her she'd been sneaking around with Dec. She wasn't sure how Kate would take it, that she'd kept this from her.

"Uhm, hi," Bree said.

Kate dropped her fire red shopping basket and stepped closer to Bree. Her eyes dropped to Bree's stomach.

"I can't believe it, is it really true?" Kate said as she looked up with misty blue eyes. Her long chocolate hair was curled for the occasion and fell over her shoulders.

"I... I..." Bree couldn't believe her best friend found out she was pregnant in the middle of Trader Joe's.

Kate held up one hand and blurted, "I didn't mean to overhear you. I swear. But I missed you at work. I wanted to check up on you, since you said you had the flu and all. When Emmy said you'd stop by here to pick up some last-minute things for today, I figured to come and help you."

When Kate looked over from Bree to Gwenn, she added, "When I walked up to you, I heard you about hormones. I'm sorry. I should have walked away. I know you probably don't want me here right now and—"

Bree stopped her best friend's apologies by stepping up to her and hugging her close.

"Shh, I wanted to tell you so bad. I'm still reeling from the fact that I'm going to be a mom. And I even haven't had the chance to tell Dec."

Gwenn snorted and said, "Pffft. Believe me, you've had your chances."

Kate stepped out of Bree's hug and placed her hand on Bree's shoulder. "How are you holding up? Is there anything I can do for you?"

It was so great to have Kate as a best friend. She'd been there for Bree in the past months when she was lovesick. Although they only met last June, Kate felt as close to Bree as her own sisters.

"I love you, Kate," Bree blurted out before she stabbed at a tear rolling down her puffy cheeks.

"I love you too, Bree," Kate said.

A woman with a fire red shopping cart walked by and said, "Aaaah."

Bree opened her mouth to say something and then thought better of it. Kate looked over her shoulder to make sure the woman was out of earshot and whispered, "If you don't mind me asking... but how—I mean, when..." Kate said while a blush crept over her cheeks.

"Remember the night we had the welcome home party for Gwenn and Kera? I went home with Dec that night."

"Noooo." Kate's eyes went wide in shock. She looked over at Gwenn and back at Bree again. "You said nothing..."

Now it was Bree who blushed. "I know. I felt so ashamed... My feelings for him freaked me out, Kate. I got scared and didn't want anyone to know. I'm sorry."

"It's okay, Bree. I just want to be there for you. And help you where I can. Did I hear correct that Declan doesn't know yet?" Kate asked before stepping aside for a woman who snatched the last tin of the good cranberry sauce behind Kate's voluptuous bum.

"Oh, sorry." Kate said, although the sturdy woman didn't even excused herself as she wiggled her way behind Kate's butt.

The woman smiled and held the tin in the air. "No problem. Got what I wanted. Happy Thanksgiving!"

"Happy Thanksgiving," they all three murmured back.

"Shall we, eh, go somewhere else to talk?" Kate asked. Bree nodded. Now even Kate knew she was pregnant before Dec, she wanted to go home and hide under the covers.

"She's been beating around this bush for weeks now, Kate. And today, it's Thanksgiving. Maybe she should say thanks right after Pops and tell everyone at once at the diner table!" Gwenn said, probably thinking it was a great idea.

"I'm not doing that!" Bree turned and strode toward the exit.

"We haven't bought what we came here for," Gwenn said from behind Bree.

Bree didn't care. She needed to go outside. Breathe in some fresh air. Her chest felt tight and her head pounded. Gwenn showed up by her side and said, "Okay, let's get a move on. You can talk later. We're going to miss Thanksgiving. I don't think any of us would like to explain to people why we're late."

Twenty minutes later, Bree followed Gwenn into Lucky, with Kate right behind her. She searched for Declan in the throng of people, but didn't see him. The Mills, Walsh, and Ryan families were all present today, filling up the pub.

Even the Mills and Moore cousins joined them for Thanksgiving. Everyone's eyes were glued to the enormous wide screen above the pool tables on the back wall, watching the first football game of the day.

Being in the pub with family and friends while carrying this big secret made her antsy. She was certain people could tell she was different somehow. The thought of being around family had made her jumpy all day. And she felt awfully guilty because she hadn't even told Declan yet. Luckily, her family thought she'd come down with the flu, so they wouldn't think much of it if she wouldn't drink tonight.

Keenan and Aiden offered a casual "Hey" at their entrance, and Bree sighed a breath of relief. Declan was nowhere. She was about to combust if she didn't tell Declan soon. Besides her sisters Kera and Gwenn, now even Kate heard about her pregnancy before Declan.

That wasn't right. She had waited and searched for the right time to tell him. She really did. Bree followed Gwenn into the kitchen where Emmy was giving out orders like she normally did as the chef at Lucky. She clapped her hands together. "Okay. Listen up. You too, Errin." The two friends smiled at each other as Emmy liked to keep Errin on her toes.

Emmy spoke in an exaggerated game show voice. "At the back of my kitchen, we have the Ryan sisters competing. Come on up here, Bree. Join your sisters."

Bree walked over to the countertop and Fianna put her arm around her shoulders.

"This year we're going to kick some ass!" Fianna said.

"And on this counter we have the newcomers to our Thanksgiving bake-off competition: the Walsh sisters." Emmy waved her ladle toward a stainless steel table to her right. Kayla and Errin hollered for Kate to join them at their table. Kate turned bright red and shuffled around Emmy to walk over to her sisters.

"Next to the newcomers, we have our runners-up from last year; the lovely Mills girls: Briana and Deirdre." Bree smiled at Keenan's sisters, who gave each other a high five.

"On my left we have the winners of last year..." and before Emmy could introduce them, Errin booed, making everyone laugh out loud.

"These newcomers are a rowdy bunch," Caitlin said.

"Yee-ha!" Kayla cheered.

The kitchen door opened and Duncan and Declan peeked their heads around the swishing door.

"You just know the football game is shite if the girls' hollers from the kitchen drown out the men," Duncan said.

Bree's eyes found Dec's, and she quickly lowered her gaze and kept it on the tomatoes in front of her. Her face probably matched the vegetable.

"Go away. No penises aloud," Fianna shouted next to Bree.

"Does a three-inch dick count? Maybe Dec can stay?" Ronan said from behind Declan. Bree was this close to put in her two cents about his rather large size before Fianna responded.

"In that case, you'd be welcome too, if I remember correctly...." Fianna said while she vehemently chopped her cucumber with a shiny kitchen knife. She looked up at Ronan and smiled like a possessed maniac. Bree grinned at her sister.

"Okay, before this gets even more out of hand, you guys need to leave," Emmy said.

Ronan sputtered something unintelligible before the kitchen door closed.

"Where were we?" Emmy said as she tapped her index finger against her chin.

"You were introducing the winners of last year," Kayla said.

"Hmm, yes. The winners of last year... the Moore girls," Emmy said.

Emmy's four sisters cheered and clanged their ladle against their pans.

"How's that fair, Emm?" Errin shouted. "You're a chef!"

"I never take part in the cooking, Errin. I'm part of the jury. Let me introduce you to the rest of our fine jury: our mothers!" Emmy opened the kitchen doors and called out for Catherine Walsh, Joan Ryan, Melissa Mills and Shauni Mills-Moore.

"Are you okay?" Kera whispered to Bree. "You seem a little pale. Take some of these breadsticks." Bree nicked a few off of Fianna's chopping board. She nibbled on a breadstick and swayed on her feet. The aroma coming from the closed pot in front of her made her nauseous. But what could she do? Draw attention by excusing herself?

"I'd love to see what you girls make of the Irish Shepard's Pie," Emmy's mom, Shauni, said as she walked over to the workstation of her daughters.

The thought of ground lamb, onions and Worcestershire sauce made Bree turn green. She took a deep breath and gripped the counter.

Bree broke out in a cold sweat. She felt the breadstick clawing its way back up her throat. "I'm sorry, I don't feel so good," Bree whispered before she bumped into the stainless steel counter with her hip. The constant talking and fuss in the kitchen was also getting to her. She speed walked from the kitchen.

Was this normal? She hated to think she was going to be some sickly wallflower until the baby came. And what happens then? How was she ever going to do this by herself? The thought was like a hand slipping around her throat and cutting off her air supply.

She walked past the rowdy bunch of guys cheering for a touchdown. By keeping her eyes trained on the floor in front of her, she tried to slip past a few Mills brothers before entering the restroom.

A firm hand halted Bree as it gripped her bicep. "What's wrong, Love?"

Again, Declan addressed her with his new nickname for her.

Months ago, he couldn't get her out of his house fast enough when she spoke of the word 'love' and now he was just throwing it out there.

Like it had no meaning. Perhaps for him, it didn't. She narrowed her eyes at him and shook his hand off.

"Leave me alone." She stomped past him and when she finally made it inside the restroom, she ran the last bit to reach the nearest stall.

The door to the restroom opened, and Bree quickly flushed. She hadn't even had time to lock her door. A groan escaped her lips as she tried to get up from the floor inside the stall.

Soft hands slid under Bree's armpits and picked her up. Shiny, chocolate strands of hair partially falling over Bree's shoulders gave Kate away.

"Come, let's sit down for a moment." Kate brought Bree over to the small bench in the restroom.

"It's going to be okay." She stroked Bree's back and offered her a glass of water. "Just to rinse out the taste. Don't take too much or it'll come right back up."

Bree rinsed out her mouth and sat back down next to Kate.

"I hope you'll feel better soon," Kate said while patting Bree's leg.

"Thanks."

The door to the restroom opened, and Dec's worried face stuck into the crack.

"Everything okay here?"

Irritation flared through her system, like a wave crashing over her body. She had no control over her emotions. Somewhere deep inside, she knew she was being irrational. But it was like another Bree was taking over her body, and she couldn't stop it if she'd tried.

"Just leave me alone! I don't need you in here. In fact: I don't need you at all!"

Hurt marred Declan's face before he took a step back and closed the door.

Bree and Kate sat in silence for several minutes. A sob escaped Bree's lips, and Kate tugged Bree against her chest and slipped an arm around her.

"It's okay. Let it out, Bree. It's okay."

She hadn't really let herself cry over this baby. She'd thought she was being careful, but fate had decided differently. The doctor had confirmed her pregnancy. But even then, she hadn't cried. Even though she knew she would not bring this baby into a stable, loving marriage.

Something she'd always swore she would make sure of. She'd seen her mother on her worse days. When she was so heartbroken she couldn't go out of bed. Or the times she'd been so angry with Bree and her sisters because she was angry at the world.

The day Kera bought Bree a pregnancy test and Gwenn blurted out she was going to be a mom, Bree had mentally checked out. Even the last few weeks Bree acted like nothing had really changed. But she couldn't just stick her head in the sand like she usually did in these types of situations.

Bree needed to face this pregnancy head on. Make plans at work. Prepare herself mentally for becoming a parent. Fix her apartment so she could raise a child.

Oh God, she'd need to look out for another apartment. Her place was way too small and not in a child-friendly neighborhood.

Bree looked up from her lap, tears still wet on her cheeks. Kate's eyes were also red rimmed. Kate kissed Bree's forehead.

"Whatever you need, Bree. I'm here for you. Always."

Bree choked back a sob and nodded against Kate's chest. "I'm making your dress all wet and snotty."

Kate shrugged. "I meant it when I said 'whatever you need'. It seems like you need a tissue."

They giggled. After another ten minutes of hiding out in the restroom, they reappeared in the pub.

The rest of Thanksgiving turned out fine. Bree passed up on the four different Shepard's Pie. She couldn't believe that her sisters had won this year's edition. It was probably all because of Gwenn and Kera's cooking.

Long after dinner, Bree attempted to clean some dishes in the kitchen. Declan passed her without acknowledging her.

He walked out into the enclosed back alley through the back door. No one had been in the kitchen or outside. This was her chance.

She walked out of the kitchen into the alley, straight over to Declan who sat on the bench with the back of his head against the brick wall. His eyes opened when the sound of her footsteps echoed between the walls of the alley.

"Hey," he said.

Declan didn't move to make room for her on the small bench. He was waiting her out. She'd seen how Declan acted when he was angry with someone. And boy, was he *pissed*...

"I'm late," she blurted while standing in front of him.

His eyebrows shot up to the inky strands that fell over his forehead. He narrowed his eyes and said, "What do you mean, you're late?"

"You damn well know what it means."

Realization dawned on Declan. He stood from the bench and leaned in to stare into her eyes.

"Is it mine?"

Her hand shot out and smacked his cheek. Slapping his stupid face was not enough. Declan grunted but didn't move.

"Can you blame me? We fucked twice, Bree. You just said

you wanted nothing to do with me and you're still talking to that douche."

He widened his stance and folded his muscular arms in front of his chest. How could she not talk to Craig? He's her colleague!

That asshole! What did he even think of her?

"Yes. *Talking.* Moron. Not fucking," Bree sneered.

"Well, how am I supposed to know?" Declan said and Bree's upper lip trembled. She wanted to cry so bad right now. But she wouldn't let him get to her.

"I'm only telling you this because it's the right thing to do—" Bree started before Declan interrupted her.

"What do you mean? If you think I'm the father—"

Dishes clanging in the kitchen interrupted Declan. Someone was doing an awful job of making his or her presence known. He or she had to have overheard their conversation. Great. Who would be the next to know about her situation?

Errin stuck her head around the corner and gave her best fake smile she could muster. Dec was sitting down again, but the anger was still rolling off of him in waves.

Bree held one hand on her still flat belly. How in the hell did they get here? What was she going to do with Declan? He didn't even believe her he was the father of her unborn child. Out of all the scenarios...

"Hey, you guys. Everything all right here?" Errin asked.

Declan narrowed his eyes at her. "Not a word. I know how you operate, Errin."

"Dec. What is wrong with you? Don't talk to her like that! She's your brother's girlfriend for crying out loud." Bree defended Errin. She had enough of his attitude. Like things weren't bad enough already.

"Well, if Errin heard us, the news will travel our families faster than the speed of lightning. And since you were nice enough to spring this news on me with both our families sitting only a couple of feet away—"

"Ah, shut it Dec. I didn't mean to throw it all out like this," Bree said, stomping a few steps away from Declan.

"So yeah, I'm asking you, Errin. Please, not a word," Declan said in a much softer voice.

"I'm telling Brennan, because we keep no secrets between us. But other than him, not a word from me." Errin faked zipping her lips and took a step back from the doorway.

Bree nodded at Errin and turned back to Declan.

"I can't believe you had the nerve of asking me if you were the father. I feel like I don't even know you anymore..."

Without waiting for a response, she walked away from him. Gwenn stood from her seat at Bree's burst through the swishing doors. Gwenn grabbed Bree's elbow and steered her out of Lucky.

"I didn't even thank Brennan. I need to say goodbye first." Bree hiccupped while the tears kept rolling over her cheeks.

"Nah, Brennan was still upstairs. I'll go back in a bit and tell them you felt sick. But only after I'm certain that you're okay."

Gwenn unlocked the passenger door to Bree's car and opened it for Bree.

"Tell me." Gwenn said after settling in behind the steering wheel.

"I can't even talk right now." Bree shook her head and closed her eyes.

"Do I need to have a talk with him?" Gwen asked.

Bree watched her sister out of the corner of her eye and almost wished she could send her sister back inside to kick Dec's butt.

"No. I'm okay." She swallowed the lump in her throat.

After a minute Gwenn said, "We're going to be okay. With or without him."

19

DECLAN

"You can't shut me out, Bree."

With an increasing cadence that represented the rising anger inside of him, Declan battered Bree's front door with his fist.

"Sir, if you don't leave now, I'm calling the cops."

Declan eyeballed the closed door of Bree's neighbor. The elderly man yelled again behind closed doors, "I mean it."

Declan had seen the brittle man once or twice, and he respected him for standing up for his young neighbor.

Normally, it would be Declan on the receiving end of phone calls reporting a disturbance. It should bother him he might end up with guys from his precinct coming by Bree's apartment.

But since Bree had dropped this bomb on him just an hour ago, Declan was not giving a flying fuck about anything.

"You do that," Declan said.

"And tell my colleagues to bring the battering ram. Or better yet, tell them that Declan Mills from Austin PD asked for the hydraulic door blaster."

Declan wasn't about to leave. What a fuckin' mess.

Bree had ignored him for days, snapped at him, told him to leave her alone, and then dropped the bomb she was late.

Because she'd said she didn't need him anymore, he'd jumped to the conclusion that he wasn't the father.

A bolt of anger had hit his chest as the vision of Bree with another man's baby crept into his mind. He needed to be the father of Bree's child. Not someone else.

While paralyzed by hurt, all of his words had come out wrong. If he hadn't been so stupid last March, then they'd be welcoming this baby with open arms—as a couple. They were going to be a family now. No matter if they were in a relationship or not.

"Bree, I know you're home. I just talked to Gwenn at Lucky."

He had been staring at the concrete brick wall in front of him, when Gwenn barged into the back ally at Lucky's. She'd given him an ear full, and it served him right. It had been the wake up call he needed.

He leaned with his forearm over his head against the front door. Declan sighed.

"Please, let me in."

The locks turned, and Declan stepped back when Bree finally opened the door wide. She took a few steps back, waiting on his next move. Bree looked ghostly.

Her white T-shirt reached mid-thigh and matched her unusually pale complexion. He closed the door behind him and locked the door.

She directed her eyes to a spot above his head, not meeting his eyes. Her lips were cracked and her hair a mess.

"Love, I'm so, so sorry…"

Her shoulders slumped, and her bottom lip trembled. He rushed to pull her in for a hug. He always did that, engulfing her smaller body with his arms so he could snuggle his face into her unruly, shiny hair.

"Have you been sick before I got here?"

She nodded against his chest.

"Shall I make you some ginger tea? Brennan said it always helped my Mom when she was sick from chemo."

Still without words, she nodded her confirmation.

"Let's get you back to bed."

Declan picked her up, and instant worry zinged through his chest. She weighed nothing. How long had this been going on? Why had he been such an arse to her? The poor lass had been sick, and he yelled at her because his stupid male pride got the best of him.

He sat her down on her rumpled bed. "Okay. Can you sit here for just a moment longer like this?"

She cocked her head. "Why?"

He knelt before her and enveloped her hands that rested on her lap with his hands.

"I'm going to the kitchen to grab you some stuff. Will you please wait for me here... like this?"

"Dec... you don't need to—"

"I need to do this. I..." He closed his eyes for a second and when he opened them again, he met her sky-blue eyes.

"I'm so sorry for being an arse to you. I want you to know that it came out all wrong. I was shocked. But I'm not using that as an excuse for saying the things I did. I hope you know that—"

Bree pulled her hand from his and placed her fingers to his lips.

"I shouldn't have sprung it upon you like that. I'm sorry too."

He kissed the tips of her fingers and as if he'd electrocuted her; she yanked her hand back.

"It isn't your fault," he said.

She nodded. "Okay. And now?"

"And now... we're going to get some food into your belly. Because I noticed you didn't touch your food at dinner. But you need to have something, or else you'll get nauseous again. Then we're going to get you cleaned up under the shower. I'm taking off this sticky bedding." Bree slapped his chest, and he chuckled.

"And after everything is all cleaned up, then we're going to bed and—"

"We're going to bed?" Bree asked with her chin jutted out. She fisted the bedding next to her thighs.

"Yes, Love. I'm going to be big spoon and you, like always, are going to be the little spoon. Just like when we were kids."

He tapped the tip of her nose once with his index finger before he stood up. "Call out if you need me, okay?"

He left her sitting on the end of the bed, wide eyed. He boiled some water for tea and stuck two slices of bread in the toaster. He pulled out his phone to call Kera.

"Declan." Kera's voice was crisp, not how she'd normally greeted him.

"I heard what happened from Gwenn."

Declan sighed. That didn't take long.

"I fucked up. I'm working things out with Bree, but it's like I'm talking to a ghost. She seems so frail. How much longer before the puking stops?"

"There's no rule book here, Dec. No pregnancy is the same."

"I know that. I guess what I'm really asking is—is Bree still healthy? I want to get her checked out in the hospital. I don't want her to get dehydrated. We need to look out for her and the baby."

"I'm a doctor, Dec. Bree's my sister. I'll let nothing happen to them. What Bree needs now is to rest. Give her some ginger tea. I've brought her salty crackers last night. The pack is on top of the fridge. Oh, and try some toasted bread with butter."

"I'm already on it," he said.

"Good. And Dec?"

"Yeah?"

"You've acted like a total putz. Get your shit together. I know the one person Bree needs right now is you."

Declan let out a breath. He was all too aware he'd fucked things up. Multiple times.

"You've always been her rock, Dec. You're the one person Bree turned to when things went from bad to worse after our dad left. She has always depended on you for guidance. I know you can be that for her once again. Please, don't let her down again."

"She means everything to me and more. Don't worry, Kera. I'm going to do right by my girl. I'm going to show her how much she means to me. She and our little baby growing inside of her are mine. I know this will not be a walk in the park, but Bree is going to trust and love me again."

"She never stopped loving you. It's the trust you need to work on," Kera said before she hung up.

He brought back the phone from his ear and laid it on the counter next to Bree's plate. How would he get her to trust him again? After he'd fucked things up yet again. The screen turned black and if it wasn't for the toast to jump up from the toaster, he would be still staring at the screen.

Declan took out the butter from the fridge. After taking care of Bree's meal, he put everything back in its place before heading out to the bedroom.

Just like he figured, Bree didn't listen to him. The shower was running in the bathroom.

He decided to not make a big deal out of it.

"Are you okay in there?"

"Yes," she said.

He cracked the bedroom window and walked around her comfy looking bed. After changing her sheets, he went to the tiny washing room in the hallway. He put the bedding in the washer and went back to the bedroom to check up on Bree.

She had turned the shower off. She rummaged around in the bathroom so he knew she was up and about.

He wanted to look her in the eyes. To see for himself, with her sister's confirmation in the back of his mind, that she still loved him. Even though he was a big putz.

Bree stepped out of the bathroom with her wet, long curls cascading over her shoulders. Droplets of water hurried themselves to find their way in between Bree's breasts.

He looked up from her cleavage pressing against the turquoise towel. Bree's throat moved as she swallowed while he stalked closer. A curl whirled around her earring, and he took the strand in between his thumb and index finger.

Dampness clung to his fingers as he rolled the strand around. The motion had always soothed him. His gaze went to her puffy lips with their fresh coat of lip-gloss. Hmm, she smelled of coconut. The tropical fragrance made him crazy with lust for her.

But he knew he had to rail himself in. He needed to be there for her. To take care of her. Not to lust over her.

She rolled her bottom lip between her teeth and it was as if a lightning bolt went straight to his dick. He sat down on the edge of her bed and took off his shoes and socks.

"What are you doing?" she said as she held still on the bathroom threshold, clutching her towel.

"I'm staying, Bree."

He stood from the bed and unbuttoned his navy blue shirt. He pulled down his jeans and grinned at her gasp.

"Sorry, but you better get used to it. You've been making me hard even before I could spell erection."

Bree's nervous giggle transformed into a full on belly laugh, and he joined her wholeheartedly.

"This is so weird," she said as she walked over to the bed and snuggled under the covers. Bree must not want to change her clothes in front of him as she lay down in a skimpy towel.

"What is?" he said.

"You. Me... Our baby."

Bree shrugged as she took her bottom lip between her teeth. She spied him as he slipped under the covers from his side from the bed.

He grabbed her arse to pull her in. She yelped and placed her hands on his chest.

"I know we have a lot to talk about. And we will... but please let me stay."

"*Now* you're asking? You've already taken off your clothes, lying here in my bed!" she scolded him while holding back a laugh.

He thumbed the apple of her cheek and said in a soft voice. "I've fucked everything up. Twice."

"This is so good. Keep your apologies coming," Bree said, grinning from ear to ear.

"You're feeling mighty better, eh?" he said and chuckled.

She missed a beat before she softly admitted, "Yes. I think I do." Bree snuggled in close, and he rolled on his back to give her room to lay her head on his collarbone. His hand instinctively found its way to her still toned stomach. Bree took a shaky breath.

"I've got you, Love. And that goes for you too, Little Love," he said as he gave the softest pat on her abdomen.

"I don't know, Dec."

"Oh, but you know, Bree. Deep down, you know this is right. Having you here in my arms is right. Having our baby is right." A lone tear fell on his chest, and he pulled her even closer. "I know we need to work out a lot of stuff..."

"I'm scared, Dec. I need to take it slow. Just... see how it goes, okay?"

"What are you afraid of?"

She looked up at him. "I'm pregnant, Dec. Of course I'm scared! I've never been pregnant before. I'm not even together with my baby's father—"

"Not if I have anything to do with it. I want us to be together." He narrowed his eyes and held on even stronger.

"I know what you want. But I don't know if it's what I need."

"How in the world can you even say that? You're carrying my

baby. Why don't you want to raise our child together? I'm... I have no words right now...."

"I can't turn a blind eye to the past year, Dec." Bree slipped out of his tight grip and sat up in bed. She tugged her towel close to her heaving chest and looked down at Declan.

"You've hurt me," she held her hand up defensively, "I know you didn't mean to. But I tried so hard to get over you when you said you didn't love me. I don't know if I can take another round of heartbreak. Especially after having your baby."

"You still have it in your head that I'm going to leave you. I'm not your Dad, Bree."

Declan knew it was a low blow, but he needed to say it. She was hiding behind a wall of hurt, and he needed to tear down that wall to bring her over to his side.

"Well, you still haven't said what I needed to hear. So... No. We are not together. Maybe, after some time. I don't know. Just give me time, okay?"

"People are going to come at you with questions. You know that right?" Declan said as he perched up on one elbow.

"You don't have to look so happy about it!" Bree bristled, and he chuckled.

"It's just a matter of time, Bree. You, me and Little Love belong together."

"Hmm."

He kissed her shoulder. When she didn't complain, he trailed his tongue over her goose bumps upwards to the spot where her neck met her shoulders. She shuddered, and he smirked against her skin.

"I love finding all these little spots, Love."

He eased her back against the mattress and unfolded the towel from her heaving chest. She looked up with her lust filled eyes. He leaned in and whispered against her lips, "I can't believe we're having a baby, Bree. You're making me the happiest man alive."

She threaded her fingers through his black hair. He kissed the corner of her mouth.

He slipped out of his boxer briefs. Her warmth and tightness welcomed him in when he entered her. She arched from the bed with her eyes rolled back into her head.

He licked and nibbled her lips. She opened up and gasped when he picked up speed.

Unbelievable that she's carrying his child. The thought almost made him come alone.

He grabbed the back of her knee and brought her leg up over his hip. This new angle had her crying out in pleasure.

"Oh, Dec. I'm so close. I... ooooh."

He wanted to go as deep as possible. If he didn't already made her pregnant, he wanted to do it now.

"This is going to be hard and fast, Love." He was almost there with her. She shuddered and bit the back of her hand while she came. Stars appeared before his eyes and his ears drummed.

Fuck. How was it that every time with Bree got better? More intense.

When she opened her eyes, she smiled at him.

"Wow."

"I know," he said before he kissed her shoulder.

20

BREE

"Are you ready?" Declan asked as they stood hand in hand on the porch.

"Ready as I'll ever be..." Bree tried to joke.

"It's all going to be okay, Love. I'm here for you and Little Love."

He kept saying that. After barging into her apartment at Thanksgiving, he did his best to show her how happy he was with their baby growing inside of her.

They'd spent two days together in their own little bubble. It was time to tell their families. The front door opened and Bree's heart skipped a beat.

Joan Ryan remained stoic at the sight of Declan and Bree holding hands on her porch. If she minded, she didn't let it show. Joan motioned for them to come in. "Don't just stand there. Come in."

"Thanks," Declan said as he brought his hand to Bree's lower back and guided her inside.

"How long has it been that you've been in my home, Dec?" Joan asked as she walked in front of them into the living room.

Nothing had really changed in Bree's old home. Joan sure loved her red carpets, red curtains and her recently bought ruby red couch. She'd kept the rest of her living room rustic but still warm of color with sandy tones.

Bree looked over to the grand windows looking over the backyard. The Mills' tree house peeked over the hedge. Declan's dad was next on their list to visit.

"Christmas Eve last year, I think. Yeah, it had to be Christmas Eve, because on Christmas Day, Bree went along with me to my old man."

Bree stood uneasy next to the couch. When Joan went to grab drinks, Declan laughed at Bree. "You're acting so weird right now,"

"What? I'm not acting weird. You are! Acting like nothing's going on—"

"Are you sure you don't want some coffee, dear?" Joan said as she walked back in with two coffees and a tea for Bree.

"No, tea is fine, thanks."

After a few minutes of sitting awkwardly together, Joan asked, "Okay. So, are you finally together now?"

Bree's cheeks flamed, and she looked over from the calculating eyes of her mom, over to Declan, who gave Bree a lopsided grin. He'd predicted this would happen.

She hadn't been ready to give in to him then. How could she? It was all going too fast for her.

Bree cleared her throat and shifted to the edge of her seat. She placed her teacup on the table and rubbed the palms of her hands on her knees.

"Okay, so I called you today... ehm, yes... to tell you that..."

Sweat broke out on Bree's back and she felt like fainting. She searched for Declan's eyes and he took her hand in his.

"Girl, spit it out. What in the world is going on?" Joan's fiery expression could match about ten Fianna's—easily. How this woman could ever let her husband walk all over her had been the world's greatest mystery.

"Mom... I..."

"What?" Joan said. She cocked her head as she looked over from Bree's teacup to Bree's hand on her stomach. Joan narrowed her eyes at Declan.

"You did this to her? You got my baby pregnant? Why? Were you afraid she was finally over you? You needed to tie her to you?"

"Mom!" Bree gasped.

"Ma'am, you're Bree's mother," he said calmly. "You're going to be the grandmother of our child. But never, ever, repeat this shite if you want to be a part of my kid's life."

"Like you could stop me from seeing my grandchild!" Joan turned red and aggressively slid her black-rimmed glasses up her nose.

"Let me tell you something, Declan Mills. No man is ever going to tell me what to do. Ever again. How could I support this? You're not even together? Or are you?"

Joan leaned forward in her seat and dismissed Declan entirely now. She looked at Bree.

"Haven't you learned anything from me? From my mistakes? How could you be so stupid?"

"And we're done here," Declan said as he stood from the couch, pulling Bree up along with him.

"See what he's doing, Bree? It's like watching myself being manhandled all over again."

"Dec..." Bree said as she tried to slow him down by taking her hand out of his.

Declan instantly halted and turned on his heel. He held up a hand. "You, Ma'am, are poison. Your daughter is sharing the news she's pregnant and you make it all about you. Talking down to your own daughter, telling her she's stupid..."

She took two steps to her mother. "Mom, I love you. Declan's just mad you would treat me like this. Like... well, let's be honest, like you've always done whenever I didn't meet your standards."

"This isn't about meeting standards about grades or finding

the right job to become self-sufficient, Bree. This is about you getting pregnant with a man who isn't in love with you."

"Now hold on, I'm in—"

Bree shot him a pulverizing look over her shoulder and hissed, "Don't you dare say it *now*. I don't want you to say it like this. Shut the fuck up, Dec."

Declan held his tongue.

"I know I'm nothing like you. I'm not as strong as you are, or even as independent," Bree said to her mother.

"Oh, dear Bree... but can't you see? You are just like me. You're exactly how I used to be with your father. I was love struck the moment he smiled at me that first time. And let me tell you this... if he ever came knocking... I still don't know if I would close that door in his face. I see that same quality in you. You've devoted your all to him."

She waved at Declan standing behind Bree, "And now you're pregnant with his child and never going to move on."

Declan walked over to them and placed his arm over Bree's shoulder. "She's never going to have to move on, Joan."

Joan snorted.

"The times Rob told me he loved me, pffft. If I got a dollar each time he said I was it for him, I could've bought a Ferrari. And in the meantime..." Joan shook her head and looked down at her red pumps.

"What? Had he been cheating during your entire marriage? Not just at the end?" Bree asked.

"Bree...." Joan looked up and her voice held a warning.

"I think I have a right to know. You brought him into this discussion. You're even comparing Declan to that man. So tell me. All those 'breaks' you had, were they because of dad cheating?"

"I'm not having this discussion with you, young lady. This is about you and Declan. Not about me and your father."

"This is rich. Real great, Joan. First you fixate your own insecurities upon your daughter and the moment she wants you to open up about what happened to this family years ago, you clam up."

"Why are you still here? I want you out of my home, Declan Mills."

"No problem. Are you coming, Bree? I'm going next door." She shook her head, and he gave her a sweet kiss on her forehead. "Okay, I'll see you at my Dad's, right?"

"I'll be just a minute. See you there."

Declan walked out of the living room, and the front door closed with a bang.

"Are you telling Sean Jr. today? Now there's another ladies man that could blow some smoke—"

"Mom! Stop it. Sean Jr. did nothing to you. Yes, after his wife died, he slept around with a lot of women. So what?"

"It's like talking to a brick wall with you. What happened with that nice boy, what's his name?"

"That boy was so memorable you can't even remember his name. Mom, I've been in love with Dec since forever. You've been away for months and months, and now that you're back from Brazil, you want to tell me how to live my life? No. I'm twenty-six and I'm doing this with Dec. With or without you in our lives."

"Hmm. That's a first."

"What?" Bree said as she dropped her fists from her hips.

"You standing up for yourself. Must be the hormones."

"Bye, Mom. I'm going over to see Sean Jr. Let's talk in a few days. Give it some time..."

Joan tugged Bree close to her chest before she could storm out of the house. Her straight golden hair was so contrasting to Bree's dark brown curls.

Bree knew her dad's side held the olive skin complexion and dark hair. She never knew her grandparents from either side. Her mom's parents had died in a car accident when Caitlin hadn't even been born yet. And her grandparents from her dad's side had always been a mystery. She'd never met them.

Bree took a pensive step back. "Who are my grandparents? Where's Dad?"

"Oh my God, Bree Juliana Ryan! I am not doing this with you. You go now, before Declan brings out his buddies from Austin PD to retrieve you."

"Why can't you talk about it?"

"Because it hurts! I promised myself to never let him get to me ever again. And talking about him brings out all those painful memories...."

"I'm sorry, Mom. But he's my father and I want to see him."

"What? Why? He's a liar and a cheat. He's going to bring nothing but trouble to your life. Please, don't do it," Joan pleaded with Bree with her gray eyes.

Bree sighed. "I'm leaving."

Joan grabbed Bree's arm. "Promise me you won't go looking for him, Bree."

"I can't promise you that, Mom."

She walked out of her mom's house. She remembered running over this driveway to her dad when she was little. He caught her mid air and swirled her around in his arms. Bree stabbed a tear from her cheek. She reached the sidewalk and shot a glance over her shoulder at her mother's house.

Joan wasn't looking out of the window. Although she shouldn't be surprised, it still hurt. Why couldn't she be happy for her? Sure, Bree's situation was far from ideal. But Bree had been unprepared at this wave of emotions crashing down on her. Being pregnant brought her upbringing in a whole different light.

After walking up the driveway to the Mills house, she swore to never become like her mother. Even if things didn't work out with Dec, she would not turn into Joan. Never.

Pops opened the door to Sean Jr.'s home. "Aaah, there she is!"

Declan's grandfather opened his burly arms and Bree gladly snuggled up to his warm chest. His enormous belly and wildly looking locks of gray hair had made her think of Santa Claus when she was little. He even laughed like him. Although Santa didn't swear and grumble as much.

"What's wrong, lass? My boyo's face reminded me of thunder rollin' over the green grass of Ireland. But he wouldn't talk to me 'bout it. He said it's between ye and yer mother? What did Joan say to ye this time?"

Growing up next to the Mills family brought them close. She could always talk to Pops. If someone were a father figure to her, it would've been Pops.

"Stop the tears, sweet Bree. Come, let's have it all out. We all know how ye mother can get. What's up her arse this time?"

"Pops! Don't talk to Bree about her mother like that," Sean Jr. said.

Declan's dad defended Joan five minutes after Joan slighted him about being some kind of manwhore. If he only knew. Bree blinked her tears away and sat down on the black leather sofa.

"What time is it, son?" Pops said.

"Not whiskey time yet, Dad."

"Phsst. It's almost four. I have me lass cryin' against me shoulder. Me boyo is doin' his best not to tear this place apart... Let's have a drink."

"Talking like a true bar owner," Sean Jr. mumbled before he walked over to the liquor cabinet in the living room.

"It takes one to know one."

"True," Sean Jr. said before he pulled out the whiskey and walked over to a side table where he picked up four whiskey glasses. He walked over to the couch and placed all glasses on the table. When he brought the bottle over to the glass in front of Bree, she shot out her hand and said, "Not for me, thank you."

"Aah, don't be silly. I was only joking. It's not too early for whiskey. It never is..." Sean Jr. winked. Her mother had been right when she'd said that Sean Jr. could blow some heavy smoke about just about anything. His charms never let him down before, you could tell.

"No, sorry... I...."

She felt Pops stiffen his arm around her shoulder. He nudged her with his calloused hand on her bicep.

"Nooo.... Really?" He looked from Bree over to Declan and the gleam in his eye misted over by the first tears.

"Tell me now. And don't take a piss. Are ye... Am I right to think yer...." He nudged his chin toward Bree's belly. "Now? Tell me. Make yer Pops the happiest man ever to be alive!"

Bree giggled when he gently nudged her by her arm. She turned in his arms and hugged him tight. "It is true, Pops," she whispered. "Me and Declan are going to have a baby."

"Sweet Lord in Heaven!"

"What's happening? Dec?" Sean Jr. poured the final glass of whiskey as he pulled one eyebrow.

"It's true, Dad... Bree and I... we're—"

"Don't be daft, son! Yer goin' to be a daideó. A granda!" Pops shouted over Bree's shoulder to Sean Jr.

Sean Jr. clanked the bottle on the table and walked over to Dec, who was sitting in his father's chair next to the fireplace. "Aye, is it true, son?" Sean Jr. asked while he pulled his six foot three tall son from his chair.

Declan smiled the biggest out of everyone, if it were even possible. "Yes! Yer gonna be a granda and Bree and me are finally gonna be together!"

She cleared her throat and tried to stand up from the couch, to say they weren't quite together, but Pops pulled her right in for another hug.

"Oh my sweet, sweet lass! Yous two were made for each other. I've always said so. I'll never forget that first day..." Pops let go of Bree and joined the hugging Declan and Sean Jr..

Bree took out her phone from her back pocket and snapped

a photo of these three burly Mills men, crying and hugging. What a sight to behold. She thought back to her Mom calling Bree stupid and almost wished she were a Mills girl. But then, she would be Dec's sister, and that shook her right out of her weird thoughts.

Pops walked back to the couch and grabbed his drink from the coffee table. After taking a hefty gulp, he burst out laughing as he remembered. "Ye were a six-year-old lass. Ye came runnin' out of ye house and bumped right into me boyo."

Bree looked over at Declan, who walked over to sit next to her on her other side. With an amused smile across his lips, he gave her a kiss on the cheek.

"Sweet, little Bree knocked Declan right into the nearest puddle. Ye knocked the wind right out of him, I'll tell ye!" Pops chuckled and Dec winked at Bree.

"Of course Ronan had to step in and gave ye his best potty mouth. Ronan was always making sure no one would ever hurt his brother."

"Fianna had handled him already," Bree said with a smirk, thinking back at Fianna standing up for her to Ronan.

"Hmm-hmm," Pops beamed at the memory.

"I'm so, so happy. Let's call the rest of me boyo's... Call Errin and her sisters. Lets have a party, eh?"

Bree tried to give Pops her best smile, but failed by the look of Pops.

"No? Not a good idea?"

"Pops, it's still new and Bree... we're..." Declan searched his words.

"We just came from my Mom's," Bree said. "Let's say things didn't go so well..."

"No? And why?" Pops asked before taking another swallow of whiskey.

Bree sighed. She hated to defend her mother. She knew her mother was in the wrong today by calling Bree stupid and trying to drive a wedge between Dec and her. But in her own way, her mother was trying to look out for her.

"Mom was being Mom." Bree shrugged.

"Let's leave it with that, shall we?" Sean Jr. said. "Let's share a toast to the Mills grandson—"

"Or Pops' first great granddaughter!" Declan said.

"Are you team pink?" Bree smiled at the thought of Declan with a baby girl in his arms, snuggling her close, smelling her hair like he always did hers.

He kissed her nose and whispered, "I'm team Bree."

She rolled her eyes. "You're so corny."

"I'm also thinkin' it's gonna be a girl," Pops said.

"Kera and Gwenn have a Baby Betting Pool," Bree said. "You can wager bets on due date and gender."

"Aye, that's me girls!" Sean Jr. smiled.

"Tell yer sisters Imma placin' a bet on a girl. Born on the fourth of... when's the baby due?"

"June," Declan said.

"Right... that's over..." Pops counted the months on his fingers.

"Six months from now. Pff that's going to be just as long as we had to wait for little Tommy to be born. Can't wait for Tommy to hear he's goin' to have a cousin."

"We're going to have a baby shower at Lucky," Pops said.

"And when the baby is born, we have—"

"That's enough Pops, let the kids be," Sean Jr. smiled.

Pops raised his glass and said, "To baby Mills."

21

DECLAN

"What time is our appointment? I thought it was at ten?" Declan said as he narrowed his eyes at the clock hanging above the nurse's station.

At nearly half past ten, his already fluttery nerves had him practically jumping from his plastic chair in the waiting room to go fetch a doctor.

"Shh. It's just busy. We're not going home without seeing someone," Bree said.

"Is that before or after our Little Love is born?"

They had told everyone in their families about the baby. Last week had been everything. All the love and support they got from their families and friends had been exactly what Bree needed after that awful talk with her mother.

It reminded him once more where Bree's uncertainty and trust issues came from. He hadn't helped with his stupid actions, sure. But seeing Joan spitting her venom had been the wake up call he needed.

He was going to take action. It was suddenly clear to him that calling Bree his Love hadn't been enough. He needed to make a statement. After telling Ro about the baby, he'd asked Ro to help him organize something for Bree at Christmas Day. He wanted to involve Ro in this new chapter of his life.

Bree rolled her eyes at his impatience and turned the page on some magazine with a smiling baby on its cover. Do babies even do that? Or was this kid photoshopped?

"Miss Ryan?" A young blonde woman in a doctor's coat screened the waiting room.

Declan jumped right out of his chair.

"Yes! Over here."

He couldn't wait to get to see their baby's heartbeat. The doctor smiled. "Ah, I'm guessing you're Miss Ryan's partner?"

"Yes. I'm Declan and this is Bree," Declan said as he placed his hand on her lower back.

The doctor chuckled. "I know. We've met before. How are you, Bree? Shall we go to my office?"

Bree smiled at the doctor and nodded.

"Yes, that's a good idea."

"You just love seeing me like this, eh?" Declan asked. "Out of my comfort zone."

He smiled against her hair as he pulled her in for a quick kiss on top of her head.

She held out her hand for him to take and they walked into the hallway, following their doctor.

"It's quite entertaining," Bree said.

"I hate to say this, but I think I'm suffering from hormones too. Pff I'm even having hot flashes at night."

The doctor was about to sit down behind her desk but held still mid air. "Oh no, did you really say this to a pregnant woman? Oh, you, sir, have a lot to learn."

Bree and the doctor shared a simultaneous eye roll and laughed.

"I see. So I'm just here for your entertainment." Declan sat down in his chair next to Bree and grinned.

"Oh, Bree. This is going to be so much fun!" the doctor said while picking up a pen from her desk to wiggle it around between her fingers.

"I know, Sarah," Bree said as she slapped Declan's knee in good spirit.

"Sarah, as in...."

"Sarah Michaels, your partner's ob-gyn. Nice to meet you," Dr. Michaels said.

"I've changed ob-gyn after the first doctor was no match," Bree said.

"Okay, nice to meet you too. Shall we get started?" Declan had a feeling he would not like being outnumbered by these two women during their upcoming appointments.

"It's been a few weeks since we last seen each other. Have you been still experiencing nausea?" Dr. Michaels asked while typing something at her computer.

"Why do people say morning sickness when it's all day long? It's been getting better now that I know that it's best to eat crackers all day. It seems to get worse when my stomach is empty."

"Hmm, yeah. I get this from a lot of women. Have you tried ginger tea?"

"Yes, Declan came up with the same idea."

Declan perched up on his seat, ready to join the conversation. But then Dr. Michaels asked her next topic on her list, "Have you been taking your pills?"

"Pills?" Declan said as he turned in his seat. Bree had said nothing about any pills.

Bree smiled. "Yeah. I take them every morning."

"What pills? Is something wrong?"

"It's just a precaution, Declan. The folic acid can help prevent birth defects," Dr. Michaels said.

"I haven't even thought about this stuff. How are we going to—"

Dr. Michaels waved her pen at him. "After this appointment,

I'm giving you enough reading material to make you the next baby expert. I promise. And over four weeks, we'll see each other again and then you can ask me everything you want. We still have months to prepare you both on this baby. I'm certain you're going to be the best parents to this little bean when the time comes."

Declan nodded and held his tongue. What else could he do? He didn't know shit about all this stuff.

"Bree, it's time to fill in the rest of my questionnaire. I noticed that Dr. Ulkner left out details about the baby's father and about your father's side of the family. We need to ask about the medical history of you both, and if possible, about any medical history in the rest of your family that could be of importance."

Bree shifted in her seat. "I know nothing about my Dad. I mean, I know who he is..." she tried to laugh it off, but her nervous chuckle broke Declan's heart.

That damn arsehole.

And her mother wasn't any better.

Declan had always felt protective of Bree, but now that she was pregnant with his baby, it had been multiplied by a gazillion. Bree's mom was projecting her own feelings on her daughter, filling Bree's head with all kinds of bullshit. He wouldn't stand for that. Mom or not.

"Bree hasn't seen her father in nearly twenty years," Declan said as he reached out to hold Bree's hand.

He gave her hand a little squeeze. "She also hasn't met any grandparents from her fathers' side. Her dad never talked about them."

Bree gave him a pensive smile, and she squeezed his hand in thanks.

Dr. Michaels hummed while typing on her computer. "Okay, noted. And you, Declan? Anything we should know about?"

"Healthy as a horse. My family is in good health." He cleared his throat, thinking of his mother. "Well... my mom died over twenty years ago. Breast cancer."

Dr. Michaels typed and nodded. "I'm sorry to hear that."

After a moment she said, "Okay, we're going to do some fun stuff now. Bree, can you please put on the gown I've placed for you on the exam table? Could you please lie down for me? I'll be back in a sec., We're going to see your baby for the first time. Are you excited?"

Declan and Bree smiled at each other when they simultaneously said "Yes." He leaned in and gave her a quick kiss.

Bree stood from her seat and walked over to the exam table.

"I can't believe we're going to see our baby," he said.

"I know. I can't wait."

Bree made quick work at removing her clothes, and his eyes zeroed in on her stomach. Declan eyed her flat tummy and wondered about the size of their baby right now.

He picked up the hospital gown so she could step into it. He closed the gown, and she looked over her shoulder.

"Thanks. I'm glad you're here with me. I'm so nervous. I hope everything is alright."

Declan swallowed the lump in his throat. He nodded. "Yeah. I know. I can't wait to see the baby. To have it all checked out and to know this is really happening."

She placed her hand on his cheek and leaned in to kiss him. "It's going to be alright."

"That's my line."

She giggled, and Declan helped her up on the exam table.

"Thanks, guys," Dr. Michaels said as she walked back into her office.

"Okay, so Bree already knows this from listening to the heartbeat on an earlier appointment, but I have to warn you, Declan. It can take a few moments to find the baby."

He grabbed Bree's hand, and she yelped, "Ouch!"

"Oh, sorry..." He kissed the back of her hand.

Bree and Dr. Michaels shared another look while they figured he didn't notice. Or they didn't care, anyway. Dr. Michaels exposed Bree's lower region.

"The heartbeat is about 170 beats per minute, but from here on out this will slow."

Dr. Michaels squirted gel on Bree's stomach, and Bree squeezed Dec's hand.

"Oh, sorry, it's a bit cold," Dr. Michaels said.

"It's okay," Bree said.

The doctor placed an ultrasound device on Bree's stomach and gently slid her way over Bree's slippery skin.

"Ah, found it!" Dr. Michaels said right after they heard the first ba-dum, ba-dum, ba-dum.

Hearing the beating heart of their child thickened Declan's throat. He watched the dark screen hanging on the wall. It was all grey spots and white specks.

Their child was somewhere in those pixels. He swallowed his tears away before he leaned in and kissed Bree. After their quick kiss, he looked over to Dr. Michaels before she tilted her head to the side and scrunched her nose.

"What's wrong?" Bree said, her eyebrows drawn down. Declan held his breath, trying to read the doctor's facial expressions.

Dr. Michaels held up a finger, showing she needed another moment to investigate Bree's uterus.

"Do either of you two have twins in the family?"

"I'm a fraternal twin," Declan said.

"You didn't mention this earlier," the doctor said.

"I'm sorry, it slipped my mind?" He looked at Bree lying at the table, looking like she'd seen a ghost.

"Twins?" Bree asked. "Tell me you're lying."

"Geez, Bree. What are ye talkin' 'bout? Like ye didn't know. Ye known me for two decades. Ye played hide and seek with Ro. What are—"

"Yes, I'm confirming it. Bree, Declan… you're going to have twins!"

"What?!"

Declan glanced at Bree, who lay still with her eyes as wide as two UFO saucers.

"Fuck…" Declan whispered. He looked over at the TV screen again, but it all seemed like a big blur.

"Oh, my, that's… that's…" Bree put her chin down and peered at the ultrasound device on her tummy.

"Are you sure?"

"Yes, Bree. I'm sure."

Bree nodded and tugged at Dec's hand, making him lean in.

"This is all your fault," she said.

"Isn't this the line women say in the movies when they're in labor?"

"Ouch, wrong answer, Declan," Dr. Michaels snickered.

"You and your twin! You did this to me!"

"I know this must be quite a shock. We'll schedule extra appointments and I'm going to see if we have some leaflets on twin pregnancy for you. I'll be right back."

The doctor walked out of the office and Dec turned to Bree and said, "What does Ro have to do with any of this?"

"Well, without him, you wouldn't be a twin. And I wouldn't be having twins. My God, we're going to need two baby seats, two baby beds, two—"

"Are you done?" Declan laughed and cocked his head.

"Excuse me?" Bree wiped the gluey stuff from her belly with some paper towels.

"Stop freaking out. Picture this," he said as he leaned over the exam table.

"We get to have two for the price of one. Two little Brees…" He kissed her still somewhat sticky belly and rested his head against the spot.

"Or two Declans. I don't know if I can handle this." She puffed a breath.

"Oh, you handle me just fine..." he winked from his spot on her abdomen.

She trailed her fingers through his hair, and he closed his eyes. Inside of Bree were his two children. Two! He couldn't wait to tell his family.

"Gwenn and Kera are going to have a field day with their Baby Pool," Bree said.

"Pops is going to give free rounds of whiskey at Lucky when he hears this," he said.

Bree chuckled, and Declan's head bobbed. "We're going to be all right Bree. I just know we are."

22

DECLAN

"10-9."

Declan pressed on his directional microphone's button and repeated, "10-23."

Caitlin crouched next to Declan, behind the see-through hedge that surrounded the house partially. They had just arrived at the scene. The front door stood wide open. A piercing female scream came from inside the one-story house.

"I'm going in," Caitlin said as she tried to stand from her hunching position.

Declan pulled her back down and hissed, "Stay the fuck down, Ryan. We're not flyin' off the hook and walkin' straight into trouble."

"We can't let him beat her into a pulp! I can't sit around and do nothing!" Caitlin spat at him.

"I'm not askin' ye to do nothin'. Just don't go all Rambo on me. Ye need to know where ye gettin' yerself into before ye—"

"This is not my first day on the job, Declan Mills."

She grabbed her gun from its holster and snuck closer to the front door, hiding behind two large trash cans.

"Why do I even try?" Declan said as he looked up to the morning sky. They were going to Bree's mother tonight for

Christmas Eve. Was it too much to ask for a slow day today? Or for Cait to not lose her cool?

As he followed Cait's lead, they crept under the window. Cait shook her head as they heard a booming voice inside say, "Admit it, Jess. You were taking Liv away from me, eh? Well, this is the last time!"

A soft little whimper followed, and a woman said, "Don't you dare hurt my daughter!"

Declan positioned himself next to the front door and announced himself.

Cait ran past Dec with her weapon drawn and before Dec could react, she already fired at the burly man holding a knife against the little blonde girl's throat.

The blonde woman who'd knelt at the man's feet let out a horrendous cry. The shot missed. Cait didn't waste another second and grabbed the angelic girl from his grasp.

She held the girl behind her back and gave the bastard a kick to his gut that lead him down to the floor.

"I'm going to kill you," the man shouted while he attempted to get up to reach for his knife.

As if possessed, Cait gave him another kick to the face. Knocking his lights out. Dec kicked the knife to the other side of the living room.

He did a first visual check on the woman who had snagged up the child into her arms. The child was crying, but luckily not bleeding anywhere. He then passed them to stop Cait from doing further harm.

He took Cait by the shoulders and pulled her away from the motionless arsehole. Although unconscious, the man's pulse was luckily still there. Declan also checked for any internal bleedings caused by Cait's kick to the gut. He searched the room and next to a painting was a bullet hole. The shot had gone wide.

If she'd killed him, he would be her second perp this year.

First she'd shot Kayla's stalker in March, and now this. Declan knew this would be Cait's final straw.

There would be no coming back from this incident. She'd stormed into the house, shooting at the man holding the knife to the child's throat. Although she'd saved the child, today's actions were unlike Cait.

Declan steered Cait into the small kitchen and called everything in. After receiving word from dispatch, he sat Cait down on a stool and made her promise to sit tight and to talk to no one.

He needed her to save whatever left of her sanity. The feral expression she'd showed today after kicking that man unconscious, made even Declan shudder. And he didn't get easily spooked.

He walked over to the woman. She rocked the little girl in her arms.

He checked the man's pulse again. Still steady. And still out cold.

Declan blocked the sight of the man as it was nothing for a young girl to see. My God, today hit him close to home.

He just found out he was having twins, and here he was, saving a little girl's life. How old would she be? Five? Six, maybe? She looked around the same age as Tommy.

"Thank you so much," whispered the woman.

"He would've…" she sobbed and her entire body shook as her cries increased in volume.

"Ma'am, can I please have a look at your beautiful baby girl?" he said.

The woman eyed Declan suspiciously, but he could understand the need to hold on to your child after this morning. He held out a hand and kneeled down again. "Just to make sure she's not hurt. Would that be okay?"

The woman nodded and her red rimmed blue eyes turned

on her daughter. "Liv, we've got to let this nice police officer have a quick look at you. Come, show him your face, sweetie."

"That's a good girl," Declan said. The girl had a bruise on her upper arm, probably where that man had grabbed her, but other than that, no injuries showed on the surface.

"Do you hurt anywhere, Liv?" Declan said.

He needed to make sure the girl didn't have any internal bleeding. In times like this, these small check-ups could save lives.

Liv shook her head and looked up to her mommy. "I want to go see Ryleigh."

"Ryleigh?" Declan asked, wondering if they'd missed someone during the altercation. He instantly stood and eyed all exits.

"Is there someone else present here?"

He couldn't believe they made this rookie mistake. He hadn't even cleared all rooms yet. He'd been too preoccupied with his partner losing her shit and almost killing the bastard holding a knife to this child.

The woman shook her head. "No. No, it's just us. Liv and I live here, and..." she waved a trembling hand at the man on the floor who still was knocked out cold.

"Nobody's here?"

Cait walked into the living room. "I got it." She checked out the pantry before he could even tell her to sit her arse back down in the kitchen. Just his luck if she would find another man to shoot in the bedroom. But he couldn't exactly yell this in front of the victims before him.

"Just a minute, I'll be right back. Call out for me the moment he stirs."

He followed Caitlin as she just entered the last bedroom down the hall. His eyes scanned the room, and he looked under the bed. After checking the closet, he turned to Cait, who held still in front of a chest of drawers with several pictures on top.

"Okay, the room is clear," he said and made a move to walk out of the room.

Cait stood stock-still. She trained her eyes on the bigger photo frame and her hand went to pick it up, as if in slow motion.

"Cait."

She didn't respond and trailed her finger over the picture.

"Cait!"

She picked up the photo frame and turned it to Declan.

"It's him," she said.

"Who? What are you talking about? Leave that and walk back with me to the kitchen. Stop touching their stuff." Declan was getting more agitated by the minute, and more worried. The haunted eyes of Cait shot over the photo and she picked up her cell phone.

"What are ye doin'?" Declan said as he tried to take the picture from Cait's hand.

"Stop it, Dec! It's all I have of him. I need to take a picture!"

"What are you doing in here?" the woman said as she held still outside her bedroom where Declan and Cait were playing a tug of war with her photo frame.

"I'm so sorry, Ma'am. We're coming right out," Declan said.

"Are you related to Rob Walker?" Caitlin asked. She looked from the woman to the picture and back again.

The woman pulled her eyebrows down and held her child close on her hip.

"Eh…" She searched for Declan's guidance as she must have found Caitlin acting as weird as he did.

"That's my uncle," said the little girl.

"What? He is," the girl said when she met her mother's scowl. She wormed her way down from her mother's hip and walked over to Declan and Caitlin. Her mother followed her and held a protective hand on her shoulder. Liv pointed at a middle-aged man, next to a blonde woman and surrounded by younger men and women.

"That's Rob with my auntie Brenda. Rob's my grandfather's brother."

The photo frame shook in Cait's hand and Declan quickly took it from her, afraid she would drop it.

"I can't believe it..." Caitlin whispered. "I never looked him up. I never wanted to know..."

"What do you mean?" Liv asked Cait.

Caitlin blinked a few times and crouched so she was at eye-level with Liv.

"I think we're family..."

"Cait!" Declan took Caitlin by the upper arm and hauled her out of the bedroom. "What in the world has gotten in to you?" he said.

"He's my dad, Dec. I've got to have that picture!" Cait thrashed as she tried to get out of his iron grasp.

"Wait!"

The woman speed walked after them into the living room, with Liv hot on her trail. "I'm Jessie. Let's talk in the kitchen!" She held a hand to her chest and tried to catch her breath.

Nobody bothered to look after the still unconscious body on the floor. What a cluster fuck. He was leaving harmed bodies behind and running after his partner, who was amid losing her shit.

Luckily, their colleagues arrived at the scene. An ambulance followed the squad cars and Declan lead them all into the house. Two I.A. officers took Cait and Dec separately to the side to question them about what happened.

Two female officers took care of Liv and Jessie. Declan overheard Jessie say she'd been grateful for Caitlin taking the man down like she did. Her husband had been abusive ever since he started drinking a few months ago. The man accused Jessie of taking Liv with her to see her family with the intent of never coming back.

Declan looked over to the internal affairs officer who lead Cait back into his car. He sighed and figured today had been the last day of his partnership with Cait.

A small hand on his bicep took him by surprise. "I'm so sorry, officer—about your partner. I wanted to thank you both. She did the right thing, but now she's going to be in trouble for saving us."

"It's our job, Ma'am. I'm glad we could be there for you and your daughter."

"Please, call me Jessie."

"Do you have any kids?" Jessie asked.

For the first time that morning, he took a deep breath, and it was like a weight lifted off his chest. He smiled.

"My girl is having our twins next year."

Her eyes rounded, and she returned his smile.

"That's so special. Congratulations."

"Thank you."

"Here, I have more copies of my own." Jessie handed Declan the picture of Rob Walker.

"Is this Rob's family?" Declan asked as he took the picture.

"We've always wondered about him, you know? My uncle left Brenda for a few years at a time, but he always came back. It was back and forth like that, until at some point, about twenty years ago, he stayed.... Now they're stronger than ever. It was right after the twins were born." Jessie pointed at two girls who were the spitting image of his Bree.

Bree's half sisters seemed to be around twenty years old. His eyes traveled the picture, and he counted three guys and two girls— the twins. My God, what had Rob Walker been up to all these years?

"Are you sure I can take this?" he held up the picture.

"It's okay. It's the least I can do for your partner. If she's really family—I want to stay in touch with her. She saved our lives today. No matter what people say…"

"Thank you. I'm leaving you my card. I know you've discussed with my fellow officers to call them if you need any help in filing charges against your husband. But you can call me night or day with questions about how to go from here, okay?"

Jessie's eyes teared up again, and she nodded.

"And I don't think its entirely following protocol for me to give you my card, but I'm involved on a personal level. My girl… she's my partner's sister. I'm meeting their family tonight for Christmas Eve."

"Your girl? That would make her also my cousin."

Declan nodded.

"How many siblings does she have?" Jessie asked before someone called her name. It seemed like her family had arrived to take over from here.

"My girl has four sisters."

"Oh, when my cousins find out, they—"

"Please," Declan urged. "Let's give it a moment before we go spread the word, okay? I don't know how everyone is going to take this. Let's meet up after the dust is settled. Also, with you and…"

He let his words trail. Not wanting to mention her husband. But he wouldn't let these strangers anywhere near his Bree anytime soon. Not now she was carrying their babies.

Jessie seemed nice enough. But he'd know from experience with other cases, one could never know. Jessie could take her husband back, and he wouldn't let Bree anywhere near that fucker.

"Okay," Jessie said, letting out a frustrated breath.

"But I felt that my other cousins need to know about this too," she added and gave a quick nod in the picture's direction.

"You're right, but please let them have Christmas before we drop this bomb on their doorstep."

Jessie nodded and took out her phone. She dialed Dec's number.

"Now you have my number too. Call me if you'd like to set something up. I'll be concentrating on Liv and whatever is going to happen to her father. But maybe in a few months, we could arrange something?"

"Let's stay in touch. Okay? I wish you all the best." He nodded at her watery smile and turned around.

How was Bree going to handle this news about her father? Stress isn't good for the babies. Shit. He needed to talk to Bree before Cait would.

23

BREE

Bree opened the door to a deliciously fresh smelling Declan, leaning into her doorway. Dressed in his signature dark blue jeans, black button-down shirt, he'd topped it off with his leather jacket.

"Hey."

He smiled and said, "Hey, Love."

The flutters in her belly took over the minute he'd texted he would pick her up early today. He had dodged all her questions. His only reply was that he needed to talk to Bree before they would spend Christmas Eve with her family tonight.

Throughout the day, she'd convinced herself he must have picked Christmas Eve to tell her he loved her. And this time, he would tell her he loved her in the same way she loved him.

She'd spent the past two hours in and out of the bathroom. She'd re-dressed several times until Gwenn finally picked out this sexy, mini wrap dress with fluted sleeves. Bree had left it hanging in her closet because of its color: bright red. But Gwenn insisted it didn't matter Bree would clash with her mother's ruby interior.

Declan tugged at a curl from Bree and gave her lips a sweet kiss. After backing her up against the nearest wall, he closed the door behind him and took her cheeks in between the palm of his hands.

"You. Are. Absolutely. Stunning," he said in between their kisses that heated more and more with every nibble or stroke of tongue. He leaned down and kissed her throat. A soft moan escaped her lips when he gently nudged his knee in between her legs.

Bree's ringtone from somewhere on the couch brought her out of her lust-induced daze.

"I'm so glad you could make it early today," she said.

Her phone rang again and Declan stepped aside to let her retrieve her ringing phone.

"I have to tell you about something that happened this morning," he said before she could answer her phone.

She looked at her screen. Cait was calling her.

"Did something happen to my sister?" She instantly turned to Declan to gauge his expression.

Declan swallowed. "Not in that way, Love. Your sister is fine. I just checked on her. Well, she's fine physically..."

"Tell me what happened? Is it something you can share? Or are there others involved?"

Bree knew some things that happened on the job couldn't be discussed at home. It had been this way with Cait, and with her sisters Kera and Gwenn during their deployment. Bree was getting more or less used to it.

"You better sit down for this," he said.

"You're scaring me, Dec." Bree sat down and placed her palms on her thighs. She fidgeted with the hem of her dress. It all seemed so silly getting worked up about which dress to wear...

"Your sister and I had a call about a situation this morning. It was a very intense situation where Cait had to intervene and make a quick judgment call. She saved the lives of two people today. But she also did it in a way I.A. most likely will not approve of."

"Is Internal Affairs starting an investigation?" Bree rubbed mindlessly on her wrist.

"Yes. I've checked on Cait before I came here and she told me she's suspended while waiting on the outcome of the investigation."

Bree gasped. "Oh, no... her work is her life, Dec. You know this better than anyone! They can't do this to her! Can't you do something about it?"

"I'm sorry, but they have already decided. And you know I can't elaborate too much, but I think it's even for the better. I told your sister she should seek counseling."

"I'm calling Cait." Bree stood from the couch and walked circles in her pocket-sized apartment with her phone against her ear.

"Hey, sis," Cait's voice sounded gloomy, and she slurred her last word.

"What in the world is going on?" Bree said.

"Hasn't Dec told you already?"

"No? He said something had happened, but he couldn't tell me anything."

Cait let out a humorless laugh. "Ah, so Dec's being Dec. Tell him he doesn't need to protect his crazy ex-partner anymore. I'm done."

"Have you been drinking already? It's three in the afternoon!"

Cait hiccupped and said, "It doesn't matter anymore. I've tried to shoot a bastard down when he threatened to kill his own daughter. I'll never forget the look in the little girl's eyes, Bree. Those eyes will haunt me for the rest of my life..."

"I'm coming over," Bree said.

"No need, Bree. Kera is here, and she's driving us to Mom's

house, so I'm going to take a nap now. Sleep the alcohol out of my system..."

Bree looked over at Declan while shaking her head. She mouthed, "What the fuck?"

She almost missed her sister mutter under her breath, "And I need another drink tonight when I tell you all about our brothers and sisters."

"What did you just say?" Bree held still mid circle and eyed Declan, who'd been following her one-sided conversation like a hawk.

"Ask Declan. He's even got pictures! Even made me a copy. I'm taking my nap now. See you tonight."

Bree stared at her phone in disbelief. What was that all about?

"She told you about Rob?"

Bree nodded while still looking at her screen. "She said something about brothers and sisters...."

Declan walked over to her and held out a picture.

"You have got to be kidding me!"

Bree took the picture from Declan and her eyes scanned the smiling faces staring back at her. She plopped down on her couch and Declan took a seat next to her.

She took a sharp intake of breath as she almost recognized herself in the picture. Two young women looked identical if it hadn't been for their different hair colors.

One had Bree's almost black hair color on top with some kind of pink, purple hue on the bottom of her hair. The other twin, because there was no mistaking the fact they were, had chestnut hair with blonde highlights.

"They look just like me...."

"I know, Love. It's the eyes, the chin... I mean sure, they're paler, but look at their brothers..., they all have the same hair color as you."

"I've always felt so different from my sisters. Fianna and Kera with the gorgeous red hair—"

"Your hair is gorgeous too," Dec interrupted. Bree smiled and bumped her shoulder to his arm.

"And then you have my mother with her blonde hair, and Gwenn and Caitlin who both have more of a brown hue."

She brought the picture closer to her face and said, "This one guy looks just like me. He's also got my olive skin tone."

"He seems to be the middle brother."

Declan chuckled and pointed at one guy. "This dude here is one scary motherfucker…"

Bree laughed. "Stop it, or I'm telling my brother on you." She bit her bottom lip. "I can't believe it. I never knew… I've got three brothers and two extra sisters, Dec."

"Half-brothers and half-sisters," he said.

She waved her hand in the air. "Pssht, semantics. They're blood. True, they're officially half-blood. But blood all the same."

Declan kissed the top of her hair. "I don't want you to get your hopes up just yet, Love. There's a good chance Rob's other family won't be so welcoming. I can't imagine what his wife Brenda will say about all this."

"Brenda? That's her name?"

Bree found her in the picture. She was no mistakenly Rob's wife. They looked at each other with so much love in their eyes.

Bree swallowed back her tears. She hurt for her mother. Joan had been heartbroken by this man who'd left them all behind.

Joan had to pick up the pieces and take care of five girls on her own. Bree's father never kept in touch with his own children. Instead, he got himself a whole new family.

"What kind of man does this?" Bree whispered as she glanced at her father.

Rob Walker had dark-rimmed glasses, almost black hair, and a proud stance. She remembered him vaguely, as she'd been only eight by the time he'd left them permanently.

"A stupid arsehole," Declan said.

This time they both refrained from joking. Because Declan was right. Her father is a stupid asshole. He could never undo the hurt he'd caused her family. She wasn't sure if she would be up for meeting him now.

During her fight with her mother, Bree blurted she'd wanted to see her father. But now she'd held the picture of his other family in hand. Doubts were kicking in. What kind of man was her father? Had he been keeping two families at the same time?

That scary dude in the picture seemed the oldest out of his brothers and sisters, and maybe even older than Caitlin. Bree's oldest sister's birthday is coming up. On the last day of the year Cait would turn thirty-six.

She narrowed her eyes and scrutinized the oldest brother. He had a bit of crowfeet next to his eyes. But he also had a certain darkness to him that Bree only had seen with Ronan whenever he was fighting in a cage during one of his MMA matches.

Yes, that's it. He had a smoldering rage inside of him. His raven beard and half long inky hair made him stand out in a crowd, she was sure.

"How did you even get this picture?" Bree said.

"Let's say, there was a situation at someone's house and your sister stumbled upon this picture."

"Oh… that's the reason she flipped her shit," Bree said.

"I don't think it is, Love. She'd already flipped out. But seeing this picture was the final straw. If I'm honest, she scared the shit out of me, Bree. She needs help."

"You scare me, Dec. It's not like you to say stuff like that. Not about my sister."

"There's something I haven't told you yet."

"What is it?" she asked.

"Because of their privacy, I first felt like I couldn't share any of this with you. But I've thought about it, and since Cait already told you fragments about what happened..." Declan took a deep breath and stared into Bree's eyes.

"The little girl that Cait talked about—her mom turned out to be your cousin."

"Oh, no! Are they okay?" Bree asked.

Declan nodded. "I know that Jessie, she's your cousin, wants to keep in touch. She gave me her number so we could set up a meet. She's grateful Cait saved her little girl's life, and she wants to help Cait by sharing information about your dad, I guess."

"What did she look like?"

Declan reached out to cup Bree's cheek and she leaned into his touch.

"She has a girl about Tommy's age, her name is Liv. And Jessie and Liv have both long, blonde hair. But Liv's hair is almost as white as Kayla's hair. They both have been through a lot."

He pulled her in for a hug and said, "I know. I'm sorry. I needed to tell you before she sprang this on all of you tonight."

She sagged against his chest. "Oh."

"I love Cait like she's my big sister, you know that, Love. But I won't let anyone hurt you. She may not care about anything anymore. She's about to lose her job, hell, her purpose in life, even. But I can't let her spring something this important on you."

"Thank you."

How could she be so stupid? She had been changing clothes like she was about to walk the runway tonight. She'd shaved her legs and everything else... All because she was sure he would finally tell her he loved her.

"Shall we go?" Bree said, suddenly done with it all.

"Aren't we early then?"

Bree grinned. "You really don't care much about my mom, eh?"

Declan stood from the couch and pulled her up by her hands.

"For you, Love... only for you, I'll tolerate her. I know she's not a bad person. But I don't like the way she treats you. I never have. After your dad left, she became some bitter version of Joan Ryan that I find hard to get along with."

"I get it, Dec. But I'm happy to be spending my Christmas with you."

He kissed the top of her head and she felt him nuzzling her coconut hair.

"Hmmm, I just love the way you smell..."

"Oh, so now you're just fucking with me," she said as she fisted her hands beside her.

"You just throw it out there, don't you?" Now he *loves* the way she smelled. Pfff.

He bit his lip from laughing. "Throw what out?"

"Never mind. Are you going with me or what?"

"Okay, Dec, you can do this. It's only hormones. She doesn't really want to stick your eyeballs out with a fork..." he joked as Bree turned red in the face with irritation.

"No. I want to scoop them out of their sockets with a spoon!"

His laughter rolled over her, and she had to admit she was being silly. Well, more precisely: admit to herself. She definitely wouldn't cop up to being hormonal to Dec. He was having way too much fun messing with her about it.

"Let's go, Love. After we grab some dinner at your mom's house, I'm taking you with me to my place."

"I'll probably be asleep by the time dessert is served, but sure... I'm game."

"I've read somewhere that the coming weeks are going to improve on nausea and tiredness, Love. Anyway, you wouldn't miss this for the world. I promise," he said with a gleam in his eye.

"If you say so," Bree said, yawning.

DECLAN

"When's the rest coming? I'm hungry," Gwenn said.

"They could be here any moment," Joan said, placing the last plate on the festive table.

Homemade decorations and centerpieces decorated Joan's Christmas table. She intertwined sprigs of the same red flowers at the table with the enormous tree in the living room.

Joan loved to go all out during the holidays. He's been to almost every Christmas celebration at the Ryan's since they moved next doors. Normally, Joan's decorations made you feel the warmth of the season the moment you walked through the door. How very contradictory to Bree's mother's attitude today.

Joan still gave them both her famous cold shoulder. While he studied Bree's mother with her cropped up anger, he suddenly felt sorry for all that Joan had been through that made her this way.

The picture of Rob Walker with his 'new' family popped into his head. By the look of things, Rob's other family wasn't so new at all... He wasn't sure, but it seemed like Rob had first two sons with Brenda even before Cait had been born.

"Shots fired!"

Declan jumped from his seat on the couch at Gwenn's voice.

He'd zoned out a bit and now Gwenn was handing him his arse. He worked his thumbs over his controller, but he was too late.

"Yes. I win! Want a rematch?" She quirked her brow and her eyes sparkled.

"Yeah, okay." Declan smiled at the youngest Ryan girl. He was glad she was back safe and sound. Not only because now he had someone to play video games with so, he could avoid Bree's mother.

"Mom, it's Christmas Eve.... Don't you think it's time to talk things out? I've been losing sleep about what we said." Bree said. Declan looked over his shoulder and listened in on their conversation, not caring if it was rude.

"There is nothing to talk about, Bree. You made your choice. Declan is here, isn't he? Even though I'm not happy about the way he talked back to me, I still invited him into my home for a Christmas celebration. So please, I've taken a big step here. Don't expect me to be all cheery. It's going to take some time to get back to how things were."

He made a move to get off the couch, but Gwenn's hand on his shoulder placed him back in his seat.

"Let them have this talk. It's long overdue," Gwenn said.

He nodded at Gwenn and watched again over his shoulder to see if Bree needed his help.

"I don't want to talk about it today... it's Christmas. Can't we be civil for one day?" Joan glared over her thick-rimmed glasses to Bree and walked out of the dining area into the hallway. Bree walked over to Declan and he tugged her onto his lap.

"I'm sorry, Love."

He placed his arm around her waist so he could stroke her belly with his thumb. It was a new thing to do. It hit him he wanted to do this with Bree every day. Stroking her tummy. Watching it grow with his children inside.

She shrugged and said, "I don't know how to deal with any of this. She's my mom, and I just want her to be happy for me. For us."

"She'll turn around. You know she always does," Gwenn said from beside them.

The doorbell rang, and Joan opened the door for Kera, Caitlin and Fianna. Since Cait had both sisters living with her at her apartment, they'd carpooled. If it hadn't been such a sad day for Cait, he would have laughed at her for entering the house with her sunglasses on, and her hair sticking out to all sides.

"Finally. Can we eat now?" Gwenn threw her controller on the couch and stood.

"Phsst, you know you don't need to worry someone is going to steal your bowl of porridge if you don't scarf it down immediately?" Fianna said.

"I was in the military, Fi. Not in prison, Geez." Gwenn rolled her eyes as she took a seat at the table.

"Just checking," Fi said as she winked at Bree.

He sat down at the dinner table and held Bree's hand under the table, on top of her thigh.

Being the only guy at this flowery Christmas table wasn't something he'd recommend to any of his brothers or friends. What a bunch of cackling, loud talking chicks. And he was being nice, because he loved them.

Seeing Bree surrounded by her sisters made him smile, though. Their babies were going to be engulfed by love. True, Joan still had to warm up to the fact she was going to be a grandma.

He was glad he could convince Bree to tell their families about the twins tomorrow.

Both families will be at his dad's house tomorrow, supposedly for a gender reveal. Bree and him don't want to find out the baby's gender, but they would surprise their families by revealing they were having twins. Bree had joked that it gave everyone time to amend the bets in the Baby Pool.

He also had an entirely different surprise planned, especially for Bree. He smiled as he looked over his shoulder to his love. She had no clue.

He peered across the table and studied Joan, talking with Fianna about her duties at the farm. As if she'd felt his eyes on him, she shot him a look that could make the best of man piss his pants.

After contemplating the facts that turned up today with the picture he'd got from Jessie, he now also had inside information on Joan's history. It made him see why Joan was so adamant to teach her girls to never rely on any man.

Declan nudged Cait's knee with his. After the day they'd had, he was glad to still be able to sit next to her. Things could have been a lot worse.

But he understood Cait didn't see it that way. She'd shuffled through the door tonight smelling like Lucky at a Friday night. Every loud laugh made Cait cringe like her head would explode.

Cait looked up from her stacked white and ruby red plates, topped with half eaten entrees. She took the matching napkin from the linen table runner and wiped her mouth.

"I'm so happy for you both, Dec. You know I kept rooting for you two."

"Thanks, Cait."

"There's one upside to all this, you know... When we're no longer partnered up, I don't have to listen to you calling me 'Ryan' all the time."

He knew what she was trying to do, and he gave in to her need to make light of the situation. He nudged her shoulder with his and said, "Damn. Well, maybe if it's a boy, we're naming him Ryan. That way I can still yell at one Ryan to move it along..."

"You wouldn't! Pfff. Ryan Ryan. That's awful."

He laughed. "No child of mine is having another surname than Mills, Cait. Get your facts straight."

"I always wondered why my father had a different surname..." Cait said as she mindlessly whirled the water around in her glass.

The conversations at the table all stopped at Cait's words.

"We're not doing this today. It's Christmas," Joan said in a final tone. She picked up her plate and made a show out of picking up Fianna's plate, sitting next to her.

"Hey! I was still eating that!"

"Ah, hush child. Your horse will thank me for this."

Fianna rolled her eyes. "Whatever."

Joan walked behind Fianna's chair and reached out to take Gwenn's plate, but Gwenn snatched it from the table and fully extended her arm in the other direction, out of her mother's reach.

"You're not taking my plate, Mom," Gwenn said. "Nobody's even finished yet."

"This is ridiculous. You're eating like you've been living on the streets for the past couple weeks. Doesn't Bree give you any food at her place?"

"Mom! Stop making us all feel like shit just because you do. We've had enough!" Cait said as she stood from her chair. She banged both fists on the dinner table, making the liquid in the glasses ripple.

"No need to be so violent. No surprise they suspended you from your job."

Caitlin took her hand to her back pocket. She was the only one wearing jeans during Christmas Eve. She looked like she'd just rolled out of bed with her hair sticking out on all sides. She probably slept her buzz off in these clothes.

It hadn't surprised him that not one sister had made a remark like they normally would. Cait had informed her sisters about the events of the day that led up to her suspension. They all had understood.

Except for Joan. She just had to make a remark.

"What I hadn't told you all about today was this," Cait said as she took her copy of the picture of Rob Walker and his second family out of her back pocket. She laid it in the middle of the table.

Joan leaned over Gwenn's shoulder to snatch it off the table, but Fianna had been faster.

"What's this?" Fianna said with her brows drawn.

"That is our dad, Fi." Fianna's emerald eyes shot to Cait above the picture and back down again.

"You've got to be fucking kidding me..." Fianna said.

"Language..." Joan singsonged.

"How you can still give etiquette lessons is beyond me. Tell me something, mother... Did you know that Rob Walker was fucking another woman at the same time he was with you?"

"Cait! I will not stand for this. I'm going to the kitchen and when I return, there will be no more talk about any of this. Do you understand?"

Nobody replied Joan. She turned on her heel and stormed into the hallway.

"Let me see," Gwenn said as she leaned in over Fianna's shoulder.

"Damn. Are those our half-brothers?" Gwenn said.

"Yes. And sisters," Bree said.

"Too bad we're related. Look at them..." Gwenn whistled.

Declan stretched out his arm and placed it on the back of Bree's chair. He ran his fingers through her curls and played with her hair. She looked up at him and gave a small smile.

Declan leaned in. "You know they had to know, Bree," he whispered. "This is good. Now your family can finally get some answers. Maybe even closure."

She nodded and gave him a peck on the lips. "I know," she said.

Kera had walked over from her side of the table and hovered

over Gwenn's shoulder. She looked up at Cait with tears in her eyes.

"I don't understand..." she said.

Cait got up and placed her arm around Kera.

"I know, Ker. Look at those two men. They're probably my age or even older," Cait said.

"But... how?" Fianna asked.

Like a whirlwind, Joan speed walked her way back into the dining room. She held her heavy, ceramic gratin dish in between her crimson oven mitts and clanked it on the table.

"Who wants a roasted rack of lamb?"

Nobody reacted.

"No? Nobody? Fine!" Joan picked up the red dish and threw it on the floor.

The dish exploded into several red and white pieces, flying around the floor. Pieces of lamb got stuck under the nearest Christmas tree.

Gasps from all around the table followed. Declan looked around and the Ryan sisters all sat back, flabbergasted, staring at Joan losing her shit.

"Mom!" Kera said and hurried her way over to her mother.

"So much for etiquette lessons," Gwenn mumbled as she sat wide-eyed in her chair.

"Oh, you want some lessons, do you?" Joan sneered. She eyed her daughters and held out one oven mitt when Kera tried to put an arm around her shoulders.

"Lesson number one," Joan said as she picked up a side dish with parsnip and carrots. "Never let a man screw with your head."

She held the white dish with a Christmas tree decoration on the side above her head and smashed it on the floor in front of her. Parsnip and carrots skidded to a halt against Bree's chair leg.

That was enough. Declan needed to protect Bree and their babies from this crazy person. In the utmost calm fashion,

Declan stood from his chair. He turned to Joan with both hands up. His shoe crunched something underneath, and he winced. Probably a rack of lamb.

"I'm not one of your perps, Declan Mills. You don't need to intervene here...." Joan warned before she eyed the table for her next dish.

"Joan... I just want to talk to you. We all want to hear your side. Nobody is judging you, Joan. We all love you—"

Joan snorted and pointed a red oven mitt at him. "Pssht. I don't believe for a minute you love me. You hate my guts. Like I hate yours!"

"Mom!" Bree gasped from behind Declan.

He cocked his head at Joan, admitting she'd hated him. Bree's mother seemed shocked by her own words and placed her mitt against her mouth. She shook her head.

"Sorry, Dec. I don't mean that. I don't mean that at all. I don't know what's gotten into me..."

Joan looked around her and started crying. "Oh, my lamb racks!"

Gwenn busted out laughing and said, "This Christmas is epic. I can't wait for next year with all our half brothers and sisters around."

Her mother sniffed. "I'm not spending my Christmas with Brenda Walker. Or any of her children. Over my dead body!"

"So you know her then?" Cait said.

Declan smiled as he witnessed Cait in action. How was she going to handle not being a cop anymore?

"Yes. I know her."

Joan stepped over the broken dishes and plopped down in a vacant chair. She took off the mitts and held out a hand.

"I know you girls want answers. I've been putting this off because I know that after tonight... you'll never look at me the same."

25

BREE

Joan brought a shaky hand to her glass of wine and drank from it like it was her lifeline. She peered over the rim of her glass at each daughter. Bree held her breath for what was to come.

"When I was eighteen, I fell in love with a boy who was everything I've always dreamt of. You girls know what I mean. Tall, dark and oh so handsome.

"And we could talk for hours. He told me about his Irish granda and how he'd loved to see my belly swell with his kids someday." Joan snorted.

"I was looking for love in all the wrong places. My parents had died in a car crash. They left me some money and because I was eighteen, I was on my own. I stayed in my parents' home and Rob quickly moved in with me."

She shook her head and traced the crimson table runner over the white tablecloth. Joan smiled as if remembering something.

"Rob said, 'I'm your family now. It's you and me, kid.'"

Bree took a drink from her water to take care of her dry throat. Her sisters all sat stock-still, listening closely to each word their mother said. Joan was finally giving them the answers they all been craving for, ever since their father had left them.

"After a while, I ehm, noticed things… you know, him coming home late. Staying away all night. We fought all the time."

Joan shook her head and sought Bree's eyes across the table. "I got pregnant with Cait, even though I knew in my heart that something wasn't right between us. That's why I reacted the way I did. And I'm sorry, Bree. Thinking back to our conversations…. I shouldn't have said all the things I did."

Bree stood from her chair and hugged her mom. She gave Joan a kiss on her cheek. "It's okay. I'm so glad you see that now. And I want you to know that we're here for you. No matter what you tell us about the past, okay? We love you."

"Yeah, we love you, Mom," Fianna said.

Gwenn, Kera and Cait held still and waited the rest of Joan's story out.

Bree took her seat next to Declan, who laid his hand on her thigh under the table. He squeezed once, and she smiled up at him. She was so grateful he was here with her tonight. She couldn't imagine going through this night without her best friend. Without the love of her life.

Declan had always known every single thing there was to know about her. She needed him to hear this part of her life too.

"I got this call one day when I was eight months pregnant with Cait… a woman named Brenda shouted and called me every name she could think of… 'home wrecker', 'whore'…"

Joan cringed at the last word.

"I should have suspected something earlier. Asked questions. Or, I don't know, followed him around. I knew in my gut Rob was unfaithful. But I never expected that someone would call my home to call me out for being 'the other woman'."

"What an asshole," Gwenn said. Bree gave a small smile and watched how her mother slumped in her seat.

"It broke my heart. But I was eighteen years old, had no family left and was pregnant with my first child. And I was so in love with Rob. That man could walk the moon in my eyes. He was the one who took care of me. Sure, he lived in my house, but he also provided for me.

"I came home from therapy shopping after that phone call from Brenda, and he had a surprise for me. He showed me the nursery he'd made that day. He'd painted the room, laid out a nice fluffy carpet, Cait's name on the wall, surrounded by smiling giraffes... everything."

Bree swiped her tears from her cheeks. She witnessed how Cait cried at the other side of the table. She'd seen her sister only cry on maybe three other occasions.

"In that moment, I knew I could never leave him. He was my family. He would be such a loving father. How could I deny my child their father? So I said nothing about the phone call. And although I suspected Rob knew Brenda had called me, he never brought it up."

"Mom... so you knew all along about Brenda?" Kera said.

"Yes. After having Cait, things were good between your father and I. I got pregnant with Kera and I really thought that by that time, Rob had left Brenda. He'd been around for everything. Cait's first tooth, her first steps..."

Joan wiped a tear and held Cait's eye. "Your first word was da-da."

Cait took a napkin from the table and wiped her nose. Tears tumbled down her cheeks.

"But the pink cloud I was on turned dark real soon after I told Rob I was pregnant again. He said he was happy, but I was losing him. I felt it to my bones. He came home one day with lipstick behind his ear. I guess Brenda was making a point by then, she was still in the game. Except it wasn't a game to me. Brenda might think because Rob married her, that she was the love of his life and I was a mere distraction. But it wasn't like that."

Bree sighed and traced the tablecloth with her finger. She'd never suspected her mom to be the other woman. Sure, they knew her parents had their up and downs. But this was shocking. Finding out that everything she knew about her childhood had been a lie, stung.

Declan traced her cheek with his thumb. She wasn't aware she'd been crying. He kissed her cheek, and she closed her eyes. His touch soothed her. Declan always felt like home to her. Home.

She narrowed her eyes at the thought of her childhood home. What a farce it all had been. She turned towards her mother when she continued her story.

"I kicked him out of my house. It was the first time I confronted Rob about this. He tried to tell me some story about being overwhelmed with the baby news that he had a one-night-stand with some girl he'd met at a bar. But when I threw Brenda in his face, he'd stopped lying. He finally told me he'd been married to Brenda ever since he was eighteen. She was his high school sweetheart, and he'd gotten her pregnant. Brenda's parents made them marry, and he said I was a breath of fresh air to him."

"But after that, you still stayed with him?" Cait said in a high-pitched voice like she couldn't believe it. Just like Bree couldn't believe it either.

"You even had Fianna, Bree, and Gwenn together?" Cait crossed her arms in front of her chest and narrowed her eyes.

"I told you, you girls were going to judge me. And you're right to do so. Even though I wouldn't ever change having you girls, it's true that I regret some of my actions. I should have stayed strong when I'd kicked him out the first time. But he always knew how to draw me back in.

"He came along with gifts for you girls, helped me out when

I was so tired of getting little to no sleep because Kera was teething. I didn't know what to do, so I called him for help. I was all alone and at my wits' end."

Bree's heart broke for her mother. She couldn't imagine going through her own pregnancy alone and even raising five girls on her own. She placed her hand on her abdomen and prayed that the twins were still safe and sound swimming together in her belly. Declan gave her a reassuring squeeze on her thigh.

"We'd been keeping in touch about the girls while he lived with Brenda. Then one day, Rob stood on my doorstep with all his bags packed. He said he was done with Brenda and that he was going to file for a divorce. I couldn't believe it at first. But he promised me that this was what he'd wanted. He wanted to be with us girls."

Joan searched for Cait's eyes again, but Cait stared at her fingers tracing the tablecloth. Bree looked from Cait over to Kera, who seemed shell-shocked with her mother's story.

"I let him back into my home, into your lives and into my heart," Joan said.

"That's why I don't have a lot of memories of Dad when I was younger," Cait mumbled.

"Yes, you were seven when Rob came back, and Kera was almost four years old."

"And then you got pregnant with me," Fianna said.

Joan nodded.

"Yes, two years later we had Bree and Gwenn made our family complete two years after that."

"Really mother?" Gwenn said. "I completed this family? He had a complete other family on the side, didn't he? Oh wait, we were the ones on the side. The bastards. Not them."

Bree winced at Gwenn's words. But they were true, weren't they? Rob hadn't married their mother. So they were the bastards and not his other children.

Gwenn shoved her chair from the table. "I'm going for a smoke."

"Are you still doing that? Think of—" Joan said.

"You are in no position to tell me what I should or shouldn't do, Mom," Gwenn spat. Bree cleared her throat theatrically, trying to diffuse the situation. But Gwenn waved her hand around the room.

"I think that's the moral of this story today. You always held us to such high standards. Pushing us to reach further and to make something of our lives. I always wanted to make you so proud. I hated to let you down if I failed at something. You're such a hypocrite!"

Joan stood from her chair and leaned on the table with both hands flat.

"Young lady, I am still your mother. I can still call you out on smoking if I please to do so. My mistakes of the past made me into the woman that I am today. I know that I've hurt Brenda by sneaking around her back with her husband. But I've hurt you girls the most. I was lost after Rob told me he was going back to her. He told me she was having twins, and he needed to be with her. I know I checked out on you girls for a long time after that."

Bree tried to get out of her chair to hug her mother. But Declan clasped his hand on her thigh. He lightly shook his head. He probably was worried for her. Her mother had acted like a crazy person, throwing dishes around. Or maybe he realized Joan needed to get this all of her chest first.

"And you know what? I picked myself up. I got a degree online. I crawled out of the darkness that surrounded me and made something of myself as a PA to a billionaire. I can proudly say that I can support not only myself but also any of my five girls if you need me to. You'd rather sleep on your sister's couch instead of staying with me. But that's not the point."

A soft smile ghosted Gwenn's lips as she looked over at Bree. Bree smiled back at her sister, knowing they both felt their powerful connection. No matter what Joan had done in the past, or would tell them now. As sisters and best friends, they would forever have each other's back.

"I'll never want or need another man. Never again. And I made damn sure that my girls didn't make my mistakes. I got on your nerves to get you girls independent. You are so strong. And I am so proud of you. Of all of you..." Joan said while looking at every one of her daughters.

Bree swallowed the lump in her throat. She nodded when her eyes met her mother's eyes.

Gwenn sat back down in her chair. "I don't get it. Why would he do this to us?"

Her shoulders shook as she cried. Fianna placed her hand on Gwenn's shoulder and hugged her.

Declan kissed Bree on her cheek. "I'm getting the desserts ready for you girls. Leave you some time to talk without me."

"There's chocolate in the fridge, Dec. And.... Thank you..." Joan said. Declan nodded before he gave Bree's mother a soft smile.

Bree watched this handsome, caring man walk out of the dining room to get her and her family chocolate. It was at that moment she realized he didn't need to tell her. His actions spoke louder than words. Declan Mills is in love with Bree Ryan.

Rob may have said he'd loved her mother, but his actions told a completely different story.

After this night, she was going for Declan without playing it safe. No need to guard her heart, like her mother would have advised her. No. She was no longer listening to people warning her about how one sided her love for him is.

What the hell did her mother know about love, anyway? She had this sick relationship with an egomaniac. How dare she compare Declan to that man?

She willed her breathing to slow down. There was still one thing she needed to know. After taking a couple of sips of water,

Bree joined the side of the table where Joan sat on her own. She fixed her mother a glass of wine.

"Have you ever had contact with Rob since he'd left us?" Bree asked.

Joan shook her head, but something in the way her eyes widened told Bree she was lying.

"Mom, now is the time to tell us everything. It's okay," Bree urged.

Joan took the glass of wine that Bree had poured and brought it to her lips. She took her time before answering.

"He contacted me once in a while for the first two years after he'd left. I told him we didn't need him."

"Mom!" Cait gasped and shook her head in disbelief. Bree's lip trembled. She was about to burst out in tears. All this time, she thought he'd just left them. Unbelievable.

"And all these years I thought my Dad didn't want me," Cait said. "That he never loved me because he never looked back."

"Cait, he loved you. He loved all of you... but he loved himself more. And I couldn't let him hurt you like he' hurt me. I needed to protect you from him."

Bree placed a hand on her abdomen. She wondered if she would have done the same. Joan had been convinced she'd done it to protect her daughters. She was so glad she wouldn't have to worry about any of that with Dec being the father of their twins.

"Protect us from our own father?" Gwenn said, crumpling a napkin.

"You'll see what I mean If you'll ever meet him again. You'll see that I was right for what I did when you were kids."

"I was eighteen and needed my father! I totally lost it that summer he left, and I slept with four guys in one week!" Cait yelled as she slammed her palm on the tabletop, making a small vase jump on impact.

Bree jumped in her seat. She felt for her oldest sister. She had seen their parents at their worst during all of their fights and break-ups. And when Cait said she'd needed her father, Bree realized how much she'd missed him growing up. Her chest tightened.

"Sounds like one hell of a summer, sis," Gwenn tried to joke.

"I lost my virginity to Robert Jackson," Cait said. "The guy that in the same night took two other girls upstairs. All because I wanted to prove to myself that someone liked me!"

Gwenn had the decency to look down. "Sorry. I didn't know."

"We all carry our hurt differently," Cait said. "This has affected every one of us on some level. It's not right you made those decisions for us, Mom. We—I—needed a father figure..."

"I can't change the past, sweetheart. I know my decisions caused so much pain. But I still think I saved you girls from much more heartbreak in the end."

"Declan told me that our cousin Jessie wants to meet us," Bree said.

"Jessie?" Cait instantly straightened her stance.

Declan walked in with a tray filled with chocolate muffins, vanilla ice cream, whipped cream and chocolate chip cookies.

"Finally, something to eat," Gwenn said.

"Yes! I couldn't even finish my entrée," Fianna said, throwing a look at her mother.

The sisters took back their spots around the table while Declan served them their dessert.

"Thanks, Dec. You're the best," Gwenn said.

"No problem. I'm glad to give you your fix," he said. He smiled at Bree and she mouthed 'thank you' to him. He winked back.

"Dec, did Jessie tell you she wanted to meet us?" Cait asked, mindlessly making circles with her spoon in her ice cream bowl.

"How do you know this Jessie person?" Joan asked.

"We met her today on the job that went wrong. I can't tell you about anything of it. Just leave it at that." Cait said, dismissing her mother. "And? Did she?"

Declan laid down his spoon and wiped his mouth with his napkin. He nodded. "She said she wanted to help you. That's she's grateful for what you've done today."

"Can anybody tell me what the fuck is going on here?" Gwenn said.

"Fine! Dec and I were on a call to check out a critical situation. As you all know, I went off my rockers and totally flipped when I saw a man holding a knife to a child's throat."

The sisters took a sharp intake of breath around the dining table.

Bree placed her hand on Dec's hand. She searched his eyes, but he held his emotions to himself. She wanted to be there for him. To ask him more, but she knew he wouldn't tell her with everyone around at the table.

Declan leaned in to say something, but Cait said, "It's all on me. I take responsibility if it ever comes out I told anyone. I'm quitting anyway."

"So I kicked this asshole unconscious—"

"Cait!" Joan scolded.

"Sorry Mom, I mean when I served this rather unsavory fellow my foot to his face."

Joan didn't respond but rolled her eyes.

"And then I heard Declan say we forgot to clear all rooms—"

"What the fuck?" Gwenn asked. "Was it your first day on the job or something? You always clear the premises first. *Always.*"

"I'm not even going to answer that. So I walk into this bedroom with clothes thrown on the floor like there had been an altercation. I don't see anyone there, so I search for signs of drugs lying around, for other weapons... I look at some pictures of several families. The next thing I know, I see a picture of a guy with his family. A guy that looks awfully a lot like the asshole that left us behind all those years."

Bree's eyes zoomed in on the picture of Rob in the middle of the table. Although almost twenty years older, she would also have recognized her father.

"And he's smiling. He's happy with his three sons and two beautiful daughters. He had his arm around his wife and one around one of the girls. I wanted to be that girl in the picture." Cait cleared her throat and Bree brought a hand to her chest, understanding Cait's pain.

"I may have been a bit out of it and told the victim we're related after she told me that the guy in the picture was her uncle Rob. So yeah, that's that. I'm suspended from my job. I found out my Dad has a whole other family, and I saved my newfound cousin and her young daughter from a man that was threatening to kill the little girl."

Cait grabbed her wine. "So, yeah. I said to myself today: 'Fuck it all.' Yes, I got drunk this afternoon. And I don't see any reason I shouldn't drink now. Cheers!"

"Drinking is never the solution, sis," Kera said.

"No. I know that. But for me, on this day? It's a great escape from reality."

"Until come morning and reality hits you right in the face," Fianna said.

"Just let me have this night, okay?" Cait said. "Tomorrow, I'm going to be your responsible big sister again. Not tonight."

26

DECLAN

Waking up with his nose stuck in Bree's curls was Heaven. Last night had been very emotional for Bree.

Being there for her at one of the lowest nights for her family had meant everything to him.

He'd noticed the shift in Bree right after her mother's revelations. After she'd finished her dessert, she got up and sat down on his lap. She'd taken his cheeks in her hands and kissed him in front of her family.

Joan cleared her throat, but unlike her normal self, she didn't even make a snide remark. Bree had broken their kiss and had whispered, "Thank you for being you."

He couldn't wait to tell her today how much he loved her.

Her sweet little snores made him smile. He traced lazy circles with his finger on Bree's soft tummy.

Good morning, Little Loves.

He still couldn't believe they were having twins. Twins! He should have thought about the possibility, since he was part of fraternal twins.

A ping alerted him of an incoming text. He slipped his arm

from under Bree and grabbed his phone. He muted the device before he read the text.

RO: Everything is ready.

Declan smiled.

DECLAN: Thanks, bro.

RO: It's still not too late. I can take everything down and hide the evidence.

While Declan thought about the right reply to set him straight, Ro sent another text.

RO: Nah, I'm not doing that. Not even if you asked me to, G.I. Joe. She's good for ye.

It was a good thing Ronan was now supportive of Bree and him. It felt right.

RO: If ye don't make her yers, I'm swoopin' in. And ye know how all the ladies like me better...

Declan rolled his eyes and snorted. Bree turned around and brought her arm around his waist.

She kissed his shoulder before she laid her head down. "Good morning."

"Morning, Love."

"What were you snorting over here for?" She tried to spy his texts.

He placed the phone back on his bedside table and rolled her so she rested with her back on the bed.

"Hmmm, someone needs to be taught a lesson," he said.

She laughed like she couldn't believe he'd said that. "Ooooh. I'm so scared. Are you going to cuff me to your bed?"

Well now, there was an idea.

He kissed her nose and shot off from the bed. Her footsteps followed him for a moment before she turned right to the bathroom. Declan went into his spare room where he kept a safe with a spare gun and some extra cuffs.

His cock jumped at the thought of having Bree at his mercy.

He locked the safe and went back to his bedroom with the keys in one hand and the cuffs in the other.

Bree surprised him by sitting ready for him on the edge of the bed, with her hair in a messy bun. Some toothpaste residue stuck next to her bottom lip, and he wiped it for her. After sucking the residue from his finger, he rolled the taste of peppermint over his teeth.

"Have you been naughty, Miss?"

Bree giggled and a cute blush crept over her chest, peeping from under her black camisole. Seductive black lace stopped halfway her juicy arse cheeks. He itched to give her a few slaps there.

He stopped trailing his finger over Bree's arm and said, "Shit. I don't think I can do this."

Bree cocked her head. "Why not?"

"I want to slap yer arse so bad, Bree. I want to watch yer flesh jiggle and turn red with my handprints. But I can't... not while yer..." he sighed and took a step back.

Bree stood from the bed and placed her warm hand on his bare chest.

"Oh, Dec..." she put her bottom lip between her teeth as she tried hard not to laugh at him.

"Don't laugh."

She did exactly that.

He grunted.

"But it's so funny. We can still make love. It won't hurt our babies."

He shook his head. "I want to fuck you. I want to possess you and make you come over and over again. I want you to scream my name. To plead for me to stop spanking ye so hard, even though it makes ye cream yer pussy. I want to *ride* ye, Love. Fuck ye senseless."

She got him so worked up he ended up talking with a thick Irish brogue.

Bree's breathing picked up and his eyes drew to her heavy tits that moved with every breath. Her nipples saluted him through the fabric of her camisole.

Declan groaned as he trailed his index finger around the nipple imprint, never touching the exact spot. Bree moaned while she closed her eyes.

"Oooh, keep doing that."

"I want to suckle them, Bree."

"Oh God," she said while she almost buckled.

He picked her up and placed her in the middle of his bed.

On his way down to the edge of the bed, he took her underwear with him. Bree slipped out of her camisole and threw it into the room somewhere.

"Tell me it's okay... Tell me I can fuck you. Right here, right now."

Bree whimpered as she pushed her hips from the bed. She searched his hands, his body... his dick. But he would not let her. He was in control.

He softly turned her on her stomach and positioned her on all fours. "Stay like this, Love."

She waved her pink pussy in the air like she'd been doing it her entire life.

Slap!

A fine red imprint showed on her right cheek.

"Hmmmm," she said.

Slap!

Bree arched her back. "Yes!"

"Hmm, you like that, eh?"

Bree swayed her hips, enticing him to take the next step. He leaned in and bit her juicy round cheek. Not to draw blood, but hard enough to make it count. She yelped, but after licking the sting away, she said, "I want you... Dec, take me..."

"Not yet," he said.

He walked over to the side of the bed, and she looked over to him.

"Come, take me in your mouth, Love. I need to feel your lips around me."

Bree turned on the bed and wanted to place her hands on his thighs.

"No, not yet. First without hands."

She opened up for him and stared wide-eyed as he stuck his hardness in her mouth.

"Fuck, yeah."

She licked the underside of his dick and sucked him further in.

"So good, Love."

He fisted her messy bun and pushed further into her mouth.

"Mmm, this feels so good."

After a few more pushes and pulls, he slipped out of her mouth. "I need to stop for a moment."

She sat up on her knees, making her small growing belly protrude remind him of their babies.

"Fuck, you're beautiful."

"Dec..." Bree blushed and wanted to cover her belly.

"I want to feel you grow every day, Love. Place my hand over our babies and feel them kick. I want to make love to you."

"I thought you said you wanted to fuck me?" She smirked.

"Can I compromise?" he said as he tugged at a curl that had tumbled out of her bun.

Bree cocked her head to the side.

He leaned in and said, "Can I make real-hard-love to ye?"

"That's not even a word!"

"It is now. It's our word. I'm going to make the hardest love to you..."

She giggled, and he picked her up in his arms. He leaned over her and aligned himself before her entrance. He stared into her eyes.

She beamed at him.

He closed his eyes and pushed into her warmth. They both groaned at the sensation of him making his way through her channel. She immediately clamped down on him and he moaned.

"That's it, Bree. I want to feel you everywhere. I need you."

He kissed her lips, and she opened them. She moaned while feathering her hands over his back. He gave another hard push, and she ran her nails down his back.

He looked down at her, worried that he might hurt her, but she seemed in total ecstasy. Her eyes closed while she swiped perspiration away from her upper lip with her tongue. Declan leaned in to kiss her and she tugged at his hair.

"Oh yes, it's so good," she whispered.

He grabbed the back of her knees and pushed her legs further open. "I know."

She grabbed his ass cheeks with both hands. He kept rocking into her. Sliding in and almost all the way out. She looked up at him with passion and longing. He slid his hand between them and cupped her breast. He rolled her hard peak with his fingers and she clamped down on him.

They both came. Hard.

With his heart pounding against his chest, he had to lie down to catch his breath. When he turned his head, he instantly found her light blue eyes, smiling at him.

He almost slipped up and told her...

But it had to wait until later.

At the end of the afternoon, he drove them in his truck to his dad's house.

"I can't wait to tell everyone we're having twins," Bree said. She put the visor down and pulled out some lip gloss from her purse to color her already pink lips.

"I can't wait to sit at a dinner table where I'm not the only guy stuck in between six women," he joked.

Bree glanced over her shoulder and back at the mirror of her visor. It was Christmas Day. The day of the 'gender reveal party'. Except there was no gender reveal. No, they were surprising everyone today with the news that they were expecting twins.

She smacked her lips, and his dick twitched in his jeans.

Today they matched. He wore a black button-down shirt with his sleeves rolled up to his elbows, and Bree had a sexy little black dress on. It wasn't too short. It came well over mid thigh, but it accented those strong thighs, and her firm arse clung to the fabric of her dress.

"I'm so nervous, Dec. You'll have to tell them about the twins. I'll just stand next to you and smile."

He laughed and shook his head. She was in for a surprise. That made him also nervous as hell. He glanced over once more. "Okay, Love," he said.

He parked the truck behind Duncan's truck and walked over to Bree's side to help her out.

"Come, Love."

She put her hand in his, and he fetched her out of the truck by supporting her.

"Thanks, Dec."

"Anything for my lovely ladies."

"Oooh, did you place a bet in the Baby Pool?" Bree smiled.

"Not yet, but after tonight I will. I'm sure Pops will agree. I have a feeling about us having two girls. I can't wait to have them in my arms. And to chase all those boys away."

She stood on her tiptoes and kissed his smiling lips.

"What's that for?"

"For being such a loving father already. After last night, you know how much it means to me I can count on you."

His heart pounded and he couldn't wait to get her inside and out into the backyard.

"What's wrong?"

He cleared his throat and took a slight step back. "Nothing, absolutely nothing, Love."

Bree narrowed her blue eyes at him but held her tongue.

He grabbed her hand and led her to the front door where he rang the doorbell. As they waited for someone to open up, he checked his phone one last time.

RO: Where are you?

RO: We're freezin' our arses off while ye and yer missus are still rollin' 'round in bed?

RO: It's a good thing we're only doin' this once.

"Who's that?" Bree said as she nudged her chin toward Dec's phone.

He quickly put it back in his jeans. "Oh, nothing."

She whirled around and just as she was going to lay it on him thick; the door opened and Errin greeted them.

"Yay, there you are! Come inside, we've been waiting all day! I'm soo betting on a boy!"

"Hello to you too, Errin."

"Hi, Dec." Errin winked at him while giving him two thumbs up. He willed her with his eyes to act normal. As normal as Errin could act, that is.

"What's going on with you, Dec?" Bree asked.

"Nothing, Love."

"If you say 'nothing' one more time, I'm going to scream." Bree hissed while they followed Errin out into the backyard.

Declan peered over the top of Errin's head and noticed that everyone already stood in position. His heart rate picked up and a wave of nausea followed. He cracked his neck and glanced over his shoulder at Bree. She shook her head at him like he'd lost it.

Errin stepped aside and as pre-arranged, this would make way for Bree to look out into the backyard.

Only she didn't. Declan still annoyed her, and she wanted to make sure he knew. She stared him down like he needed to tell her right now what he's been hiding or else she was going to kick his arse. When he tugged her hair, she blinked once, and she finally noticed their families standing in the backyard.

Declan searched for Brennan who stood next to Pops who'd already been tearing up. Declan smiled, and then he locked eyes with Ro. His twin nodded and smiled the biggest smile he'd ever seen him give.

Declan gently took Bree's bicep in his hand and directed them to the middle of the backyard, surrounded by their closest family and friends. Joan and her daughters had mingled in between the Mills family. Aiden and Keenan stood under the tree house where Tommy was hanging from the rope to go down. The Walsh sisters had found their spot next to their Mills' boyfriend.

This was it. Bree would think he would tell everyone they were having twins. But first he wanted to surprise his love. After a quick nod at his Dad, Declan went down on one knee.

"Ooh my..." Bree put a hand against her mouth. He heard Errin starting with "Aaah," followed by several other women present.

He raked a hand through his hair before he took her hand in his. Her hand trembled just like his. He closed his eyes to take a calming breath.

"My sweet, sweet, Love.... As you can see, we've pimped the tree house for this special occasion."

He followed Bree's eyes as they went over to the tree house. On top of the tree house hung a golden banner with the red velvet text:

I love you, Bree. Marry Me?

27

BREE

Bree blinked away the tears that threatened to fall and ruin her mascara. The text on the golden banner had everything she could ever wish for. Finally. Bree realized how she'd longed to hear those words from him.

Declan squeezed her hand and when she looked down into his gray eyes, he said, "You were six when you knocked me off my feet. You came around the house, talked for hours with Pops. Played video games with all of us. And you even climbed onto the roof of the tree house."

"I dare you to do it again," Ronan shouted. "Well, when you're not pregnant, that is."

Brennan cuffed him on the back of the head to shut up. Bree let out a nervous laugh and shook her head at Declan's twin.

"Anyone who's ever been up there, has seen our initials: B + D. It has always been you, Bree. You are the most precious, funny, sweet, kind... and sexy—"

"Now we're talking!" Aiden shouted, making everyone laugh. Bree blushed so hard her cheeks hurt.

Declan smiled at her. "You are the most important person in my life. I made a mistake last March by not letting you in. I was afraid of losing you. Of losing us."

She nodded, and a tear fell from her chin. A weight lifted off her shoulders. The past didn't matter anymore. Him declaring his love for her in front of their family and friends was all that mattered. He had his eyes on their future and that was exactly what she was going to do.

"During the months that followed, I've been a total wreck. And—"

"And an arsehole..." Ro snickered at his own joke but stopped at Fi's icy glare. Bree stared down at Dec sitting on one knee in front of her. His watery eyes matched hers.

"And I never, *ever*, want to miss you from my life again. I can't wait to start our own little family. All my dreams are coming true, but there is one last thing. Will you please do me the honor in becoming my wife? Make me the happiest man alive?"

She took his face in-between her palms and leaned in to kiss him.

Their friends and family cheered so loud, the neighbor's dogs howled.

He whispered against her lips, "Is that a yes?"

She leaned back and shouted, "Yes!"

He stood up from the one knee and whirled her in his arms. He kissed her and held her close. His warmth engulfed her, and she almost forgot they stood surrounded by their friends and family. Right. The twins.

She stopped the kiss. "There's something I'd like to say."

Declan winked at Bree, giving her the spotlight to bring the news.

"Everyone, shut yer face. Bree wants to talk!"

"Thanks, Ro."

Ronan winked at her, and she grinned. It seemed he was warming up to her again. Well, he'd better, because she wasn't going anywhere.

"Thank you all so much for surprising me today! It means so

much to me." Bree smiled at Kate, who wiped tears from her cheeks with a white handkerchief.

She glanced at Declan as he put his arm around her. "I should say to *us*. We'll never forget this moment for the rest of our lives."

Some people started clapping and cheering, but she wanted to say one last thing. Bree held up a hand, and when it didn't work, she looked over at Ronan.

He put two fingers in between his lips and let out a shrill whistle, silencing the whole backyard again.

Bree looked over the crowd and tried to keep the nervousness out of her voice.

"For anyone that has already placed their bet with Ker or Gwenn about the gender of our baby... I'm sorry, but we don't want to know the gender before birth," she said.

Joan stepped out of the crowd and said with her brows pulled down, "What's that for new age bogus?"

Bree busted out laughing. Only Joan. Leave it to her mother to vent her opinion like that.

"Perhaps it is, Mom. But we would like to share something else with you all.... we're having twins!"

Pops immediately engulfed Bree with his burly arms and kissed the top of her hair. She let go of Declan's hand and hugged Pops back.

"My, My. What a day. You bring so much joy and happiness into our lives, sweet Bree. I'm so proud of me boyo that he's goin' to be a da, and he's finally goin' to marry ye. I feel like me heart is overflowin'. And Twins!"

She snuggled into his chest like she did when she was a kid.

A pang of sorrow shot through her as she realized her father would not be a part of her children's life. He was missing out on so much already. He wasn't here today. Most likely will not be at the wedding... Or when the twins would be born.

Bree cried for all the things her father already had skipped. School plays, graduations... Pops held on even stronger.

"What's the matter, lass?"

"I was thinking of my dad. Sorry, didn't mean to cry all over your shirt, Pops."

"Nonsense."

He leaned in and whispered against her hair, "It's okay, lass. Let it all out. I'm here for ye. I may not be yer da, but I love ye just the same. Ye hear?"

She sobbed and nodded.

"Can I steal my girl for a moment?" Declan asked, his hand on her waist.

"Sure, boyo. Ye keep an eye out on me, lass, eh?"

"I will, Pops. Always."

She looked into the dark grey eyes of Declan. He was trying to read her.

"Are you okay?"

She swallowed and tried to hold herself together. "Yes, I'm okay, Dec. It's just those damn hormones."

He whispered against her ear, "You don't need to be so damn strong all the time, I'm here for you. Share your pain with me. Maybe I can help."

"It's my Dad. I have such mixed feelings about everything..."

He kissed her bare shoulder. "Maybe we should get together with Jessie. When everything has cooled off with her situation, that is. I'm not letting you near her while that husband of hers is still walking free."

Before Bree could ask, Kate interrupted them. "I'm so, so happy for you both!"

Donovan walked from behind Kate and hugged Declan. "This is such good news, Dec. I can't believe you're having twins."

Kate and Donovan switched places, and Donovan hugged Bree.

"Congratulations," he said, swallowing down his emotions. Which took her by surprise, since the reserved Donovan never opened up to anyone. Well, except Kate.

"Thank you, Donovan."

"I'm so happy for you both. And thank you for making me an uncle."

"Is it my turn now?" Ronan boomed from behind Donovan.

Ro picked her up and whirled her around, just like his twin had done when she'd accepted his proposal.

"Bree... what can I say? I've been an absolute arse. I know it. But I love ye like yer my sister. I've only got one twin and we're pretty tight... but ye can hang with us."

"Thanks, Ro. You're so kind." She joked and poked his bicep with her fist.

Declan shoved Ro playfully. "Shut up, Ro."

"I mean it, Dec. I took my own experiences and said some stuff that—"

"Alright, Ro. Bree and I are together now, so it's all water under the bridge."

"I love you, man." Ro said as he pulled Dec in for a hug.

"Love you too." Bree watched them hug it out and grinned.

Bree's sisters speed walked across the backyard and surrounded her in their huddle. Fianna started jumping up and down, taking the rest of the Ryan sisters with her.

"Our sister is getting married!" Fianna said.

Gwenn and Kera simultaneously kissed a cheek of Bree. Cait took Bree's hands in hers and said, "I'm so, so happy for you both! You two deserve each other."

"Thank you, sis." Bree looked around and felt the love from their family and friends. She grinned from ear to ear.

Pops clapped his calloused hands together and said, "Let's eat!"

"Finally," said Tommy as he ran past Bree, solely focused on getting to the tables of food inside.

"Tommy Aiden Mills, get yer butt over here!"

Tommy looked over his shoulder and gauged his father's distance from him. Bree realized he was debating if he should risk it or should listen to his father.

"Hey Tommy, good to see you." Bree said.

"Yes?" Tommy eyed Bree wearily as his father was on his way to him.

"First, you congratulate Miss Bree, then you can go inside." Keenan said.

"What for?"

"Because she's getting married and having twins?" Keenan said, exasperated.

"Not right now?" Tommy eyed Bree's stomach like they could pop out any minute and could take out an eye from him.

Bree giggled and leaned in. "No, it's still going to be a few months."

"Is that why you're not always at school?" Tommy pointed at Bree's stomach.

She nodded. "Yes, I felt sick for a while."

"Did the baby make your head hurt? My Dad's head hurts a lot."

Bree stood up straight and gave Keenan a reassuring smile. "I'm sorry to hear that, Keenan."

"Can I go eat now?" Tommy shifted his weight from side to side.

Keenan nodded, and Tommy leaped through the back door.

"How are you holding up, Keenan? Is there anything I can do for you?"

"We're not having this conversation now, Bree. This should be a fun day. You just got engaged!" Keenan patted her shoulder to dismiss the discussion.

"I know, but I'm your boy's teacher and you are one of Dec's best friends. Please, let me help."

Keenan smiled. "My Cuz did good in tying you down. You

are one special lady, you know that? Always looking out for others. The way you are with Tommy…"

Keenan put his hands in the pockets of his slacks and kicked a small rock. "I feel like I'm fuckin' everything up, you know? Working overtime, helping Aiden and Dad to smooth out the takeover from Dad's company."

"I heard you had some problems with finding a good nanny… I'll keep my eyes and ears open, okay? Maybe I can—"

Keenan leaned in and kissed Bree on her cheek. "It's going to be alright. I've got an interview with someone in a few days."

Bree placed his hand on his shoulder. "That's good, Keen. I hope everything turns out all right."

Joan stepped up and Keenan excused himself, leaving Bree alone with Joan. Before Bree could greet her mom, Joan tugged Bree in for a tight embrace.

"Congratulations, my sweet Bree. I know I haven't been your biggest supporter but when Dec called me last night—"

Bree turned and beamed up at Declan, who had joined them. "You called my mom?"

Declan pulled her in to his side and put his arm around her shoulder. "Yeah. I had to ask your mom for your hand in marriage, didn't I?"

He smirked at her confusion. She rubbed at her eyebrows that squished together.

She turned at her mother, who said, "Yes. It was the right thing to do. Giving you kids my blessing was the right thing to do. I only say this once: don't mess it up. I know where to find you, Declan Mills."

Bree giggled, but her mother seemed as serious as a heart attack with her lips pursed and narrowed eyes.

"I know Joan. But that will not be necessary." Declan said with a smile in his voice.

"Good. Now. I'm going to see if I can get a plate to eat before

Ronan devours everything." Bree rolled her eyes before she watched her mom walk inside the Mills house.

"Let me see the ring!" Errin said from across the yard on her way over.

"Shit." Declan said beside Bree. His arm around Bree's shoulders stiffened.

Bree glanced at Dec and broke out in laughter.

An engagement ring. Declan hadn't given her a ring. Declan let go of her shoulders and rummaged around in his pocket. Sweat trailed down the side of his face. He clenched his jaw.

"Shit," he said again. His other hand went into his other pocket.

Bree bit on her bottom lip to keep from laughing.

"Yes!"

Declan pulled out a black velvet box and waved it in the air.

"Found it."

Bree giggled at Declan, who pressed a palm to his heart. He shook his head smiling and said, "Am I allowed to have this one and final fuck-up?"

She stepped into his open arms and hugged him close. She leaned her head back and stared into his eyes.

"I don't think this will be your final fuck-up, Dec."

He cocked his head and waited for her to explain. She smiled up at him and said,

"Even if you are a putz, I will still love you forever."

EPILOGUE

Declan

August

"Fuck. They're here already?" he said.

"Who is?" Bree asked while stacking the second laundry basket full with folded clothes. Declan shot a glance at the array of white, pink, yellow and blue baby clothes.

"I asked you yesterday if it was okay for Jessie and Liv to come over for Sunday brunch so they could meet you and the twins, Bree."

He chuckled while taking the laundry basket from her.

"It's like I still have my pregnancy brain." Bree shook her head while dumping the pile of unfolded clothes on top of the basket.

"I'm still in my pajamas! I hate to make a first impression like this. Can you open the door? I'm changing real quick."

He kissed her nose.

"Sure."

Declan had been in touch with Bree's cousin via email and

texts. They'd arranged this first meeting for Bree to meet Jessie and Liv.

Bree had expressed her hope to bond with Jessie and to see if she could perhaps meet some of her half siblings in the future.

Not every Ryan sister had been enthusiastic about this meeting. But Bree didn't care. His wife simply followed her heart and did what felt right. He loved calling Bree his wife. It had been a shot-gun wedding at the courthouse.

But non of it all mattered. They would have their big celebration at Lucky in a few months. Bree didn't want to get married while pregnant. So they compromised.

Luckily, the doorbell didn't wake up the twins. He picked up the two baby monitors and spotted the two dark-haired babies still sound asleep.

He searched for the frizzy black hair to pick out the first-born, little miss Ava. Bree had said that she got her curls after she was eighteen months, and she was sure their daughter's hair would turn out just like Bree's.

Dean made a sudden move in his sleep like he had a bad dream. He hit himself with his tiny hand in the face and woke up crying. A cute little putz. A true son after his father.

He smiled at the monitor when he heard Bree's soothing voice and saw her arms picking Dean up. Dean had also been born with thick, dark hair. He was going to be a heartbreaker. Best to keep him far away from Ro.

Declan sat the monitors down on the table next to the front door and opened the door. Liv took a step back behind her mother and clung to Jessie's leg.

"It's okay, Liv. Do you remember that nice police officer? It's all right. Come, sweetie." Jessie gave Declan an apologetic smile as she tried to peel Liv from her leg.

"I'm sorry, it has been so long since we've seen you. And it wasn't in the best of circumstances," Jessie said to Declan.

He understood. The hell they have been through would have

caused a lot of trust issues for Jessie's daughter, Liv. Especially since he was a stranger to her.

Liv shook her almost white blonde head against her mother's jeans, and Jessie sighed. She got on her haunches and took Liv's shoulders in her hands.

"Please come inside, Liv. Just for a moment. We're going to meet Mommy's cousin and her two little babies. They're just three months old. They must be so sweet and tiny."

Liv peered from behind Jessie's leg, but the moment she didn't find a woman with babies but a six-foot tall man standing there, she whiffed her head.

Declan got on one knee. "Hi Liv. I don't know if you remember me, but I am so glad to see you again. The twins are waking up from their naptime. We're about to have pancakes. Do you like pancakes?"

Liv's eyes widened for a second, but she still clung to Jessie's shirt. She tugged her mother down. "Do they have syrup?"

"I don't know, sweetie," Jessie smiled. She looked over at Declan and cocked her head, "Do you have syrup?"

Declan opened his mouth to answer her, when he felt a warm hand on his bicep. Bree made her presence known so he wouldn't accidentally knock her over by turning around.

"Hey! Did I hear someone say syrup? I love syrup. But do you know what's also awesome on a pancake?" Bree asked with her eyes solely focused on Liv.

Liv eyed Bree for a moment as she stood there, holding Dean in her arms. Their son was grabbing a hold on one of his mom's curls. Bree winced when Dean yanked a curly strand down. Declan quickly untangled his son's fingers from Bree's hair.

Declan met Bree's smiling face and gave her a quick kiss. He turned around and watched Liv relax a bit at the sight of baby Dean. Liv let go of her mother's shirt and took her mother's hand.

"I like peanut butter and banana on my pancake," Bree said.

The five-year-old scrunched up her nose. "Yuck!"

Bree laughed and said, "I know! I've got the weirdest taste buds since I've been pregnant. It's till not back to normal."

"Ooh, I remember! I used to eat scrambled eggs and bacon every day while pregnant with Liv. In the middle of the night sometimes. Now I can't stand the smell."

"Oh," Declan said, because he was about to serve exactly that. Scrambled eggs with crispy bacon were his favorite. It probably was the only thing he was good at making.

Bree giggled. "We have other things, don't worry. Please come inside! I'm Bree, by the way. And this is our son, Dean."

Before Jessie could respond, she turned around at a yell from across the street.

"Tommy Aiden Mills! Get your butt over here, now!"

Declan noticed Tommy storming off towards them, like a broken free puppy. Declan smiled while figuring the only thing missing was his tongue hanging out the side of his mouth.

"Hey, Tommy. I think I heard your dad calling out your name. Am I right?" Bree said in her teacher's voice.

"Yes, Miss Bree."

"You need to listen to your father, Tommy," Bree said.

Tommy held still before Liv and said, "I know you."

Liv stuck out her chin. "Oh? Never seen you before."

"Nuh-ah. You go to Miss Kate's class." Tommy put his thumb against his chest and said, "I'm in Miss Bree's class. She lives here. And I live there," he pointed across the street where his father was stomping on the asphalt to get his son back into the house.

"But Miss Bree had two babies. And I had Mister Craig. But after the summer, I'm getting Miss Bree again."

"You had Mister Craig?" Liv asked. She looked like she wanted to say something of the likes of feeling sorry for Tommy, but withheld. She grabbed her Mom's leg again the minute Keenan had reached their gathering in front of Dec's front door.

"Didn't I tell you to never cross the street without looking? *And* that you always need to tell me first whenever you want to go see Miss Bree or the babies? You can't go over here all day, every day."

"Keen. It's okay," Bree said. She ran her hand over Tommy's golden hair while holding Dean firmly in her other arm. Declan wanted to remember this sight forever.

"Oh, I'm sorry. We just interrupted you. I'm Keenan Mills, Dec's cousin. And this tornado chaser is Tommy."

Keenan held out his hand for Jessie, who eyed the tall Mills cousin up and down. She giggled at Tommy being introduced as a tornado chaser. Keenan wore grey sweatpants and a white, simple T-shirt with a V-neck, like he'd just got out of bed. His inky hair stood to all sides, so it made sense.

Jessie blushed as they shook hands. "Hi, I'm Jessie Walker. I'm Bree's cousin."

Keenan looked over from Jessie to Dec and cocked his head.

"It's a long story," Bree said.

"An endless story," Jessie added, giggling.

Bree took a step back and said, "Now, please come inside everyone. I hear our daughter Ava is waking up."

"Oh, we were just leaving," Keenan said and furrowed his brows because he probably already knew what was coming next.

"But, Dad..." Tommy whined.

"It's okay, Keen. You can stay. We're just having brunch. It's all very casual. Just so we can have this awkward first meet over with." Bree slapped a hand before her mouth.

"Oh, I didn't mean it like how it sounds. I meant that first dates are always awkward. But with the kids here, we can all sit around and relax. You know? Get to know each other without it becoming a job interview."

Jessie giggled again. "Oh, I like that, Bree. You have no idea how nervous I was."

"Mom dropped a vase this morning," Liv said.

Declan laughed as he could see Jessie being fidgety. He turned and took a few steps back to make room for everyone to enter their home.

"Well, that was this morning. Now we know we have nothing to worry about," Jessie said, smiling to Liv before guiding her daughter inside.

Bree placed Dean on the baby play mat and he reached out his hand for the mirror that hung above his head.

"I'm getting Ava, be right back," she said. He nodded at Bree and turned to ask what everyone wanted to drink.

While getting the drinks, he watched Keenan and Jessie having small talk and Tommy and Liv sitting at the table ignoring each other. Bree walked back into the room with Ava in her arms. "Come kids, who wants to watch the twins play?"

Liv and Tommy both jumped from their seats and ran over to Bree. Declan could never grow tired of the cute baby sounds. Jessie oohed and aahed as she joined Bree and the kids.

Keenan joined Declan in the kitchen to whip out scrambled eggs and bacon. Jessie came into the kitchen looking for some juice to give to Tommy and Liv.

"If it's alright with you, that is?" Jessie asked Keenan while raking a hand through her long blonde hair.

"Sure," Keenan said as he kept on flipping strips of bacon.

Declan smiled as he sliced an apple in four pieces. His cousin was unaware of the appreciative looks Jessie was giving Keenan.

Jessie bumped her hip into the counter, and Keenan still didn't look up.

"You are one hard nut to crack, Cuz," Declan said.

"Nah."

"I think after Evangeline, the only time you've shown interest in someone had been that time with Errin." Declan remembered how angry his oldest brother Brennan got when Keenan's showed his interest in the youngest Walsh sister.

"I just liked her spirit, you know? Errin tells it like it is. And she got that whole sexy angel thing going on."

Declan stilled his slicing and pulled a brow when he looked up at his cousin.

"You know I would never go there now, come on. But when I first saw her standing there in Lucky? Yeah... she's my type, all right."

Declan leaned in and said in a low voice, "And Jessie isn't?"

Keenan shrugged. "Didn't get the vibe. You know... that tingle. She seems sweet."

"Ah, come on, man." Declan felt the need to defend Bree's cousin. When a guy said 'she seems sweet' it usually meant she looked like princes Fiona from the Shrek movie—the green version of the princes.

"I could see you two together."

"Dec, you're just being like Pops. You see two single people in one room together and you figure they're meant for each other."

Declan grinned but returned his attention to slicing another apple.

"Didn't you tell me she got major issues with some ex? I don't want Tommy—"

"That's been handled. He's in jail for at least a decade, and the divorce is almost final. I asked Donovan to keep tabs on him in jail. You know how my brother will keep on following him when the asshole gets out."

"Well, that's something at least. But I mean it, Dec. I need to get knocked upside the head. Get a kick in the gut. But I just didn't feel it. So, just leave it at that."

Declan nodded. They walked back into the dining room and the laughter from Tommy and Liv, while playing Go Fish, welcomed them. Bree sat with a big smile on her face, watching them play.

Jessie looked up at Declan but had only eyes for Keenan when he entered the room. Declan smirked at how uncomfortable Jessie's looks made his cousin. Seeing him squirm was fun.

"Keenan, I heard from Bree that you're looking for a nanny?" Jessie said as she placed her elbows on the table and rested her head on her clasped hands.

Keenan sat down next to Tommy and said, "Yes. Do you know of anybody who could do four weekdays?"

"My sister Ryleigh would be perfect for the job," Jessie said, not noticing that Liv tugged on Jessie's shirt again.

"Mom?" Liv said.

"Yes, sweetie?"

Liv leaned in and tried to whisper, but everyone could over-hear her say, "I don't want Ryleigh going to Tommy."

Jessie stroked Liv's long hair from her face and said, "Ooh, but you'll still see Ryleigh, sweetie. Ryleigh is always going to be your aunt."

"Why can't I have Ryleigh as my nanny?" Liv said as she looked up hopefully at her mom.

"Well, we live with grandpa and grandma now, and grandma loves to help me with picking you up from school and taking you to dance classes."

"But I want Ryleigh," Liv said as she shoved her plate forward.

"We'll talk about it when we get home," Jessie said, and she gave a final nod. Liv pursed her lips and walked back to the twins. Tommy followed and Bree got up from her seat too to join them.

Jessie cleared her throat and passed a card over the table to Keenan.

"This is my sister, Ryleigh. She's been real great with Liv. My absolute rock. I'm staying with my parents now, so my mom is eager to help with Liv. But Ryleigh is the best you could ever find as your nanny."

Keenan perked up in his seat after picking up the card from

Jessie. Declan glanced down at a postcard with a picture of Jessie sitting on a bench in the park, sitting and laughing with a younger woman.

Their faces seemed so similar, like they could have been twins. They both had wide, corn blue eyes, high cheekbones, and a pert nose. But if this was Ryleigh on the postcard, she had shiny, long red hair instead of blonde hair like Jessie.

Ryleigh's hair wasn't as fiery red like Bree's sister Fianna. No, it was a more carroty red. With a copper undertone, making it more red than orange.

Keenan's thumb caressed the side of the postcard, flicking over and over a laughing Ryleigh as he studied the card. Keenan cleared his throat. "How old is your sister?"

"She just turned twenty-one," Jessie said.

Declan glanced over at Jessie, who studied Keenan the same way as Declan did. She held out her hand for Keenan to return the postcard. "But maybe you're right, she's young..."

Keenan didn't look up from the postcard. "Could you give me her number?"

"Eh, well, I... I don't know if she'd like that. I can give you *my* number? To eh, set up a meet?"

Keenan held out the postcard and held on a bit too long when Jessie grabbed it.

"Give her mine and please have her call me." Keenan brought out his business card and placed it on the table. He stood and thanked Declan for brunch.

"It would be great to have some help with Tommy, Jessie," Keenan urged.

"I'll give her your number. It was nice meeting you," Jessie said as she also stood from the table.

It didn't escape Declan how his cousin tested Ryleigh's name on his lips as he walked out the door. Bree walked back to the table with Ava in her arms.

"I've never seen Keen like this," Bree whispered. She

searched Declan's eyes to get a read on his thoughts of Keenan's odd behavior.

Declan's upper lip pulled. Keenan Mills has just been knocked upside the head and kicked in his gut, with just one look at a picture of Ryleigh Walker.

THANK YOU FOR READING DECLAN! If you're ready for more of the sexy, heartfelt and funny Lucky Irish series, continue with book 5 in the series: **Keenan** (coming spring 2021)

HAVE you heard of the spin-off series Winter Peaks? Caitlin Ryan is moving to the mountains of Colorado. You can order book 1 Adam now.

IF YOU ENJOYED DECLAN, would you please consider leaving a review? It's reviews from fans like you that help spread the word about my books, giving me the opportunity to keep writing the series.

THANK you so much <3

ADAM - WINTER PEAKS

If **Caitlin Ryan** had known Pops' grandsons in Colorado were freaking hot with an equal amount of irritating traits, she'd picked another place to overthink her life. **Adam Mills**, the oldest brother of the family that agreed to take her in, has an unnerving sexy confidence and overall hotness. And the former snowboard star has his eyes set on her.

As an Olympic gold medalist on the half-pipe, Adam Mills has seen and done it all before. He's finally ready to give his heart to a woman and settle down. But can Adam win over Caitlin's heart?

Welcome to Winter Peaks, Colorado! A small tourist town where all year round, people come and go to enjoy the mountains. But the families of the Winter Peaks series have made the town their home.

ღ Small town romance
ღ Strong heroine & steamy alpha man
ღ Funny, relatable family members

ADAM is book one in the **Winter Peaks series** about the ups and downs of several families in a small tourist town in Colorado. The series is a spin-off of the sweet and sexy Lucky Irish series, about several close-knit families in Austin, Texas.

Each book is an interconnected standalone. As we read a new sexy romance, we can also catch up with favorite characters throughout the series.

Although the heroine, Caitlin, comes from the Lucky Irish series, it's not required to read those books first.

This book can be read as a standalone.

Winter Peaks series:
Adam (Book 1)

ACKNOWLEDGMENTS

A huge thank you to all of the amazing readers out there who took a chance on reading one of my books! It means the world to me that you enjoy the characters like I do. Some even fell in love with the series and I'm happy to keep popping out Lucky Irish books for you! :)

Thank you to all the reviewers, ARC readers and bloggers who've helped me to get the word out! I'm so grateful for all your support!

Thank you, Tiffany Grimes from Burgeon Design and Editorial, for working with me on the fourth book of the series. It was again such a pleasure working with you. And your coaching helped me so much! I'm so happy that I've found you!

Dear Emilie of InkSlingerPR, thank you for being there for me! It's so good to have you in my corner! And it's so cool that you know a few Dutch words! *Dankjewel voor alles :)*

I loved writing about the five Ryan sisters and their family dynamics. I want to dedicate this book to Eline, my sister.

We drove the rest of our family of five mad with our bickering and petty little fights over who got the best spot in front of the mirror, while lip-syncing a song with our hair brushes in hand.

As we got older you turned into my true big sister who's not only my rock, but also one of my best friends. <3

To my family, my husband and three daughters, you give me so much inspiration on writing about love and strong-willed heroines in particular. Every day, you make me feel so loved, and I can only hope that I'm making you proud.

ABOUT THE AUTHOR

Anna loves to write heartfelt and steamy romance series. She falls in love with her characters as they go through their ups and downs. Anna often laughs out loud behind her laptop as she writes the banter between siblings. Sometimes, she cries as a result from the real talk that comes with family. There's no hiding from a nosy Pops ;-) Her books are for mature readers only because of their steamy content.

Anna Castor lives in a small town near Amsterdam, The Netherlands, with her husband and their three young daughters. When she's not writing and has some time left between bringing her kids to school and picking them up from play dates or volleyball practice, she's glued to her e-reader.

Anna is a former wedding photographer turned author. While photographing weddings, Anna loved being a part of the couple's special day to tell their (love) story through her pictures. Each wedding had a different story to tell: the histories of the bride and groom, their family dynamics, their challenges in life, and of course, how they met and fell in love.

And now Anna takes her readers through the troubles and hardships her characters may come across on their journey to a happily ever after.

Anna loves to hear from her readers <3. Follow her online to get updates on new releases, ARC opportunities, freebies and more!

Connect with her online:
>   Website: www.annacastor.com
>   Newsletter: www.annacastor.com/subscribe